Matt Jensen:
The Last Mountain Man
The Great Train Massacre

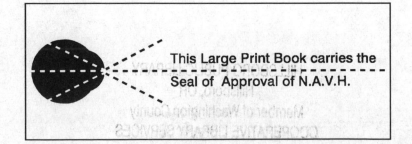

MATT JENSEN:
THE LAST MOUNTAIN MAN
THE GREAT TRAIN MASSACRE

WILLIAM W. JOHNSTONE
WITH J. A. JOHNSTONE

WHEELER PUBLISHING
A part of Gale, Cengage Learning

GALE
CENGAGE Learning

Farmington Hills, Mich • San Francisco • New York • Waterville, Maine
Meriden, Conn • Mason, Ohio • Chicago

GALE
CENGAGE Learning®

6096 4698 10/16

LIBRARY OF CONGRESS CATALOGING-IN-PUBLICATION DATA

Names: Johnstone, William W., author. | Johnstone, J. A., author.
Title: Matt Jensen, the last mountain man : the great train massacre / by William W. Johnstone with J. A. Johnstone.
Other titles: Great train massacre
Description: Large print edition. | Waterville, Maine : Wheeler Publishing, 2016. | Series: Wheeler Publishing large print western
Identifiers: LCCN 2016018077 | ISBN 9781410491916 (softcover) | ISBN 1410491919 (softcover)
Subjects: LCSH: Large type books. | GSAFD: Western stories.
Classification: LCC PS3560.O415 M464 2016 | DDC 813/.54—dc23
LC record available at https://lccn.loc.gov/2016018077

Published in 2016 by arrangement with Pinnacle Books, an imprint of Kensington Publishing Corp.

Matt Jensen:
The Last Mountain Man
The Great Train Massacre

CHAPTER ONE

On board the Western Flyer

The train was heading south on the Denver and Rio Grande Railroad. It was a little past four in the morning, and from Spruce Mountain the train was a symphony of sight and sound. Red and orange sparks glittered from within the billowing plume of smoke that was darker than the moonlit sky. Clouds of steam escaped from the drive cylinders, then drifted back in iridescent tendrils to dissipate before they reached the rear of the engine. The passenger cars were marked by a long line of candescent windows, glowing like a string of diamonds.

There were ninety-three passengers on the train, counting Matt Jensen. Matt was more than just a passenger, because he had been hired by the Denver and Rio Grande Railroad to act as a railroad detective. It wasn't a permanent job, but the D&RG had been robbed too many times lately, and because

7

Matt had worked with them before, they offered him a good fee to make one trip for them. They didn't choose the trip arbitrarily — they had good information that the train would be robbed somewhere between Denver and Colorado Springs.

Matt accepted the assignment but under the condition that no one on the train, except the conductor, would know about him. He had boarded the train in Denver as a passenger, taking a seat, not on the Pullman car, but in one of the day cars, doing so to keep his official position secret. He had turned down the gimbal lantern that was nearest his seat, which allowed him to look through the window without seeing only his own reflection. At the moment he was looking at the moon reflecting from the rocks and trees when the train suddenly ground to a shuddering, screeching, banging, halt. So abruptly did the train stop that the sleeping passengers were awakened with a start.

"Why did we stop in such a fashion?" someone asked indignantly.

"I intend to write a letter to the railroad about this. Why, I was thrown out of my seat with such force that I could have broken my neck," another passenger complained.

Because Matt could see through his window, he saw some men outside, and it gave him a very good idea of what was going on. He pulled his pistol and held it close beside him, waiting to see what would happen next. He didn't have to wait but a short time before someone burst into the car from the front door. The train robber was wearing a bandanna tied across the bottom half of his face, and he was holding a pistol, which he pointed toward the passengers.

Although the passengers were shocked and surprised at this totally unexpected interruption of their trip, Matt was not. He had been told to expect a train robbery between Denver and Colorado Springs, and it was now obvious that the intelligence had been correct.

"Everybody stay seated!" the train robber shouted. He was holding a sack in his left hand, and he handed it to the passenger in the front seat.

"Now, if you are churchgoing folks, I know you understand what it means to pass the plate. Just pretend that this sack is the plate that gets passed around in church, only don't hold back on your donations like you do with your preacher. Gents, I want you to drop your wallets into the sack. Ladies, if you got 'ny jewelry, why, that would be appreciated, too."

"Look here, what gives you the right to . . ." a man started, but before he could finish the question, the train robber turned his gun toward him.

"This gives me the right," he said.

Another gunman came on to join the first. "How is everything going?" he asked.

"Nothing I can't handle. Is everything under control out there?"

"Yeah," the second gunman answered. "We've got the engineer covered, and we're disconnecting the rest of the train from behind the express car."

"How will I know when you're pullin' the express car away? I mean, what if you fellas leave and I don't know you're gone? I'll be stuck back here."

"We'll blow the whistle before we go."

"There's no need for you to be worrying about that. You two won't be going anywhere," Matt said.

"What? Who said that?"

"I did," Matt replied. "Both of you, drop your guns."

"The hell we will!" the first gunman shouted as he fired at Matt. The bullet smashed through the window beside Matt's seat. Matt returned fire, shooting two times. Both of the bandits went down.

During the gunfire, women screamed and men shouted. As the car filled with the gun smoke of the three discharges, Matt scooted out through the back door, jumped from the steps down to the ground, then fell and rolled out into the darkness.

"Walt, Ed! What's goin' on in there?" someone shouted from alongside the track. "What was the shootin' about?"

"I'm afraid Walt and Ed won't be going with you," Matt called. Matt was concealed by the darkness, but in the dim light that spilled through the car windows, he could see the gunman who was yelling at the others.

"Drop your gun and put your hands up!" Matt called out to him. "I've got you covered."

"I'll be damned if I will!" the train robber replied. He realized he was in a patch of light, so he moved into the shadow to fire at the voice from the darkness. He may have thought he would be shielded by moving out of the light, but the two-foot-wide muzzle flash of his pistol gave Matt an ideal target, and he fired back. A bullet whistled harmlessly by Matt, but Matt's bullet found its mark, and the outlaw let out a little yell, grabbed his chest, then collapsed.

Matt stood up then and moved toward the

side of the train to try and get a bead on the one who had been separating the express car from the rest of the train. One of the passengers poked his head out to see what was going on.

"Get back inside!" Matt shouted gruffly.

The passenger jerked his head back in quickly.

The train robber peered cautiously around the corner, trying to see his adversary.

"Mister, you are the only one left alive," Matt called out. "And if you don't drop your gun and come out here with your hands up right now, you'll be as dead as your partners."

"Who the hell are you?" the outlaw called back.

"The name is Jensen. Matt Jensen."

"Matt Jensen?" The outlaw's voice suddenly took on a new and more frightened edge.

"That's my name."

There was a beat of silence, then Matt saw a pistol tossed out onto the ground. A moment later the would-be train robber emerged from between the cars with his hands in the air.

"We can go on ahead, Mr. Engineer," Matt called up. "It's all over now."

"Yeah, but the track ain't clear," the

engineer called back down from the cab window. "Look ahead, 'n you'll see what it is that made me stop so fast."

Matt saw that a tree had been felled across the track.

"We're goin' to have to get that cleared away before we can go on."

By now the conductor, hearing the conversation and realizing that the danger had passed, came down to see what was going on.

"I'll get some volunteers to clear the track," the conductor promised.

"You think you can get enough people to volunteer?"

"I'll offer them a refund on their train tickets," the conductor said.

Matt looked at the man he had captured. "What's your name?"

"Dockins," the man replied. "Art Dockins."

"Dockins, you and I will ride in the baggage car with your three friends."

"Are they dead?" Dockins asked.

"Oh, I expect they are," Matt replied easily.

The conductor employed the two porters to load the bodies into the baggage car, while passengers from the train made quick work of the tree trunk that was lying across the track. Within an hour after the train's unscheduled stop, they were underway again.

The sun was fully up by the time they reached Colorado Springs, and the platform was crowded with family and friends who were there to meet the arriving passengers as well as departing passengers and those who were there to tell them good-bye.

"We was held up!" someone shouted as soon as he stepped down from the train.

"Held up?" one of those waiting said.

"No, we wasn't actually held up," another said. "Though some folks did try to hold us up."

"What do you mean, tried?"

"I mean tried. Some men tried to hold us up, only they didn't get away with it. Three of 'em's dead now, 'n the fourth one is bein' held prisoner in the baggage car."

"You mean one of 'em's still alive? Let's string 'im up. There ain't no better lesson given to would-be train robbers than to see one of their own with his neck stretched."

Inside the car, Matt sat with his prisoner, Dockins, and the bodies of the three outlaws he had killed.

"Oh, Lord!" Dockins said. "They're

a-fixin' to hang me."

"No, they aren't."

"Yes, they are. I heard 'em talkin' about it."

"They'll have to get you away from me first," Matt said. He opened the door to the baggage car, then stood there in the opening.

"Mister, is it true you're holdin' one of the train robbers prisoner in there?" someone called up to Matt.

"I am. I'm holding him for the law."

"Ain't no need for you to be a-doin' that. You can turn him over to us."

"I don't think so," Matt replied.

"You'll either turn him over to us, or we'll take him from you."

Matt drew his pistol.

"I don't think so," he said again.

"There's at least twenty of us. There's only one of you. Do you think you can stop all twenty of us?"

"No, that wouldn't be possible. I've only got six bullets in my gun. But before you get him, I'll kill six of you." Matt pointed his pistol straight at the loudmouth. "And I may as well start with you, right now."

"No!" the man shouted, holding out his hands. "Now, just a minute, mister, you got no call a-doin' that."

"Then I suggest you start trying to calm down all your friends. Because I will kill the first person who makes a step toward this car, then I will kill you."

"Hold it, fellas, hold it!" the loudmouth said, talking to the others in the crowd. "Let's just let the law handle this."

"Thanks, Jensen," the surviving train robber said.

By that time the sheriff and his deputy were pushing their way through the crowd toward the mail car.

"Get back," the sheriff was saying. "Get back, ever'body. Make way! Let me an' my deputy through here!"

When the sheriff reached the train, the messenger climbed down from the express car.

"You want to tell me what happened here?" the sheriff asked.

"We were beset by train robbers," the messenger said.

"I had a bank shipment coming. Did they get any of the money?" The question was asked by a very thin, clean-shaven, bald-headed man who had a prominent Adam's apple. This was the banker.

"No sir, Mr. Underhill," the messenger said. "I'm proud to say that the money is all here."

"We got three bodies on board, Sheriff," the conductor said. "What do you want to do with 'em?"

"They the ones that tried to rob the train?" the sheriff asked.

"Yes, sir."

"I've got a prisoner for you, too," Matt said.

"You've got a prisoner? Who are you?"

"His name is Jensen, Sheriff," the conductor said. "The railroad hired him to look after the money shipment. He's the one that killed the three and captured this one."

"All by himself?" the sheriff asked in disbelief.

"All by himself."

The sheriff turned to his deputy. "All right, get 'em out of the car and lay 'em on the platform," he said. "Let's take a look at 'em."

Soliciting help from a couple of men in the crowd, the deputy soon had the three bodies out and lying on the brick platform. Drawn by morbid curiosity, the crowd moved in for a closer look.

"Hey, Sheriff, I know a couple of them boys," the deputy said. "That's Walt Porter and Ed Stiller. They used to cowboy some for the Bar T."

"Yeah, I know them, too," the sheriff

17

replied. He pointed to the third one. "I don't know that one, though."

"That's Bing Baker," Dockins said. "Me 'n him used to ride together up in Wyomin' some."

"Who are you?"

"Dockins. Art Dockins."

"He's the prisoner we've got for you," the conductor said.

"Prisoner? How come he's not tied up or anything?"

"There was no need to make him uncomfortable," Matt said. "He wasn't going anywhere."

Chapter Two

"The Denver and Rio Grande thanks you," General William Jackson Palmer said to Matt. General Palmer was president of the railroad.

"And, in addition to the agreed-upon fee of two hundred and fifty dollars, I am proud to present you with an additional fifty-dollar bonus."

"General, I thank you," Matt said.

"Let me ask you this, Mr. Jensen. Do you have any interest in becoming a full-time private detective?" Jefferson Emerson asked. "The pay is good, and you would be a natural for it."

Emerson owned the Emerson Private Detective Agency, and provided contract security service not only for the D&RG, but the Denver and New Orleans, as well as the Union Pacific Railroad. Emerson's headquarters was actually in San Francisco, but he had come to Colorado Springs to discuss the renewal of his contract with the Denver and Rio Grande Railroad.

"Well, Mr. Emerson, I do thank you for the offer," Matt said. "But I have the feeling that steady work like that would be a little too confining for me. Over the years I've developed the habit of moving around. I'm afraid if I stayed in one job too long, I'd wither up like a piece of rawhide."

Emerson and General Palmer both laughed.

"Well, we can't have you withering up, now can we?" Emerson asked. "But I wonder if I could call on you from time to time, to handle a specific job for me? At a mutually agreed-upon payment, of course."

"Yes," Matt said. "I see no reason why I couldn't take an occasional assignment."

"That's good to know, but, if you're going to be moving around, how will I get in touch with you, if I need you?"

"Isn't your home office in San Francisco?" Matt asked.

"Indeed it is."

Matt smiled. "Well, that's where I'm heading now. I'll be there within two weeks, so, why don't I just check in with you when I get there?"

"Wonderful!" Emerson said.

Lucas Conroy had a fine office on the top floor of the Solari Building on Jackson Street. He had a rich red carpet on the floor and a George Catlin painting on the wall. A vase dating from the Ming dynasty sat on a table in front of the window. At the moment, he was meeting with a potential client.

"You have to be specific in telling me what you want," Conroy said. "I don't deal in generalities."

"I, uh, have to know just what it is you are willing to do before I can be more specific," Conroy's visitor said.

"I arrange things."

"What kind of things do you arrange?"

"Look around my office," Conroy said. "Everything you see here cost a great deal of money. I can afford expensive things, because my business is very lucrative. And my business is very successful, because I am willing to arrange things that most people won't do, either because they can't, or they are too frightened."

"Does that include things that may not be within the law?" his client asked.

"Yes."

"Suppose someone came to you . . . uh, this is just a question, mind you, but, suppose someone came to you and said that he wanted someone killed?"

"That would cost you a great deal of money."

"I didn't say I was the one who wanted someone killed. I was posing a hypothetical question."

"I have no time for hypothetical questions. If a hypothetical question is the only reason you have come to see me, then I must tell you that this meeting is over. So please, get to the point."

"All right, I will get to the point. I represent a consortium of businessmen. And I believe, that is, the consortium believes, that our businesses, and indeed many businesses that we don't represent, are being hurt by the ruthless practices of someone who is concerned only for his own self-interest. We believe that this person's ruthless business practices put at risk the jobs of thousands of people. He is much too powerful to take on in the courts. We believe the only solution is to have him killed. So you see, Mr. Conroy, that wasn't purely a hypothetical question. Can we arrange to have that done?"

"Yes, you can arrange that. But it is going to cost you a great deal of money."

"You will guarantee success?"

"Of course. I could not stay in business unless I guaranteed my clients success."

"Very good. I would say, then, that we wish to become your client."

"Who is the person you want killed?"

"Actually, there are two of them that we want killed."

"Two? You mean you want to arrange two separate operations?"

"No. The two I want killed are always together, so it will be only one operation. Do you think you can handle that?"

"Yes, I can handle it. But whether or not it is one operation or two separate operations, the fact that you want two people killed will double the cost. A human life is a human life, after all, and one doesn't kill without some compunction."

Conroy's visitor smiled. "I'm glad to see that your misgivings can be set aside, for a price," he said caustically.

Colorado Springs

Matt was awaiting his turn in the Model Barbershop on Lamar Street. The barber and the customer in his chair were having a discussion. As it turned out, they were discussing him, though neither of them knew that the subject of their discussion was present at the time.

23

"Jensen faced down all four of 'em," the man in the barber chair said. " 'Throw up your hands, or prepare to meet your Maker,' he called out to 'em.

" 'It's you that'll die,' one of the three men said. Then the pistols commenced a-blazing, 'n the next thing you know, why, three of them bandits was lyin' on the floor of the railroad car, 'n the fourth one got scairt and throwed up his hands."

"That's pretty amazing," the barber said.

"Yeah, well, if you knew Matt Jensen as well as I do, you wouldn't think nothin' of it. I told him, I said, 'Matt, you keep gettin' yourself into situations like this, one of these days you're just liable to bite off more'n you can chew.' "

"What did Jensen say when you told him that?" the barber asked.

"Why, what did you expect him to say?" the talkative man replied. "He said, 'The outlaw ain't been born who can get the best of Matt Jensen.' Yes, sir, that's what he said. And me 'n him knowin' each other as well as we do, why, I figure he's prob'ly right." Overhearing the conversation, Matt chuckled quietly, then picked up the newspaper and began to read.

From the *Colorado Springs Gazette:*

GILLESPIE ENTERPRISES ACQUIRES NORTHWEST FINANCIALS

John Bartmess Gillespie announced this week that his company, Gillespie Enterprises, has acquired Northwest Financials, the largest investment firm between San Francisco and Chicago. In making the acquisition, Gillespie beat out Whitehurst Commercial Development, the Kansas City–based company that was also bidding for the investment firm.

Northwest has its main office in Denver, but there are subsidiary offices in a dozen cities. Northwest has been losing money over the last two years, and it is believed that Gillespie will completely reorganize the institution.

"That'll do it, Mr. Allman," the barber said, taking the cape from his customer.

Allman looked at himself in the mirror, ran his hand through his hair, and smiled. "You done a good job, Milt," he said, handing the barber fifteen cents.

"Hello, Mr. Allman," Matt said as the customer walked by.

"Do we know each other?" Allman asked, made curious by Matt's greeting.

25

"I heard the barber call you by name."

Allman nodded, then left the shop.

"You're next, sir," the barber said.

Matt lay the paper aside and walked over to get into the chair.

The barber put the cape over Matt, unaware that Matt had drawn his pistol and was now holding it in his lap under the cape. It was a suggestion that his mentor and friend, Smoke Jensen, had made a long time ago.

"Matt, I have a feeling that, like me, you're going to wind up making some enemies, more than likely, a lot of them," Smoke told him. "In addition, there will be some men who aren't particularly enemies, but would be happy to kill you just for the reputation. One place where you are always vulnerable is when you're sitting in a barber's chair with a cape tied around you. That's when your enemies will see you as a prime target. But you don't have to be vulnerable there. If you'll just pull your pistol and hold it in your lap, you'll turn the situation around. Then, it will be you who will have the upper hand."

"That fella that just left here sure gets around," the barber said. "You heard him talking about Matt Jensen, didn't you?"

"Yes, I did."

"Yes, sir, well, Matt Jensen ain't the only one he knows. He's good friends with Smoke Jensen and Falcon MacCallister too. He also knows Wyatt Earp, and he knew Wild Bill Hickock. Yes, sir, that fella really gets around."

"Some men just have a knack of making friends, I suppose," Matt said, swallowing a laugh.

"Find anything interesting in the newspaper?" the barber asked as he began building up a frothy lather in the shaving cup.

"I was just reading about Northwest selling out," Matt replied.

"Yeah, what do you think of that?"

"It doesn't look like they had much choice," Matt said. "According to the article, they've been losing money for the last couple of years."

"I guess that's right," the barber said. "It's just that I hate to see it go to Gillespie."

"Why? What's wrong with Gillespie?"

"Oh, I don't know as there is anything wrong with him. It's just that it don't seem right for one man to have so much money. Why, they say he's as rich as some countries." The barber was sharpening his blade on the razor strop.

"There's nothing wrong with being rich,

as long as you have come by it honestly," Matt said.

"Well, yes, sir, I reckon that's true. Maybe I'm just jealous 'cause he's got all that money, and I don't."

"Are you married?" Matt asked.

"Yes, sir, I am. I got me a fine wife, two kids, a boy 'n a girl, and another one on the way."

"And a nice business where you provide a service for people who need that service," Matt commented.

The barber was quiet for a moment, then he chuckled. "You're a pretty intelligent man, mister. You're right. Now that I think about it, I've got all a man needs to be happy."

The barber whistled a contented tune as he began shaving Matt.

After the shave and haircut, Matt walked out front, untied his horse from the hitching rail, then swung into the saddle.

"Spirit, we're going to San Francisco. I know that's over a thousand miles, but you won't have to walk the whole way. I'll find a place for us to catch the train before we get there."

CHAPTER THREE

San Francisco, the Gillespie Building

Drew Jessup stood just at the open door of John Gillespie's office and knocked lightly on the door frame. At the knock, John looked up from his desk and smiled.

"Drew, what can I do for you?"

"It's not what you can do for me, John, it's what I can do for you," Drew replied. "Well, for you and for Mary Beth." Drew, who was the vice president of Gillespie Enterprises, walked into John's office with an envelope in his hand. Smiling, he put the envelope on the desk in front of John.

"What is this?" John asked.

"Didn't I hear Mary Beth tell you last week that she wanted to go see the Junius Booth play?"

"Yes, as a matter of fact I believe she did say that."

Drew pointed toward the envelope.

"There are two box seat tickets there," he said.

"Why, Drew," John said, picking up the envelope. "What a wonderful thing for you to do!"

"What good is it to be friends if one friend can't do something for the other friend from time to time?" Drew asked.

"I'll keep that in mind," John said. He waved the tickets. "And I'll have to find something nice to do for you someday."

"I already know what I would like for you to do for me," Drew replied.

"What's that?"

"When you go to Chicago next month, you can bring back a souvenir. Have you told Mary Beth yet that you are going?"

"No, I was waiting for the right time."

Drew pointed to the ticket envelope. "Can you think of a better time to tell her than when you are both at the theater?"

John shook his head. "Why, that's a wondeful idea, Drew. Yes, the theater would be an excellent time to tell her."

"Do you still plan to invite her to go with you? The reason I ask is, I will need to know, so that I can make all the arrangements for your travel."

"Thank you, Drew, I appreciate that," John said.

San Francisco, the Solari Building on Jackson Street

"You don't have to worry, Mr. Conroy, I'll take care of it."

"If you can, make it look like an accident," Conroy said.

"Yes, of course, I have it all worked out. I know exactly what I'm going to do. All you have to do is just have the money ready. You do have the money, don't you?"

"Yes, I have the money, but I don't intend to pay you until afterward. And then I will pay you only if you succeed," Conroy said. "I don't make a habit of paying for failure."

"I understand."

The Alcazar Theater

John Bartmess Gillespie and his twenty-three-year-old daughter, Mary Beth, stepped out of the theater, which was on O'Ferrel Street between Stockton and Powell. They had just seen a performance of *Julius Caesar* starring Junius Brutus Booth Jr.

"Thank you so much for bringing me to the theater, Papa," Mary Beth said. "I thought it was a lovely performance, and Mr. Booth played the role of Brutus so eloquently, don't you think?"

"He was good, but not as good as his

father was. Now, there was a brilliant actor. To be honest Junius Jr. wasn't even as good as his brothers, Edwin, or John Wilkes," John said.

"John Wilkes? Papa, surely you aren't praising the man who assassinated President Lincoln?" Mary Beth asked, shocked by her father's comment.

"Give the devil his due, sweetheart. A murderer and scoundrel he may have been — he was, nonetheless, a very talented actor."

"Well, I feel sorry for Mr. Junius Booth, having to live with the shame of knowing what a horrible thing his brother did."

"It wasn't his fault, and the theatergoers have accepted both him and Edwin, without ascribing to either of them any guilt by association. I have spoken with him about it, and he is reconciled to the shame John Wilkes brought to the family."

"Shall I summon your coach, Mr. Gillespie?" a young man asked.

"Yes, if you would, please," John said, handing him a fifty-cent coin.

"Yes, sir!"

"By the way, Mary Beth, what do you think about your father being invited to give a speech at Northwestern University in Chicago?" John asked, after the boy hurried off to summon the coach.

"Really, Papa? Oh, what a wonderful honor that is! But then, the university should be equally honored to have you. You are going to accept the invitation, aren't you?"

"Yes, indeed. It has been a long time since I was last in Chicago. I've asked Drew to make the arrangements to have my private car attached. Would you like to come with me?"

"Oh, yes, Papa, I would love to!" Mary Beth replied enthusiastically. "When are we going?"

"We'll leave here next month. I thought maybe we would spend a week or ten days there."

"Does Uncle Drew know you are planning to be gone for that long?"

Drew Jessup wasn't actually Mary Beth's uncle, but he was as close as family. Many years ago Drew and John had been classmates at the University of Pennsylvania and were still friends. Drew was now vice president of Gillespie Enterprises, a far-flung operation that included shipping, mining, and commercial properties. John also had investments in railroads, railroad sleeping cars, and oil. He was exceptionally wealthy and was often mentioned with such men as

Cornelius Vanderbilt and Andrew Carnegie.

"I've no doubt but that there will be receptions to attend, and you can act as my attendant. Your mother used to do that for me, you know."

"Yes. I know she teased you about it, but I think she actually enjoyed doing it."

"I think she did as well." John was quiet for a moment. "I miss her so much, Mary Beth."

"I know you do, Papa." Mary Beth moved closer to him, and he put his arm around her.

"I would give every penny I have to have her back. I don't know if I could stand it if it weren't for you."

"Oh, here comes the coach," Mary Beth said, speaking cheerfully in hopes of breaking her father's melancholy.

"I'm glad to see that Mr. Chan is giving the young man who summoned him a ride back to the theater," John said.

Mary Beth giggled and pointed to the driver. "Look at Mr. Chan in his new red jacket. I think he really likes it."

The young messenger, who had ridden back on the driver's seat, jumped down and opened the door to the coach. He helped Mary Beth enter and held the door open for John, closing it behind him.

"Thank you," John said. "All right, Mr. Chan, we're all ready," he called up to the driver.

The coach drive from the theater to the Gillespie home would take about half an hour. They were near the top of Eureka Peak, the north hill of Twin Peaks, when they heard Chan give a yell in alarm.

"Mr. Chan, what is it?" John asked, and looking out the window he saw the team of horses running away. Chan was lying facedown in the road, and the coach was picking up speed and heading for the edge of the cliff.

"Mary Beth, jump!" John shouted.

Fortunately, Mary Beth didn't take the time to question him. Instead, she opened the door to her side of the coach and jumped, as John did the same thing on his side. They slid and rolled along the road but stopped short of the precipice.

There was a low fence, but it did nothing to impede the momentum of the coach, which crashed through it, then started down. They heard the splintering sound as it hit the side of the mountain, then tumbled over and over, leaving pieces of it strewn along the way until it came to rest on the ground, eight hundred feet below.

"Mary Beth!" John shouted. "Where are you?"

"I'm here, Papa!"

John saw Mary Beth sitting up slowly.

"Oh, no!" Mary Beth said in a pained voice.

"What is it? What's wrong? Are you hurt?"

"My dress is a mess! It's dirty and torn."

Despite himself, John couldn't help but laugh. "If all you're concerned about is your dress, you're all right," he said, relief evident in his voice.

"What happened? Where is Mr. Chan?" Mary Beth asked.

"Chan!" John said. He got to his feet then and ran to check on the Chinese driver, who was lying in the middle of the road groaning in pain.

The Gillespie Building, two days later

Drew Jessup poured two glasses of bonded whiskey and handed a glass to John Gillespie. John was in Drew's office.

"You were lucky you weren't killed," Drew Jessup said. "And to think that the accident happened in the worst possible place. What if you and Mary Beth had not been able to jump from the coach when you did? Why, you would have crashed all the way to the bottom of Eureka Peak and, no doubt, been killed."

"Yeah," John said. "There's no way we would have survived the crash, that's for sure."

Drew shivered. "Let's not even consider such a thing. Lord a'mighty, John, do you have any idea how many people depend on you? If you had been killed, it would not only have been a personal disaster to me for losing a close friend, it would have been an economic disaster to more than a thousand families."

"Ahh, you could have kept it going," John said. "If I didn't think so, I would have never made you vice president."

"How are you and Mary Beth doing? Any the worse for wear?"

"No, we were very lucky, a few scrapes and bruises, is all. It was Mr. Chan who was hurt."

"Yes, I should have asked about him. How is he doing?"

"He has a broken collarbone and a broken leg, but he is recovering."

"Well, you give him my best, will you?"

"Yes, and I'm sure he will appreciate it."

Drew smiled and held his glass out toward John, who touched his glass to it.

"Well, I would say be more careful, but

accidents by their very nature are accidents."

"Yes," John said. "I suppose so."

"I have made the arrangements for your trip. You will be leaving San Francisco in about four weeks, and your car will be attached to the *Conqueror.* That's the fastest engine on the line."

"Thanks, Drew. You always have been good with making arrangements like that. I have to confess, when I have to take care of details, I don't know whether to wind my watch or scratch my ass."

Drew laughed. "Well, John, it has always been my observation that a man can never go wrong by scratching his ass."

John laughed with him.

"I believe you said you asked Mary Beth, and she will be going with you?"

"Yes, you were right. The play was the perfect time to ask her. I think she is very much looking forward to it."

"I don't blame her. It will be a good trip for her. And Chicago is an interesting city. I'm sure she will enjoy it."

"Drew?"

"Yes, John?"

"This accident has started me thinking. It's like you said, accidents by their very nature are accidents, and you never know when something like that might happen. I guess what I'm trying to say is . . . if something were to happen to me, I want you to look out for Mary Beth. She's a bright young woman, but there's no way she could run this entire company all by herself. I would want you to do for her what you have been doing for me all these years, but probably even more so. Can I have your promise that you will do that?"

"I'm flattered that you would ask, and I would be glad to," Drew replied. "But let's not talk about such things. I don't like to think about you being gone."

"Oh, and thanks again for the tickets to the play. Mary Beth and I had a wonderful time." He chuckled. "Except for the accident, of course."

The Solari Building
"I told you," Conroy said. "I don't pay for failure."

"I didn't fail. You said you wanted me to arrange an accident, and I arranged an accident. Hell, you saw what happened. The carriage went over the edge and fell two or three hundred feet. If they had still been in the coach when it went over, both of them would have been killed."

"Perhaps that is so," Conroy agreed. "But we will never know, will we? Because they weren't still in the coach when it went over."

"It was just dumb luck that they managed to get out before the coach went over the edge."

"When you set out to do a job, you are supposed to take everything into consideration. And that means everything. There is no room in this business for something as arbitrary as 'dumb luck,' I believe you called it, to get in the way."

"Look, I did what you asked me to do. I arranged the accident, and now I think I should be paid."

"I didn't ask you to arrange the accident," Conroy said.

"The hell you didn't. You told me to make it look like an accident."

"I told you to kill both Gillespie and his daughter, and to make that look like an accident. And since you didn't kill them, the accident makes no difference."

"But I . . ."

"Please," Conroy said interrupting him. "If you ever intend to work for me again, just accept that you failed with this assignment and put it behind you."

"All right, I'll do it. It don't seem right to me, but I'll do it."

CHAPTER FOUR

Office of Jeff Emerson, private detective
"You were right to be suspicious, Mr. Gillespie," Jeff Emerson said. "What happened to you and your daughter wasn't an accident."

"I had a feeling it might not have been. But how do you know to say so, so definitely?" John asked. John had hired Jeff Emerson to investigate the wreck of his coach.

Emerson opened the middle drawer of his desk and pulled out a piece of metal for John's examination.

"I had to do a lot of climbing and poking around in the wreckage of your coach, but I found this."

"What is it?"

"It's the tongue pin. Or at least half of it."

"The tongue pin broke in two?"

"Yes, but it had help," Emerson said. "Look at this."

Emerson held the tongue pin, broken end

toward him.

"As you can see, it was sawed three-quarters of the way through. The wonder is that it held long enough to even get you to the top of Eureka Peak. Someone wanted to kill you."

"Damn," John said.

"I'm curious, Mr. Gillespie. You said you had a feeling that it might not have been an accident. May I ask why? Are you aware of any particular enemies?"

"I'm not aware of anyone specifically," John said. "But, as you know, my name is often in the news, and I do business in a dozen states. It seems to me very unlikely that I wouldn't have an enemy somewhere. Probably more than one enemy, and someone might feel enough of a grievance toward me to want to do something like this."

"I understand that you are going to take a train trip to Chicago."

"Yes, Mary Beth and I will be leaving in a few weeks."

"You will be taking your daughter with you?"

"Yes."

"If you don't mind, I'm going to suggest that you hire someone to go with you to act as your bodyguard."

"Surely, it hasn't come to that? Don't you

think this was a one-time thing? I mean they failed, do you really believe that whoever it was would go so far as to follow me onto the train?"

"If he wanted you dead badly enough to do this," Emerson emphasized his comment by holding up the sheared pin, "then, yes. He might very well follow you to Chicago."

"But where would I find a bodyguard? Why, I wouldn't have the slightest idea as to where to start looking to find such a person."

"I have someone in mind who would be excellent for the job, and as it so happens, he'll be here in San Francisco before you leave for Chicago. His name is Matt Jensen."

"You have confidence in this Matt Jensen, do you?"

"Oh, yes, my confidence in him is absolute," Emerson said with a nod of his head. "Matt Jensen is one of the most capable men I have ever known, or even heard of."

"All right, get in touch with this Mr. Jensen. I'll hire him."

"I will do so. That is, if he will agree to take the job."

"If he will agree? What do you mean if he will agree? Just how particular can a bodyguard afford to be?"

"He isn't a bodyguard."

"But I thought you said . . ." John started to say, but his response was halted by Emerson's raised hand.

"I said I had someone in mind who would be excellent for the job, I didn't say he was a bodyguard. For all I know he has never been a bodyguard before, but if we can talk him into taking the job, I feel confident in saying that you and Miss Gillespie will make the trip safely."

"Do you think he will take the job?"

Emerson smiled. "I believe we can convince him to do so."

When John stepped into Drew's office a short time later, Drew looked up.

"Ah, John, good, there you are. Carmichael was in here a few minutes ago, and he wanted to know if we would like to take a position on a shipment of copper ingots to Hong Kong. I had to make a quick decision, so I told him we would. It's not too late to change our minds, though, if you think we shouldn't take it."

"No, I think that would be fine," John said. He took something from his pocket and lay it on the desk. "Take a look at this."

Drew picked up the piece of metal.

"I don't understand. What am I looking at?" he asked with a puzzled expression on his face.

"One-half of the tongue pin," John replied. "It was found in the wreckage of my coach."

"Ah," Drew said, shaking his head. "So, this broken tongue pin is the culprit for your accident."

"Yes, but it didn't break, and it wasn't an accident."

"What do you mean it didn't break? I'm holding no more than half of it in my hand."

"Look at the end of it."

Drew turned the pin around and examined the broken end. He gasped.

"I'll be damned, someone cut this," he said. He held the tongue pin out. "You're right, John, your accident wasn't an accident."

"Yes," John replied. "They cut it just enough for it to give way at exactly the right time."

"Why this is unbelievable! Well, no, it isn't unbelievable, I mean I'm holding the evidence right here in my hand. But it is awful. Who would do a thing like that? Do you have any idea who it might be?" Drew asked.

"No, but Drew, you and I both know it could be just about anyone. Some disgruntled employee in one of our operations, maybe even someone who was put out of business by one of our companies."

"Are you still going to Chicago?"

"Yes. I can't just quit my normal life, Drew," John said. "Anyway, I doubt that whoever it was will try again."

"And you still plan to take Mary Beth?"

"Oh, yes, I wouldn't dream of leaving her behind. Jeff Emerson is arranging for me to have a private security guard make the trip to Chicago."

"One of his men?"

"No, I don't think so. I gathered from our conversation that the man he intends to send with me is not in his employ. It is someone named Matt Jensen."

"Matt Jensen? Who is he? I don't believe I've ever heard of him," Drew said.

"I haven't ever heard of him either, but Jeff told me a little about him. Apparently he is very well known back in Colorado. He is what they call a gunman."

"A gunman? Good Lord, John, you don't mean to tell me that Emerson wants to hire an outlaw to protect you, do you?"

John laughed. "Maybe gunman isn't the right word. What I mean is, he is exceptionally good with a gun and had been tested many times. Most recently, I understand, he stopped a train robbery by killing three of the bandits and capturing the fourth. And he did this all by himself. As I said, he is very well known in Colorado, and, I was told, feared by all the outlaws there. Apparently he is sort of a paladin."

"He is a what?"

"He is a champion of the defenseless, against men of evil who would attack them."

Drew nodded. "Well, I think you should listen to this . . . champion." Drew set the word "champion" aside from the rest of the sentence. "I am sure that I would feel a lot more comfortable knowing that you and Mary Beth were being well looked after. But be careful, would you?" Drew smiled. "You and I have been friends for far too long now. If something happened to you, I don't know if I would be able to make a new friend."

John chuckled and put his hand on Drew's shoulder. "I can understand how you wouldn't be able to make a new friend. Hell, I can barely stand you myself," he teased. "So I guess I will just have to be careful."

"That's not true. I seem to remember having a friend once," Drew said, laughing in response to John's tease. "Oh, by the way, I have telegraphed ahead and have made reservations for a suite in the Palmer House. I think Mary Beth will enjoy being there, right in the middle of the city."

"Thank you, Drew. And I take back all

47

those bad things I've been saying about you."

"*All* the bad things?"

"Well, most of them, anyway. You still sound like a heifer with her foot hung up in a wire fence when you try to sing."

Drew laughed, then he wadded up a piece of paper and threw it at John. "Get out of here before I find something heavier to throw."

"If it was any heavier, you couldn't pick it up," John said, returning the banter.

The Solari Building

The man who represented the consortium was back in Lucas Conroy's office.

"I have just learned that John Gillespie may hire Matt Jensen to act as his body-guard."

"Who is Matt Jensen?"

"I have done some research on him. He is someone who is very well known, respected by lawmen, and feared by outlaws. And according to everything I have been able to find out about him, he is also a man of considerable skill with a gun."

"And you say Gillespie has hired him?"

"He hasn't been hired yet, but I think you should operate as if he will be hired."

"Is he here, in the city, somewhere?"

48

"He is supposed to come here, I think, but he isn't here yet. He travels around, but he spends most of his time in Colorado."

"All right, I will instruct my people to be aware of him," Conroy said.

"I think you should do more than that."

"What do you suggest?"

"What I am really saying, Mr. Conroy, is I think you should take whatever steps you need to get Jensen completely out of the picture. We need to get rid of this man before we can put the rest of our plan into action."

"You mean kill him," Conroy said.

"Yes."

"That's going to be rather hard to do. You say he travels around a lot and may be in Colorado. Even if he is in Colorado, and you don't even know that for sure, I wouldn't have any idea how to find him. In fact, I don't even know who he is. I had never heard of him until you mentioned his name."

"It doesn't matter that you have never heard of him, a lot of people have heard of him and would recognize him on sight. We can use that to our advantage."

"Use it how?"

"Do you have access to a printer that you can trust?"

"I have my own printing press."

"Print this," his visitor said, sliding a piece of paper across the desk.

Conroy examined the piece of paper, then looked back up at his visitor.

"You think this will do the trick, do you?"

"I don't know, but I think it is certainly worth a try. It's like I said, Conroy. Your job is going to be a lot easier if you can get Matt Jensen out of the way."

"All right, I'll give it a try," Conroy agreed.

Later that same afternoon Conroy pulled a sheet of paper from the Washington hand press and examined it. It contained the exact wording his client had suggested, enough to interest the bounty hunters, but nothing that would indicate that the law actually had anything to do with it. Now all he had to do was get the flyers distributed.

He had decided to distribute the flyers in Colorado and Nevada only so he wouldn't have to worry about dealing with the California authorities. He had two men who, for fifty dollars apiece, would post them for him. And since it was more than three weeks before Gillespie was scheduled to go to Chicago, there would be plenty of time for the wanted dodgers to be posted, and more important, time for the bounty hunters the

50

posters would attract to do their job.

He couldn't help but wonder, though, if something like this really would work. He liked to be directly in control of all the jobs he accepted, and putting a bounty on Matt Jensen's head seemed, to him, to disconnect him from the operation. But, it was his client, and not he, who came up with the idea, so he was willing to give it a try. After all, if it failed, it wouldn't be his fault.

CHAPTER FIVE

Central Colorado

Matt Jensen was on his way to San Francisco when he saw a paper nailed to a tree. He knew what it was, because this was the third one he had seen in the last two days, and as he had done with the other two, he pulled this one from the tree. Unlike the other two, which he had destroyed, he folded this one up and stuck it down into his pocket.

WANTED FOR MURDER
MATT JENSEN

500 DOLLAR REWARD PAID
for *Proof* of His Death

Contact: *Solari Building, San Francisco*

Whatever it was, he knew that it was not an official wanted poster; it didn't bear the mark of any law agency, and besides, he knew for a fact that there was no paper out on him.

On the other hand, he knew that from time to time outlaws, wanting to get him out of the way, had put out their own wanted posters on him. But always before those posters had been hand printed and sometimes barely legible.

This poster was professionally printed and that gave it the look of authority, so much so that bounty hunters might act upon it first and ask questions later.

"All right, Spirit," he said, slapping his legs against the side of his horse. "How would you like to spend the night in a nice, comfortable stable? I know I'd like to sleep in a bed tonight. What do you say we stop at the next town we see?"

Matt had ridden no more than another mile and was about to cross a swiftly running stream when the hair pricked on the back of his neck. Someone had the drop on him. Suddenly, and unexpectedly, Matt threw himself off his horse, doing so just as a rifle boomed and a bullet cracked through the air at exactly the place where his head had been but a second earlier.

"Sumbitch! How'd you do that?" he heard someone call out.

Matt had hit the water feetfirst, and now

he was running through the stream, splashing silver sheets of spray as he headed for the bank on the opposite side. He zigzagged as he ran, and a second rifle boomed, the bullet striking the water nearby.

As he dived into the tall grass on the bank of the stream, then wriggled on his belly toward the protection of a large rock about ten yards away, he realized that there were at least two ambushers after him.

He lay in the grass, but this was not a good place to be. He was concealed, but there was no cover, nothing to turn away a lucky shot.

"What do you men want?" he shouted. "I'm not carrying enough money to make shooting me worthwhile."

"You're Matt Jensen, ain't you?" one of the men said. "I know you are, 'cause I seen you oncet before."

"I'm Matt Jensen."

"That means you're worth five hunnert dollars."

"No, I'm not. That dodger isn't real. The law isn't after me, and whoever is just wants me dead. He has no intention of paying five hundred dollars to anyone."

"He'll pay." This was a different voice, confirming Matt's belief that there were at least two of them.

Matt found a fairly long branch and put his hat on the end of it. Then, thrusting it out as far away from him as he could, he lifted the hat up out of the grass. Two rifles boomed, and Matt used that opportunity to slither through the grass until he reached a boulder. Getting behind the large rock, he took a few deep breaths and relaxed. Now, he had cover, and he could take the time to search out his attackers.

"Do you see the sumbitch?" a voice called.

"No. I wonder if we kilt 'im. Why don't you go down there 'n take a look? I'll keep you covered."

"The hell with that! You go take a look, 'n I'll keep *you* covered."

"No need to look, I'm right here," Matt called. He had hoped his answering them would cause them to shoot at him so he could locate them by the wisps of gun smoke, but he got no response.

There was a long moment of silence from the two men, then Matt heard the sound of horses hooves, and when he raised up to have a look, he saw that the two men had mounted and were now galloping toward him. Both had pistols in hand and they were shooting at Matt as they approached. The bullets were close enough that he could hear them buzz and pop as they flew by him.

Matt returned fire, and he saw a puff of dust rising from the vest of one of the riders and a spray of blood from the head of the other. The one he hit in the chest pitched backward out of his saddle. One foot hung up in the stirrup and his horse continued to run, raising a plume of water as he was dragged through the stream. As the horse tried to climb the bank out of the water, the shooter's foot disconnected from the stirrup and he lay motionless, half in and half out of the water.

Matt ran over to him, surprised to see that he was still breathing, though he knew he wouldn't be alive much longer.

"How the hell did you know we were there?" the shooter asked.

"Just a feeling I had," Matt replied.

"That's some feelin'. I'm dyin', ain't I?"

"I expect you are."

"I'll be damned."

Those were his last words. He gasped two more times, then died.

Matt looked over his shoulder as he led the two horses across the swiftly running stream. Each of the horses was carrying a body, belly down across its back. He didn't really know which body belonged to which horse, and he didn't care; he had just tossed the two dead men on, first come, first served.

He had been underway for about half an hour when he realized that two more men were following him. They weren't exactly following him, it was more like they were keeping pace with him, riding parallel, and keeping a ridge between them. They were pretty good at what they were doing, but Matt was better.

Matt rode on for a couple of miles more, waiting to see if they would make their move, then decided not to wait any longer. He would make the first move.

The opportunity presented itself when the trail led in between two parallel rows of hills. Once into the defile he dropped the lines to the two horses, knowing that they would continue at the pace he had established and, because they were in a draw, they couldn't wander off. Then he galloped ahead about two hundred yards until he crossed over the ridge line, which put him ahead of the two men who were following him. Dismounting, he climbed onto a rocky ledge to wait for them to appear.

It didn't take long. He waited until they were right on him, then he suddenly stood up. He realized then that he hadn't chosen the best place to confront them, because he was staring right into the setting sun.

"Hello, boys, don't you think it's about time we met?"

"How'd you get here?" one of the riders shouted as he started for his gun.

"Don't do that!" Matt shouted, holding his empty hand out toward the two riders.

The rider pulled his hand back. "Who are you?" he asked. "And what are you doing here?"

"I expect you already know my name," Matt said. "That's why you're following me, isn't it?"

"You're Matt Jensen, ain't you?"

"I am."

"They's paper out on you, Jensen."

"It's worthless."

"The hell you say. It says you're worth five hunnert dollars."

"It's not a paper put out by the law," Matt said.

"Hell, Jensen, I don't care whether the law put it out or not. Five hunnert dollars is five hunnert dollars, no matter who pays it."

"If you try and collect it, you won't live long enough to ever see it."

"Did you kill them two bodies that's belly down on their horses?" the other rider asked.

"I did."

"What did you kill 'em for?"

"I killed them because they were trying to kill me."

"Do you know who they are?"

"No."

"One of 'em is Enos Walker, 'n the other one is Jake Breen. They was friends of our'n."

"Like you, they were trying to collect a phony reward. If you two are smart, you won't make the same mistake. I'd advise you men to just walk away now."

The talkative one laughed. "That's real funny, you talkin' about us walkin' away. Like I told you, you're worth five hunnert dollars. That means we ain't goin' to be walkin' away from this, 'n neither are you."

"Oh, I think I will," Matt said easily. He lifted his hand to block out the sun.

"Ha! Sun in your eyes, is it?" the talkative one asked.

"I'll admit, it is a little bothersome," Matt replied.

By then the sounds of the hoofbeats echoed through the draw. "That'll be the two horses with . . . who did you say they were? Walker and Breen? So if you boys will excuse me, I'll gather them up and be on my way."

Matt turned away from them and as he did so, he looked at the shadows of the two men, which were cast against the rocky wall in front of him. As he thought they might, both men made a grab for their guns.

Matt drew and whirled around, startling the two men with the quickness of his reaction. He fired two times in rapid succession. Only one of the two men managed to even get off a shot, and because it was a wild shot as he was going down, it hit the rock wall, then careened off down the canyon. Both men were knocked from their saddles and both were mortally wounded.

Matt now had four horses to lead, each horse bearing a body, but it took less than half an hour to reach a town that was identified at its edge by black letters on a small white sign.

GRIZZLY FLATS
Population 508

Just inside the town limits a dog started running alongside the four horses, yapping at the bodies that were draped across the horses' saddles.

"Look at that! Them's bodies, ain't they?" someone asked.

"Yeah them's bodies. What else would they be?"

"Who are they? Does anyone recognize 'em?"

"Whoever they are, they ain't nobody I've ever seen before."

"Who are them men you're a totin' there, mister?" someone shouted.

"Did you kill 'em?" another asked.

Matt neither responded to the shouted questions, nor glanced toward the questioners. Instead, with eyes straight ahead, he continued to ride on into town. He saw a water pump on one side of the street, and realizing that he was thirsty, he headed toward it, leading the four body-laden horses. There was a young boy standing at a pump, and though he had been filling a bucket with water, he stopped pumping the handle and just stood there, staring in morbid fascination at Matt and his gruesome load.

"Son, are you finished with the pump?" Matt asked.

The boy didn't give a verbal reply, but he did nod.

"Good. Would you mind filling that dipper with water and handing it to me, please?"

Matt flipped the boy a quarter, and when

61

boy saw the coin, the look of shock on his face was replaced with a big smile.

"Yes, sir!" he said, and lifting the dipper from its hook, worked the pump handle a couple of times, then handed it to Matt. Matt turned the dipper up and began drinking, allowing the water to cascade down each side of his mouth and wet his shirt.

"Would you point out the sheriff's office?" Matt asked as he took the dipper down.

The boy pointed to a building about halfway down the street. By now, several people, seeing or hearing about a strange man riding into town with four bodies draped over horses, had come outside to see for themselves. Then a man came out of the building that had been pointed out to him by the boy, and Matt saw a flash of reflective light from the badge on the man's shirt.

Matt dismounted, took a canteen down from his saddle and held it under the mouth of the pump, then began working the handle, filling it. The man who was approaching him looked to be in his late forties or early fifties. He was rawhide slender, with dark hair that was laced with ribbons of gray. He had dark eyes and a big curving moustache.

For just a moment the man stood there

without saying a word. The silence was broken only by the sound of the clacking pump handle and the gurgle of water. Finally, the man with the badge nodded toward the four bodies, then he spoke.

"These here bodies. This your doin'? Or did you find 'em on the trail?"

"It's my doing," Matt answered as he continued to work the pump handle.

"Are you telling me you killed all four of 'em?"

"All four of them."

"Do you know who they are?"

"I know the names of two of them," Matt said as he closed his canteen. "One of them is Walker, and one of them is Breen. Or, so I was told. I don't know which is which, and I don't know their first names."

"Were you also told that there was a reward on them?"

"Is there a reward on them?"

"You a bounty hunter?" the sheriff asked, without answering the question.

"No. But if there is a reward on them, I'll take it."

"Tell you the truth, mister, I don't much hold with bounty hunters. They'll go after someone that's got a dead or alive price on their head, and they most never bring 'em in alive. More often than not, they'll sneak

63

up on 'em and shoot 'em in the back."

"Check them out, Sheriff. You'll see that the holes are in front," Matt said, easily. He turned the canteen up and took a long drink, as the sheriff checked out the bodies.

CHAPTER SIX

The sheriff checked the bodies, then nodded. "You're tellin' the truth. All four was shot in front. You said Walker and Breen. You know who the other two men are?"

"I don't have the slightest idea."

"If you don't know who they are, why did you kill 'em?"

"For the same reason I killed Walker and Breen. They were trying to kill me."

"Well, this one," the sheriff said, pointing to the one who had been so talkative, "is Ross Martell. And this one is Pete Dooley. They've got a price on their heads, too. For someone who doesn't claim to be a bounty hunter, you've done pretty well for yourself today. There's two hundred and fifty dollars reward on each one of them. That's a thousand dollars you've made in one day, which is a whole year's salary for me. Why would they be trying to kill you?"

Matt smiled. "As it turns out, I have a

price on my head as well."

"What? Look here, mister. Who are you, anyway?"

"The name is Jensen. Matt Jensen."

The frown on the sheriff's face was replaced by a smile and he stuck out his hand.

"Matt Jensen! Well, I'll be damned! Why didn't you say so in the first place? I've heard of you, Jensen. Hell, I don't know many people who haven't heard of you. I'm Sheriff Ben Curtis. Listen, it will more than likely be a couple of days for the reward to be paid. I hope you'll stick around town until we can get the funds transferred."

"For that much money, I'll be glad to stay around," Matt said.

"Wait a minute. Did you say you had a price on your head?"

Matt reached into his pocket and took out the folded piece of paper. "I've seen a few of these posted around," he said, turning over the poster he had taken from the tree.

"This here says you're wanted for murder, but, even though it's printed up real nice, I don't see no lawman's name on it."

"That's because it's not official. I've seen such flyers before, though I've never seen any that were printed up as nice as this one," Matt said. "From time to time someone will take it on himself to get revenge if

I've killed a relative or a good friend. Not long ago I was working as a railroad detective, and I stopped a train holdup, and I had to kill three of the robbers in the attempt. I expect this is related to that."

"Yeah, I wouldn't be surprised. I don't see how somebody can just take it on hisself to put out wanted posters though."

"It says contact the Solari Building in San Francisco," Matt said. "I don't know what that is, but I doubt there are any of these posters in California."

"I reckon you're right. Let's get these stiffs delivered to Potashnick. He's the undertaker here. Then come on down to the Anderson's Saloon with me, and I'll buy you a beer," Sheriff Curtis said.

"I should be the one buying, Sheriff. I'm the one that's going to get the reward."

"Ah, don't worry about it," Sheriff Curtis said with a dismissive wave of his hand. "It won't be me buyin' you a beer anyhow. It'll be the town."

Half an hour later Matt was in the Anderson's Saloon, being introduced by Sheriff Curtis to the others, as if the sheriff and Matt were old, and longtime friends.

"You might remember them fellers that held up the stagecoach last month and kilt

67

the driver," the sheriff said. "Well, I'm happy to report that all four of 'em are down at the undertaker now, 'n Matt Jensen is the one who put 'em there."

The four men Matt shot were on display for a short time in front of the Potashnick Undertaking Parlor. They were wearing the same clothes they had been wearing when they were brought in, and because the town wouldn't pay any money for embalming, they weren't embalmed. The only accommodation made for them was a rough, pine box, and all four boxes were standing up. There were several people standing around staring at them, and there was a hat on a table in front of the four boxes and a sign that read:

Everyone deserves a Christian burial.
PLEASE DONATE.

Matt put twenty dollars into the hat.

"Do you think you can buy off your conscience with twenty dollars?" someone asked.

"My conscience isn't bothering me," Matt said.

"I understand you'll be getting blood money for killing these men."

"Yes, one thousand dollars, or so I've been told."

"Mister, you didn't even give these men a chance to come in and stand trial. Everyone deserves a fair trial."

"You've got that right. I couldn't agree with you more," Matt said.

"Then why didn't you bring them in so they could stand trial?"

"Why would I have done that? I didn't even know they were wanted."

"What? You mean you killed them for no reason?"

"Mister, do you know who you are talking to?" one of the others asked. "You're talking to Matt Jensen."

"I don't care who he is, everyone deserves a fair trial."

"As I said, I agree with you," Matt said, refusing to be agitated by the heckler. "Everyone deserves a fair trial."

"But you didn't give these four gentlemen a fair trial, did you?"

"Well, if you put it that way, I guess I didn't," Matt said.

One of the men in the group who had been listening to the exchange between Matt and the obnoxious heckler turned and walked away from the others. When he was some distance away, he pulled a piece of paper from his pocket and looked at it. It was exactly like the paper Matt had shown the sheriff the night before. It was a five-hundred-dollar reward.

He walked into the Muddy Bottom, which was somewhat rougher in character than the Anderson's Saloon. There, he joined two other men who were sitting at a table in back of the saloon. A bar girl was on the knee of one of the two men.

"What do you think, Jed? Ira thinks this girl has fallen in love with him," the man without the girl said by way of greeting.

"You're just jealous, Andy, 'cause she ain't sittin' on your lap."

"Leave," Jed said to the girl.

"What?"

"I said leave." Jed made a gesture with his thumb.

"Well, I . . ."

"You better go," Ira said, pushing the girl off his knee.

"Well, don't expect me to be back here soon," the girl said in a huff as she walked away.

"We don't have to worry 'bout Breen 'n his bunch gettin' to Jensen before we do," Jed said.

"Why not?"

"They're all four standin' up dead down at the undertakers, that's why not."

"All four of 'em? What happened to 'em?"

"Jensen kilt 'em."

"I don't believe that. I mean, he couldn't 'a possibly kilt all four of 'em. Could he?"

"Kilt 'em, 'n is goin' to collect a thousand-dollar reward for 'em."

"I'll be damned."

"Unless we collect it first," Jed said.

"How are we goin' to do that?"

"We'll accuse Jensen of stealin' them bodies from us and use that as our excuse to pick a fight with Jensen. If we provoke 'im, we can kill 'im in broad daylight, 'n there won't be no murder charges. Also, oncet he's dead, we'll push our claim to the sheriff that we was the ones that kilt Breen, Walker, Martel, and Dooley. 'N with Jensen dead, there won't be nobody to say otherwise. We can collect that thousand, and the five hunnert for killin' Jensen, 'n that'll give us five hunnert dollars apiece."

"You're forgettin' one thing," Andy said.

"What's that?"

"He kilt Breen 'n the others, 'n they was four of them. If he could kill four of them, what makes you think he couldn't kill three of us?"

"You know damn well he didn't kill all four of 'em at the same time. What he done, no doubt, was sneak up on 'em one at a time. There are three of us, 'n only one of him."

"Yeah, but what if he just gets one of us?" Ira asked. "I ain't all that willin' to be that one."

"Ira's got a point," Andy said. "What good does the money do if you're dead? And what if he does just get one of us? I don't want to be that one either."

"Yeah," Jed said, stroking a week's growth of whiskers on his chin. "Yeah, I see what you mean. I don't want to be the one that gets kilt neither. We're goin' to have to think on this for a bit."

"Well, I got an idea as to what we can do," Ira said. "What if the three of us was to go over to the sheriff right now, 'n tell him we was the ones that kilt Breen 'n the others, 'n we're the ones that should get the reward money?"

"What good would it do us to tell him that?" Andy asked. "Jensen is the one that brung 'em in."

"Well, who knows, there's three of us 'n only one of him. Even if the sheriff don't give us the money right off, he'd more 'n likely not give it to Jensen neither, till he figured out who was lyin'."

"He ain't goin' to believe us," Andy said. "I can tell you that right now."

"I don't know," Jed said. "Seems to me like it wouldn't hurt us to try."

"All right," Andy agreed. "We can at least try."

Sheriff Curtis was in his office, sitting back with his feet propped up on his desk. He was drinking coffee when the three men came in. He put his feet down and sat up straight.

"Yes, sir, what can I do for you boys?" he asked.

"You can give us the reward for them four men you got standin' up down at the undertaker's place," Ira said.

Sheriff Curtis frowned in confusion. "What? Why would I do that?"

"On account of 'cause we was the ones what actual caught them four," Jed said. "We had been trackin' 'em for a long time, 'n we finally caught up with 'em 'bout ten miles west of here. We got the drop on 'em, 'n we tied all four of 'em up to a tree."

"Then we left 'em there whilest we went huntin' 'n fishin' to get us somethin' to eat, seein' as we was all out of food by then," Andy said.

"But when we come back, they was all four gone," Ira said.

"We thought they'd all got away from us,"

73

Andy said. "We figured, maybe we didn't tie 'em up too good."

"So we come here, thinkin' to get some more grub 'n go out lookin' for 'em again," Jed said.

"Only, that's when we seen 'em standin' up down there at the undertaker's. Now, what we don't none of us understand is, how'd them four get theirselves kilt, 'n wind up here," Ira finished.

Sheriff Curtis took the final swallow of his coffee before he answered. "Now, boys, that's quite a story you've just told," he said.

"Yes, sir, I reckon it is," Andy said. "Onliest thing is, we still don't know how it is that they wound up dead, here."

"That is, unlessen they all four come into town 'n you kilt 'em," Jed said.

"I reckon we didn't think about that. If you kilt 'em, of course, there ain't no reward in it for us," Ira said.

"Did you kill 'em?" Andy asked.

"No, I didn't kill them," the sheriff replied. "They came into town belly down across their saddles."

"Who was it brought 'em in?" Ira asked. " 'Cause whoever it was, Sheriff, they just flat-out stole 'em from us. 'N more'n likely what they done is, they shot 'em down in cold blood, too, seein' as we already had

74

'em tied up 'n ever'thing. Are the men that done this still in town?"

"It wasn't men, it was a man. Just one."

"One man brung 'em in, all by hisself?" Andy asked.

"Andy, that wouldn't be too hard when you stop to think about it," Jed said. "Remember, we had 'em all tied up 'n ever'thing. It wouldn't 'a been that hard for one man to just come in there 'n shoot 'em dead. It would be that easy." Jed snapped his fingers.

"Let me see if I understand this," Sheriff Curtis said. "You are saying that you had these four men tied up, and Matt Jensen came into your camp while you were fishing, killed all four of them, then brought them in for the reward?"

"Yeah."

"I don't believe you."

"Why don't you believe us? It's our word against his'n, and that makes it three to one, don't it?" Ira asked.

"Just because three people are telling the same lie, that doesn't make it true," the sheriff said. "Anyway, it doesn't matter."

"What do you mean, it don't matter?" Jed asked.

"Possession is nine-tenths of the law," Sheriff Curtis said.

"What does that mean? I ain't never heard of such a thing," Andy said.

"That means that Matt Jensen brought the four bodies in, and it would take an overwhelming preponderance of evidence to deny him the reward. Word of mouth, even from three others, is not enough. I'm sorry, gentlemen, but the reward will be paid to Mr. Jensen."

CHAPTER SEVEN

Leaving the jail, the three men returned to the Muddy Bottom Saloon.

"We ain't goin' to get no reward money from the sheriff," Andy said. "So what do we do now?"

"I know how to get it," Ira said.

"How?" Jed asked.

"We just wait for Jensen to get the money, then we'll kill 'im, 'n take it from him."

"Uh, uh, we done talked about that, remember?" Jed said. "I don't plan on facin' that son of a bitch, even if it is three of us to his one. He's bound to get one of us, 'n there ain't none of the three of us that want to take a chance on bein' that one."

"Who said anything about facing him down? We'll wait until he leaves town, then we'll shoot him from ambush," Ira said.

"How are we going to collect the reward for killing him?" Jed asked. "You plannin' on takin' his body all the way to California to prove that we kilt 'im?"

"Yeah, come to think of it, how *would* we prove we kilt him?" Andy asked. "I mean, even if we had got to 'im before he kilt Breen 'n the others, there wouldn't 'a been no way we coulda proved that we kilt 'im."

"That don't matter none now, anyway," Ira replied. "I mean, once we kill him, we'll take the thousand dollars offen his dead body, 'n just forget about the reward money."

"Yeah," Jed said. "Yeah, let's do it."

Two days later Ira came into the Muddy Bottom Saloon and dropped a newspaper on the table in front of Jed and Andy.

"Look at this."

"Look at what? You know I don't read all that good," Andy said.

"This here newspaper says that Matt Jensen has done been paid the thousand dollars reward."

"All right," Jed said. "So it's just there for the takin' now."

"Yeah," Ira replied with a smile.

"So, how do we do it?"

"He told the newspaper that he was on his way to San Francisco. He said he wanted to have a look around at the big city," Ira said.

78

"When's he goin'?"

"He's still here, 'cause I seen 'im over at Mama Belle's Café, but I reckon he'll be leavin' pretty soon. If he's actual' goin' to go to San Francisco, there's only one road he can take out of town. And when he takes it, we'll be a-waitin' on 'im."

Two hours later, Ira was lying on top of a flat rock, looking back along the trail over which he, Andy, and Jed had just come. He saw the lone rider half a mile behind them.

"Is Jensen still a-comin'?" Jed asked.

"Yeah," Ira growled. He climbed back down from the rock and ran his hand across the stubble on his unshaven cheek. "He's still there."

"I'm gettin' tired of waitin' on 'im. Let's hurry up 'n kill the sumbitch and get it over with," Jed said.

"Come on, I know a perfect spot," Ira said.

"Do you think he knows we're here?" Andy asked.

"No, I don't think he suspects a thing," Ira answered. "I mean, we ain't showed ourselves even once. There ain't no way he could know."

Matt knew that there was someone ahead of him, and he knew they were watching for him. There had been little hints that most people wouldn't have noticed, but Matt had learned from his mentor, Smoke Jensen, who had learned from his mentor, Preacher, and Matt had picked up a lot of trail wisdom on his own. He stopped at a creek and dismounted to let Spirit get a drink while he studied the lay of the land.

Horse droppings told him that there were three men ahead of him, and he saw footsteps leading over to an elevated flat rock that overlooked the back trail. One man had climbed up there for a look, while the other two waited.

But why? What was their interest in him? Were they actually going to try to collect on the reward that had been put out on him?

Just ahead, the trail led into a canyon, and Matt knew that if anyone was planning an ambush, that would be where they would do it. When he reached the canyon, he pulled his long gun out of the saddle holster, then dismounted and started walking, leading his horse. The horse's hooves fell sharply on the stone floor and echoed loudly back from the canyon walls. The canyon made a forty-five-degree turn to the left just in front of him, so he stopped.

"All right Spirit, run, and keep your head down," he said, speaking quietly. He slapped his horse on the rump and sent it on through.

Matt's suspicion that someone was waiting to ambush him was validated when the canyon began echoing with the sound of gunfire. The bullets of the ambushers whizzed harmlessly over Spirit's empty saddle, raising sparks as they hit the rocky ground, then ricocheted away, echoing and reechoing in a cacophony of whines and shrieks

From his position just around the corner from the turn, Matt saw the gun smoke of the three ambushers rising from behind a rock. He couldn't see them, but he knew they were there.

The firing stopped, and after a few seconds of dying echoes, the canyon grew silent.

"Where the hell is he?" one of the ambushers asked, and though he may have thought that he was speaking quietly, the concave canyon walls amplified the voice, and Matt could hear the last two words repeated in echo down through the canyon . . . *is he, is he, is he?*

Matt waited, knowing that eventually his ambushers would get impatient, and at least one of them would raise his head for a better look. Bracing himself against the rock wall, he aimed just over the rock where he expected the assailant to appear.

He didn't have to wait long. Less than thirty seconds later, someone popped up to peruse the canyon. Matt's rifle boomed loudly, and he saw a little cloud of blood spray from the man's head. The thunder of the detonating cartridge picked up resonance through the canyon, doubling and redoubling in intensity.

"Son of a bitch! He kilt Andy!" a frightened voice called.

"Where did that shot come from?" another voice asked.

"How the hell do I know? The sound was comin' from everywhere!"

"I'm down here, boys," Matt called. He stepped out into the open, holding the rifle in his left hand.

"Shoot 'im 'afore he can get that rifle up!" one of the two men shouted, and both of them stood up with pistols in hand.

Matt drew his own pistol and fired twice, doing so quickly and accurately. Both of his adversaries went down, one falling back and the other tumbling over the rock they had been using for cover, and slid to the bottom of the canyon.

Matt didn't know whether there was a reward on the three men or not, and he didn't care. Even if there was a reward on the three men, he doubted that it would be enough to make it worth his while. He certainly hadn't set out to kill them, and he didn't intend to take any more time with them.

Retrieving Spirit, he continued his trip to San Francisco. He didn't intend to ride all the way; he had promised Spirit he wouldn't ride him the whole way, and now with the one thousand dollars, he could afford to catch the train a lot earlier than he had planned. There was no railroad at Grizzly Flats, but he would be in Cañon City before nightfall and in San Francisco within three days.

Behind him, the buzzards began circling, wary of any wolves that might beat them to their unexpected feast.

San Francisco
"Mr. Conroy, I wonder if we might have been ill-served by listening to those who said that you could handle our situation."

"You have to give me a little time," Conroy replied to the consortium representative. "You are asking me to deal with one of the wealthiest men in America, if not in the world. There are as many people who would recognize the name John Gillespie as there

83

are who would recognize the name Grover Cleveland. This is no easy job, and I doubt, seriously, that you would be able to find anyone else in San Francisco, or anyone else in the country, for that matter, who would be as uniquely qualified to carry out this task as I am."

"So you say, but you failed on your first attempt to kill Gillespie and his daughter, and you have failed to eliminate Matt Jensen."

"Well, we don't know about Jensen yet," Conroy said. "I did distribute the wanted posters. We'll have to wait to see if they bear fruit."

"I can tell you already that they did not," the representative said. "Jensen is already in the city. He has boarded his horse at the Heckemeyer Stables, and he has taken a room at the Royal Hotel."

"May I remind you, sir, that you are the one who suggested putting out the wanted posters?" Conroy said.

"So I did. And I will take full responsibility for the failure of that plan. However, I still think it is going to be necessary for you to eliminate Jensen, if you are to succeed in your assignment."

"As I understand it, the principal concern of you and the consortium is that neither

Gillespie, nor his daughter, come back from Chicago alive. That is what you have hired me for, isn't it?" Conroy asked.

"It is."

"Then, please. Allow me to do my job."

"We will give you more time, Mr. Conroy, but I hope you realize that our patience isn't without limit."

After his visitor left, Conroy thought about the job he had undertaken. The first attempt had failed. Lucas Conroy had hired someone to cut halfway through the tongue pin, hoping it would cause an accident that would result in the death of John Gillespie and his daughter, Mary Beth. He had been surprised to learn that the consortium wanted both of them dead, but he had no qualms about killing the daughter, as long as his clients were willing to pay him enough. And that they were.

Conroy was playing a very high-stakes game, but that was what he did. Conroy had a very successful business . . . his business being to "arrange" things for wealthy clients. The kinds of things he arranged, however, could not be advertised. In the past two years, he had "arranged" for an oceangoing ship to be sunk, for a hotel to be burned down, and for a mine to be disabled by a cave-in.

Conroy was very successful in his chosen occupation. He owned a house on Knob Hill and a fine coach, driven by a liveried driver. He dined in the finest restaurants and drank the finest whiskey, wine, and champagne. He seldom traveled, because he had neither need nor desire to leave San Francisco. On those few occasions when he did travel, though, he always traveled first-class, and he stayed only at the best hotels.

Everyone was aware that Conroy was a very wealthy man, but only a very few knew the source of his wealth.

"He owns a gold mine," some said of him.

"No, a shipping line."

"I heard he owns a bank somewhere."

Conroy represented only the very wealthy, and that was necessary because he charged a great deal of money for his services. Never, however, had he charged anyone as much as he was charging for this current job. For this job he was being paid fifty thousand dollars.

The money had been placed in an escrow account, though ten thousand of it had been released to him to be used for expenses. When the job was completed, Conroy would be able to keep that part of the fifty thousand dollars that he had not used in bringing the job to fruition.

He had been willing to pay five hundred dollars to get Matt Jensen out of the way, but had thought, from the beginning, that merely putting out wanted posters was an inefficient way of doing the job. He wondered how important it was to actually get rid of Matt Jensen.

There was a light knock on his door.

"Yes?" he called.

The door opened, and Maurice McGill, a lawyer who occupied the same building, stuck his head in.

"Lucas?" he called.

"Yes, Maurice, come in, come in."

McGill believed that Conroy was an exceptionally successful freelance stockbroker.

"Lucas, there is a man downstairs who presented me with this and wanted to know what I knew about it," McGill said. He held out one of the wanted posters that Conroy had printed and circulated in his attempt to get rid of Matt Jensen.

Conroy looked at it, waiting for McGill to make the next comment.

"Do you know anything about it?" McGill asked.

Conroy shook his head. "No, you being a

lawyer, it seems like this would be more in your bailiwick than mine. You say a man gave it to you?"

"Yes."

"Is he still here?"

"Yes, he's just outside your office."

"Well, bring him in. Let's see if we can get to the bottom of this," Conroy said.

Matt was waiting just outside the office door, but he was able to overhear the conversation between the two men, including the part where Lucas Conroy asked McGill to bring him in. Matt knew Conroy's name, only because of the name on the door.

LUCAS CONROY
Business Broker

"Mr. Wood, you can come in now," McGill said.

Not wanting to identify himself as the name on the wanted poster, Matt had taken the name of one of Smoke Jensen's top hands, Cal Wood.

"Mr. Wood, this is Lucas Conroy," McGill said when Matt stepped into the office. "I have spoken to him about your flyer, and he says he knows nothing about this document either."

"How did you come by this poster, Mr. Wood?" Conroy asked.

"I found it nailed to a tree in Colorado," Matt replied.

"I see. And you are here to claim the reward, are you?"

"Suppose I am. Who would I see for the reward?"

"Did you kill this man, Jensen?"

"I don't see as I need to go any further into it," Matt said. "The point is, that dodger," he pointed to the flyer Conroy was holding, "says to come here for the reward. Well, I'm here, and I have spoken with all the other occupants of this building — Dr. Urban, the folks at Golden Gate Realty, Mrs. Pinchon of the dance academy, and Mr. McGill — but I can't find anyone who knows anything about it. You are my last hope."

Conroy shook his head. "I'm afraid I don't know anything about it."

"Mr. Wood, I believe you have been made the victim of a hoax," McGill said. "If you had examined the poster closely, you would have noticed that there is no authorizing official. I've been a lawyer for some time now, and in the course of my legal practice I have

89

been exposed to numerous reward posters. But never have I seen one issued without some validating authority."

"Do you know what I think?" Conroy asked.

"What's that?" Matt replied.

"I think someone just wanted this . . ." he made a point of looking at the name on the poster, "Matt Jensen dead, and he hoped that by printing up an official-looking dodger, someone would do the job for him. I don't believe that whoever did it had any intention of actually paying the reward. That's why he put the name of this building on the poster but omitted the name of a person to contact."

Conroy handed the flyer back to Matt.

"I'm sorry. If you have come to collect your reward, I'm afraid there is no money here for you."

"Thanks," Matt said, taking the poster back.

"I'll walk you back downstairs," McGill said.

Conroy waited until he heard their footsteps going down the stairs before he closed the door and returned to his desk. He let out a sigh of relief. If he had not learned but half an hour earlier that Matt Jensen was alive and in town, he would have questioned Cal Wood more intensely to determine whether or not Matt Jensen actually was dead. And had he done so, he would have fallen right into the trap that Matt Jensen was setting for him. And yes, Conroy was thoroughly convinced that the man who had just been here was Matt Jensen, here to find out what he could about the posters.

Chapter Eight

The Gillespie Building
Jake Fowler, John's private secretary, stepped into the office.

"Mr. Gillespie, Mr. Emerson is here to see you, sir."

"Emerson? Yes, show him right in, Jake," John said.

A moment later the private detective was extending his hand in greeting.

"Jeff," John greeted. "It's good to see you."

"I've been thinking about your trip to Chicago," Emerson replied.

"I hope you're not going to try and talk me out of it, because I am going. I don't know what this was all about. As I said earlier, it could have been anyone from a disgruntled employee to someone who is holding a grudge. But whoever it is, I refuse to change my life around out of fear. I'm going to Chicago, and I'm taking my daughter with me."

Emerson chuckled. "Relax, John, I'm not going to try and talk you out of going to Chicago. But you remember that I told you I wanted to send a bodyguard with you?"

"Yes, I remember. Someone named Jenkins, was it?"

"Jensen. Matt Jensen. He is someone with whom I have recently worked, and I was very impressed with him. I want you to hire him."

"Well, sure, if you think I should. You have faith in this man, do you?"

"I have absolute faith in him," Emerson replied. "In fact, short of having a company of soldiers guarding you, I can't think of anyone in the country who could do a better job. He is one of the best, if not the best, but it's going to cost you."

"He comes high, does he? Well, I expect someone that good would be charging a lot for his services. How much is he asking?"

"He isn't asking anything, because I haven't approached him yet. I'm the one who is saying it's going to cost you a pretty penny."

"All right, I'll go along with that. Just how do I reach this one-man army?"

"It just so happens that Mr. Jensen is in San Francisco right now, and he is staying in one of your hotels."

"All right," John said. "Approach Mr. Jensen on my behalf, and feel free to offer him whatever you think is appropriate."

"Five thousand dollars," Emerson said.

"Five thousand dollars?" John let out a low whistle. "My Lord, man, that is an enormous amount of money!"

"How much is your life and the life of your daughter worth?"

John nodded. "You have a point."

"Would you like to meet with him?"

"Yes, I think I would."

"Very well, I'll set it up for you."

"I'll walk you to the front door," John said.

The two men walked through the building with John exchanging pleasantries with the employees he encountered. Then, as John returned to his office, he was met by Drew Jessup.

"Was that Jeff Emerson?" Jessup asked.

"Yes, remember that I told you he was going to hire someone to make the trip to Chicago with Mary Beth and me?"

"Yes. I believe you said his name was Matt Jensen."

"My, no wonder you are so efficient. Yes, that is his name. You have a great memory!"

San Francisco, Royal Hotel
With 755 guest rooms, the Royal was the

largest hotel in the western United States. It was also the tallest building in San Francisco, with a skylighted open center that featured a grand court overlooked by seven stories of white-columned balconies.

Matt wasn't used to staying in such elegant accommodations. More often than not his accommodations consisted of a blanket for his bed, a saddle for a pillow, a rabbit or a can of beans for his supper, and the serenade of wind through the tree limbs, accompanied by owls and coyotes. But why not indulge himself? He had a thousand dollars in his pocket, and how often did he get to a city like San Francisco?

At the moment, Matt was lying on the bed in his room, with his hands laced behind his head, thinking about his visit this morning to the Solari Building.

Maybe the business broker was right. Maybe whoever published the poster just added the name of the Solari Building to give the illusion of it being an official document. Whatever it was, he wasn't going to worry about it. Besides, it was nearly lunchtime, and he was getting hungry. Setting up, he pulled on his boots, then went downstairs to the restaurant.

As Matt was walking through the lobby, he was approached by a uniformed bellboy.

"Mr. Jensen?"

"Yes?"

The young bellboy handed Matt an envelope. "I was told to give you this, sir."

"Thank you," Matt said. He gave the boy a quarter.

"Thank you, sir," the boy said, but when he didn't leave, Matt looked up at him.

"The gentleman who gave me this envelope asked me to stay for a moment. If you accept his invitation, I am to show you where he is."

"All right," Matt said, opening the envelope.

Mr. Jensen,

You may recall that when last we spoke, you suggested that you might be amenable to occasional employment. A situation has just presented itself. If you are interested in learning more about this, please allow the young man who delivered this note to bring you to my table.

Jeff Emerson.

"All right," Matt said. "Take me to him."

"This way, sir."

Matt followed the boy into the restaurant, and as they started toward the back corner, a well-dressed man, sitting alone at a table, stood.

"That's the gentleman, sir," the bellboy said.

"Yes, thank you, I recognize him," Matt said.

"Mr. Jensen, it's good to see you again," Emerson said, extending his hand when Matt reached the table. "Won't you allow me to buy your dinner?"

"I never turn down a free meal," Matt replied with a smile.

"Are you enjoying your visit to San Francisco?"

"Yes, I am."

"Good."

The two engaged in friendly but meaningless conversation until after they ordered. When the waiter left, Emerson looked directly at Matt.

"Mr. Jensen, have you ever heard of a man named John Gillespie?"

"Yes. Actually, my barber and I discussed him a few days back."

Emerson laughed. "That's no surprise, he is well known. He owns the Consolidated Rail Car Company, the Far West Gold Mine, McKnight-Keaton, that's a wholesale company in Wyoming, I think, Nebraska Livestock, the Assumption Coal Mining

Company, American Meat Packers of Chicago, a ranch in Texas, and several hotels, including, I might add, the very one we are sitting in."

"I believe I read that he also recently bought Northwest Financials," Matt said.

"Yes, as a matter of fact, he did."

"Does the job you mentioned have something to do with Gillespie?"

"It does," Emerson replied. "A couple of weeks ago, after he and his daughter left the theater, someone manufactured an accident that could well have killed them. I think that Mr. Gillespie could handle it if he had been the sole target, but the assassination attempt also included his daughter."

"I can see how he would find that troubling," Matt said.

"In a few more days Mr. Gillespie and his daughter, Mary Beth, will be traveling to Chicago. I told him that you and I had worked together, and I am convinced that you will be able to keep him and his daughter safe. If you accept the job, it would require that you go to Chicago with them. Would that be a problem for you? Going to Chicago, I mean."

"The only problem that concerns me would be, what would I do with Spirit?"

"Spirit?"

"My horse."

"Where is he now?"

"He's at Heckemeyer's Stables."

Emerson nodded. "I know, Matt, that Heckemeyer runs an excellent stable. I will see to it that Spirit is very well taken care of in your absence. He'll be fed well and exercised daily. And that will be part of the arrangement between you and John Gillespie."

"That sounds very generous."

"Oh, you don't know how generous Mr. Gillespie can be," Emerson said with a broad smile. "He has authorized me to offer you five thousand dollars if you will accept the job."

"Five thousand dollars? That's a lot of money," Matt said.

"Yes, it is for you, for me, and for almost everyone in America. But for a few men, men like Cornelius Vanderbilt, Jay Gould, Andrew Carnegie, and John Bartmess Gillespie, five thousand dollars is but a drop in the bucket. And it is something he would gladly pay for someone to protect him and his daughter.

"If you will agree, I'll set up a meeting for you. In the meantime, whether you decide to accept his offer or not, your stay here at the hotel is gratis as well as any meal you may eat in the hotel restaurant.

"Will you agree to meet him?"

"Of course," Matt said. "It wouldn't be courteous to not at least meet with him."

"His corporate office is on the corner of Fremont and Market. May I tell him that you will meet him this afternoon?"

"Yes," Matt said. "I'll be glad to meet with him."

"I'll set the appointment up for two o'clock. It's very easy to get there from here. Just take the car to Fremont."

"Excuse me, sir, have you the time?" Matt asked a fellow passenger on the Market Street cable car.

"I do indeed, sir. It is lacking five minutes of two o'clock."

"Thank you," Matt said. He stepped off the car at Fremont, then looked at the large building in front of him. The sign over the entrance, worked in gilded letters, read: *Gillespie Enterprises.*

When Matt stepped through the front door, a uniformed security guard approached him.

"I'm sorry, sir, but you can't wear a gun in this building."

"No, that's all right, Clyde, I'll take care of this gentleman," a man said as he approached the front door.

"Very good, Mr. Fowler," the security guard replied.

"You would be Matt Jensen?" the man asked.

"Yes."

"Mr. Jensen, I'm Jake Fowler, Mr. Gillespie's personal secretary. If you would come with me, sir."

Matt followed the rather plump, bald-headed man up a set of marble stairs. They were met on the second floor by someone whose closely cropped black moustache extended no further than the smile of his thin lips. He had dark hair, graying at the temples.

"I'll take it from here, Jake."

"Yes, sir," Jake said, obsequiously. He left silently.

"Mr. Gillespie?" Matt asked.

"No, I'm Drew Jessup, chairman of the board and chief executive for Gillespie Enterprises. John will be with you in a few minutes. Would you like to come to my office?"

Matt walked across the hall into Jessup's office. This was a large room with a huge desk as well as leather chairs and a leather sofa. The walls were filled with original art.

"Mr. Jensen, have you ever acted as a

bodyguard for anyone before?" Jessup asked.

"No, I haven't."

"What do you know about Mr. Gillespie?"

"I know only that he is a very wealthy man who owns several businesses."

"And yet, you have agreed to take five thousand dollars to protect him," Jessup said.

"No, I haven't agreed to protect him."

"You haven't agreed? Then, may I ask why you are here?"

"I have agreed only to meet with him," Matt replied.

"Assuming you do agree, do you feel you are capable of providing him and his daughter with the protection they would need?"

"I wouldn't accept the job if I didn't feel that," Matt replied.

The challenging expression on Jessup's face was replaced by a broad smile.

"Good, good. You will forgive me, please, Mr. Jensen, if my questioning sounded rather harsh to you. But John Gillespie is the best friend I have in the world, and I couldn't think more of Mary Beth if she were my daughter. I hope you can understand that I take very seriously any threat to their safety."

"I do understand," Matt replied.

"Good, good, I'm glad that you do. Well,

come with me, and I will introduce you."

Jessup led Matt down a long hall to another office. Because this office was smaller than Jessup's, Matt thought it might belong to someone else, perhaps Jake Fowler, but it wasn't Fowler who met him. The man who extended his hand was taller than Jessup, nearly as tall as Matt.

"I'm John Gillespie," he said. "Thank you for coming, Mr. Jensen."

"That is the least I could do, Mr. Gillespie. After all, you are paying for the hotel and my meals."

"Good." John glanced toward the wall clock. "I've invited my daughter here to meet you as well. She'll be going to Chicago, too, so I think it only right that she be a part of this interview process. That won't be a problem, will it?"

Matt smiled. "I've never been one to turn away from the opportunity to meet a young lady."

"Good. Drew, there's no need for you to stay," John said. "Unless of course, you want to," he added quickly. He laughed. "I don't want you to think I'm trying to get rid of you."

"No such thought, John," Drew said with an easy smile. "I have to go over the incorporation papers for Northwestern Financial anyway. Mr. Jensen, it was good to meet you, and if you accept the position, I'm sure we will meet again."

"Hello, Papa. Hello, Uncle Drew."

"Ah, here she is," John said turning toward the young woman who had just stepped into the office. She was a very attractive girl, tall and trim, with delicate facial features and rich, glowing, auburn hair.

"Hello, Mary Beth. John, I will leave you to do your business," Drew said as he started toward the door left open by Mary Beth's entrance.

CHAPTER NINE

"Mary Beth, my dear, this is Matt Jensen."

Mary Beth came toward him with her hand extended. "It's very nice to meet you, Mr. Jensen," she said.

"The pleasure is all mine," Matt replied, recalling some of the pointers in polite discourse he had learned over the years.

"Are you the man who is going to protect us on our way to Chicago?"

"Well, I'm certainly willing to discuss it," Matt replied.

"I don't know what Emerson told you of my . . . that is, *our* experience," John said, nodding toward Mary Beth. "But a little while back as we were returning home one evening the team suddenly separated from the coach, dragging our driver along the road."

"Poor Mr. Chan, he broke his collarbone and his leg, and he is still not able to be up and around," Mary Beth added.

"The coach, without a team or a driver, lurched over the drop-off and crashed to the ground, several hundred feet below," John continued. "Mary Beth and I barely escaped by jumping out."

"I gather that you don't think it was an accident?"

"I thought at first that it might have been, but, just to be on the safe side, I hired Jeff Emerson to look into the wreck for me. This is what he found."

John held out the tongue pin.

Matt took it, then ran his thumb over the smooth edge. He handed it back to John.

"This convinced me that it was no accident," John said.

"I think your analysis is correct. Do you have any idea who might have done something like this?" Matt asked.

"No, I don't. The truth is, Mr. Jensen, I have business operations all over the country, and it could be just about anyone. It has been my practice, when I buy out a business, to keep the original owner on as manager whenever I can and whenever they agree to accept my offer. It is entirely possible that there might be some residual resentment among some of them."

"Am I to understand that this attempt also included Miss Gillespie?" Matt asked.

106

"Yes, as I said, we both managed to leap from the coach just in the nick of time."

"Well, may I ask, and please don't take offense to this question, but is there any reason to suspect that your daughter might have been the target?" He looked at Mary Beth. "Let me explain what I mean. Would there be any men in your life, say from a broken relationship, who might be upset enough to try something like that?"

To Matt's surprise, Mary Beth laughed out loud. "Why, I take no offense at all, Mr. Jensen. I'm flattered that you would think I could affect someone to that degree. But the answer is no, I've had no relationships that were that intense."

They talked for about another half hour, and Matt enjoyed the conversation. John was a very engaging man, full of wit and humor, and Mary Beth was an exceptionally attractive woman, and she, like her father, was a most entertaining conversationalist.

"Well, Mr. Jensen, it's time to make a decision. Would you be willing to accompany us to Chicago?"

"Yes. I would be glad to. When do we leave?"

"We leave in five more days. At that time, my private car will be attached to the

107

Western Flyer."

The moment Lucas Conroy learned that Matt Jensen had accepted the job and would be acting as bodyguard for Gillespie and his daughter, he began researching him. He learned that Matt Jensen was a sometimes railroad detective who had also been a deputy U.S. Marshal, and on more than one occasion had been a deputy sheriff. He had tamed outlaw towns and faced down fast guns. The consortium that wanted Gillespie killed, was right to be concerned about Matt Jensen. His presence would make killing the Gillespies difficult, so the obvious thing to do would be to get him out of the way first.

Conroy had taken the consortium's suggestion of printing up wanted posters and spreading them throughout Colorado and Nevada, hoping that someone would kill Jensen before he reached California, but from the moment this tactic was first suggested to him, he had no confidence that it would work. And as it turned out, he was right. Jensen was now in San Francisco, and Conroy was going to have to try another tactic, one that was more direct.

Conroy had no full-time employees, but he did have men that he called on from time to time. Normally, he didn't expose these men to actual jobs, because they were too valuable to him. By keeping them from being directly involved, he protected them, not only from the law, but from any repercussions from the job itself.

One such man was Michael Beebe, and while Matt was meeting with John and Mary Beth, Beebe was in Conroy's office getting directions.

"I need you to find a couple of men to do a job for me," Conroy said.

"What kind of job?" Beebe asked. "The reason I ask is, I need to know what kind of men you want me to go looking for."

"I want someone killed," Conroy replied frankly. He was in his own office, and he was speaking with someone who had done similar recruitment jobs for him in the past. There was no need for him to be circumspect about what he wanted.

"But, don't tell them what I want. I'll tell them who I want killed and where they can find him."

"All right," Beebe agreed.

Because John had some business to complete, he asked Mary Beth to take Matt to the depot to show him the private car.

"Thank you, Miss Gillespie," Matt said.

"Oh, for heaven's sake, if we are going to spend the next two weeks together, it's going to get rather tiresome saying Miss Gillespie and Mr. Jensen, isn't it, Matt?"

Matt smiled. "It may, at that. Very well, Mary Beth it is."

"Would you like to have a drink with me, Matt? I know a very nice place that caters to ladies and gentlemen."

"Why, I would be honored to have a drink with you, Miss Gil . . . I mean, Mary Beth."

Mary Beth asked a lot of questions over their drink, some of them a little more personal than Matt liked to share with people he had just met. He didn't refuse to answer any of them, though; he understood that she had every right to know as much about him as she could. After all, she was about to put her life in his hands."

"Oh, my, we've spent some time here," Mary Beth said. "Papa wanted me to show you the private car we'll be riding in."

For the past few days those people who, in their daily commerce, happened to pass the Union Pacific Depot had their curiosity aroused. What caught their attention was the private railcar sitting on a sidetrack. When they had passed by one evening, the track was bare. When they passed by the next morning the sidetrack was engaged, the private car having mysteriously appeared during the middle of the night.

"There it is," Mary Beth said when they arrived.

The outside of the car was unremarkable, except for the fact that it was longer, by a third, than the average car and had a bright sheen from the thick coat of varnish.

"Shall we have a look inside?"

If the outside of the car was relatively unremarkable, the inside was anything but. The first thing Matt noticed when he stepped aboard was the car's opulence . . . the rich wood paneling, the leather trim, the carpeting, and the furnishings. It was as if the car was a cross between an elegant men's lounge and the finest hotel suite.

"Why don't I turn up the light so you can get a better look?" Mary Beth suggested.

She twisted a valve to bring instant illumination from the gaslight fixtures. Looking around the car, Matt saw a long, narrow strip of paper curling down from a bell jar that covered some sort of mechanical contrivance.

"What is that?" he asked.

"That is a teleprinter," Mary Beth replied.

"I've never heard of such a thing. How does it work?"

"It's like a telegraph, but you don't have to know the Morse code in order to operate it. Papa has a lease arrangement with Western Union. That allows him to tap directly into their wires, no matter where he is. This way he can send and receive messages without having to rely upon a third party. And, because the machine works by sending electric pulses to the proper letter-key, the message will be automatically imprinted upon the paper as soon as it begins coming in."

Matt heard a clacking sound, and a long, narrow strip of paper began curling down from the bell jar that covered the teleprinter machine.

Mary Beth went over to it, waited until the machine grew quiet, then clipped off the paper. She smiled as she read it.

"Papa wants us to meet him at the Royal Hotel dining room for supper."

"What did you think of the car?" John asked over their meal that evening.

"I've never seen anything like it before," Matt said.

"It has three sleeping compartments, so of course you will occupy one of them."

"Will there be Pullman cars on the train?"

"Yes, of course, there will be."

112

"I might be able to do a better job if I take a berth on the train and sort of not let everyone know what I'm doing."

"All right. I'll make certain that you have a berth at the end of the car that is closest to my car."

"I'm really beginning to get excited about the trip to Chicago," Mary Beth said. "I'm glad you are going with us, Matt, but I don't really expect anything to happen."

"Matt, is it?" John asked, lifting his eyebrows.

Mary Beth laughed. "Papa, you're old and don't understand. Young people don't like to call each other mister and miss. And if Matt is going to be with us all this time, we may as well be friends, don't you think?"

"And that's all right with you, Mr. Jensen?"

"I feel no need to be called mister."

John smiled. "Well, if that is the way it's going to be, you may as well call me John. Tell me, Matt, is your room at the hotel satisfactory? Because if it isn't, we can go see the clerk and find one that is to your liking."

"The room is perfect," Matt replied.

"Ahh, here is our dinner," John said as two waiters approached, carrying the plates.

113

Shorty McNair and Will Shardeen had broken out of prison in Salem, Oregon, three months ago, doing so by killing a guard who was escorting them to the dispensary. They had come to California to get away from the manhunt in Oregon, and in that time had supported themselves by petty theft and by doing jobs for various people. Most of the jobs they did were the kind that the average person wouldn't undertake, and in many cases, what they were paid to do would have been illegal.

At the moment Michael Beebe was sitting across the table from them in the Four Aces. Beebe knew that McNair and Shardeen were just the kind of men he was looking for to do the job that Conroy wanted. He knew that they had been in prison for murder, which meant they wouldn't balk at doing it again. He also knew that they were escaped prisoners and wanted men and that gave him an advantage when he approached them with the offer.

"How much?" McNair asked.

"I'm not authorized to negotiate the amount," Beebe said. "You'll have to discuss that with the gentleman who is hiring you."

"Gentleman? Ha!" Shardeen said. "I can't

114

actually see no *gentleman* hirin' us for anything."

"I can tell you this," Beebe said. "I will give each of you twenty dollars apiece just to meet with him. And whether you decide to accept his offer or not, the twenty dollars is yours to keep."

McNair and Shardeen looked at each other and shared a broad smile.

"You'll give us twenty dollars just to meet with him?" McNair asked.

"Yes."

McNair stuck his hand across the table. "All right, give us the money. We'll meet with this fella."

CHAPTER TEN

Much later that evening, McNair and Shardeen waited on the docks for a meeting. They had no idea who they were to meet, because Beebe hadn't told them. The only reason they had agreed to the meeting at all was because of the twenty dollars and the implied promise of much more money. And because the meeting was in the middle of the night, and in a very remote location, the two men were certain that the job, whatever it was, would be to their liking. It was cool and damp, and as neither of the men was wearing a coat, they wrapped their arms around themselves in an unsuccessful attempt to keep warm.

"Why the hell did the son of a bitch want to meet us in the middle of the night?" Shardeen asked.

"Probably 'cause he don't want to be seen with us," McNair replied.

"Hell, we that ugly that somebody don't

want to be seen with us?"

McNair laughed. "I'm not, but you are," he said.

Out in the harbor a bell buoy clanged, its syncopated ringing notes measuring the passage of night. On a ship close by, a signalman striker marked the time as six bells, or eleven o'clock of the first watch.

From the dark water of the bay, gossamer strands of fog lifted up to wrap around the pilings and piers as long, gray fingers of vapor blanketed San Francisco.

The night was still, and the gaslights of the streetlamps were dimmed by the heavy blanket. There was an eerie, unworldly quality to the scene that made it hard to distinguish fantasy from reality.

"Damn, why don't he come on?" Shardeen asked.

Shardeen had just asked the question when a private coach suddenly appeared, almost as an apparition materializing before them. A fog-dimmed aurora shrouded the running lamps as the coach stopped near the two men. The door to the vehicle opened, and in the spill of its inside lamplight, McNair and Shardeen could see the rich, red, velour upholstery of the interior. A well-dressed man leaned forward into the light.

"Mr. McNair? Mr. Shardeen?"

"Yeah, that's us," McNair said.

"Please join me."

The two men glanced at each other, as if asking should they do this, then they climbed into the coach. "Who are you?" Shardeen asked.

"I'm the man who asked the two of you to meet with me."

"Yeah, but, what's your name?"

"I see no need for you to know my name. Is that a problem for you?"

"Not if you pay for it, it ain't."

"Oh, you may rest assured that I will pay you."

McNair ran his hand lightly across the upholstery. "Damn, I ain't never seen no wagon like this before. I'll bet somethin' like this costs a whole lot of money."

"Indeed it does."

McNair continued to examine the coach.

"Would you gentlemen like a drink?"

"Yeah. You mean you got whiskey in here?" Shardeen asked.

The well-dressed man opened an upholstered box attached to the door and removed a cut glass decanter of whiskey. He then took out two crystal tumblers, poured them half full, and handed one to each of the two men. He watched as each of them took a preliminary sip.

"I'll just bet that you have never tasted anything like this before, have you?" he asked.

"Hell, I don't know," McNair replied. "I don't think I've ever actually tasted any whiskey. That don't mean I ain't drunk whiskey, but I ain't never drunk it for the taste of it. Only reason I ever drink it is to get drunk."

"Yeah, me, too," Shardeen said.

"This is brewed from the mist that rises off the Scottish moors," the well-dressed man said.

"I don't know what that means," Shardeen said.

"It just means that it is very good whiskey," their host said.

McNair drank it, and while he didn't have a palate sophisticated enough to determine the taste of quality whiskey, he could tell that it was better than the stomach-turning, throat-burning bile he was used to drinking.

"Let's talk about money again," Shardeen said. "Beebe said me 'n McNair could make a lot of money, if we was to do this job for you."

"Yes, and I like a man who gets right to the point."

"What do we have to do?"

"I want you to kill someone."

"Yeah, we kinda figured that. You need to know, though, that that is goin' to cost you."

"How much?"

"A hunnert dollars," McNair said.

"Each," Shardeen added. "In addition to the twenty dollars Beebe give us to wait out here in the dark tonight so's we could meet you."

"Very well, I will give each of you twenty-five dollars now, and another seventy-five tomorrow after the job is done."

"What's the name of the feller you want us to kill?"

"You don't need to know his name."

"You're big on not givin' names, ain't you? And what do you mean we don't need to know? How are we goin' to find 'im, iffen we don't even know his name?"

"It is best that you not know his name. That way, there won't be any way to connect the two of you to the killing. I'm just looking out for you two."

"And for you," McNair said.

"Yes, and for me. And as for finding him, he is in room 202 at the Royal Hotel. Here is the key."

McNair took the key.

"Wait until after midnight."

"When do we get our money? 'N how will we find you again?"

"If you are successful, meet me here at this same time tomorrow night, and I'll have the rest of your money."

"But you want this feller kilt tonight, right?" McNair asked.

"Yes."

"All right, we'll do it for you," Shardeen said. "Will you take us to the hotel where he's a-stayin'?"

"No, I don't want you to be seen getting out of my coach. The hotel is only a few blocks away. That's why I arranged to meet you here. I'll see you here tomorrow night at the same time."

"You had better be here," McNair warned.

"I'll be here."

After the two men left, Conroy leaned out of the window and called up to his driver.

"Mr. Ho! Take me home!"

Conroy leaned back in the comfortable seat, listening to the staccato clip-clop of the horses' hooves on the paving stones. He would never use such men as the two he had just met for a job that would require thought and initiative. For example, he wouldn't think of using these men to actually be the ones to carry out a contract on

121

John Gillespie and his daughter. But what he was asking them to do tonight couldn't be simpler. All they had to do was sneak into the room and kill the sleeping occupant. And he had even given them the room key.

He wasn't as convinced as the consortium was that this man, Matt Jensen, would have to be killed in order for the job to be successful. He didn't need anyone else to tell him how to do his job. He had once arranged for the assassination of a Russian nobleman who was visiting the United States, and that had gotten the American, Californian, and Russian governments involved. The case was still unsolved.

Matt Jensen was just a diversion, and whether McNair and Shardeen killed him or not, Conroy was sure he would be able to take care of John Gillespie and his daughter.

Royal Hotel

The hotel clerk was dozing behind the front desk when McNair and Shardeen stepped into the lobby. The two men walked quietly across the carpeted floor, then took the stairs to the second floor. Told that the room would be at the end of the hall closest to the street, they turned in that direction.

122

"Here it is, 202!" Shardeen said out loud.

"Shh! We don't want to wake no one up," McNair cautioned.

It was too late. Matt heard Shardeen say the number, which happened to be his room number. He also heard the response.

Matt had taken off only his boots when he climbed into bed earlier tonight. Now he swung his legs over the edge of the bed, stuffed the pillow under the bedcovers, and hearing the key being put into the lock, pulled on his boots, snaked the pistol from its holster, then stepped through the window. Because his room was on the front of the hotel, facing the street, Matt was able to climb out onto the portico roof, and he waited there to see who was coming into his room. Because of the pale moonlight, which fell in through the open window, the room was slightly brighter than the hallway. The two men could see the bed and Matt's hat and pistol belt hanging from the brass bedpost. What neither one of them noticed was that the holster was empty.

"This is goin' to be the easiest money we ever made," McNair said with a smile as he aimed at the lump in the bed.

McNair fired, and his shot was followed almost immediately by Shardeen's and, for a moment, both guns were firing, lighting up the darkness with white flashes and filling the room with thunder.

"Hold it! Quit shootin'," McNair shouted. "The whole town is likely to be in here in a minute. We got to get out of here! Check and make sure the son of a bitch is dead!"

Shardeen walked over to the bed and felt around, then gasped in surprise.

"McNair! He ain't here!" he shouted.

"What? Where is he?"

"I'm right here," Matt said from just outside his window.

With shouts of frustrated rage and fear, McNair and Shardeen turned their guns toward Matt and began firing. Bullets crashed through the window, sending large shards of glass out onto the roof. Matt had jumped to one side of the window as soon as he spoke, which meant that the bullets flew by without finding their mark. Matt leaned around and fired into the room. He hit one of the men and saw him go down. The other one bolted through the door.

Matt started to climb back in through the window but changed his mind. He was certain that the one who ran from the room would be leaving the hotel, so he decided to just wait until he came through the door and ran out onto the street. There, the would-be assassin would be in the open, and there would be less likelihood of an innocent bystander being hurt.

Matt jumped down into the space between the hotel and the building next door, then waited in the shadows, keeping his eyes on the front door of the hotel. As he expected, the door burst open a moment later, and a man ran out, the gun still in his hand. Matt stepped out into the street to brace him.

"Hold it right there!" he called out.

Matt heard a policeman's whistle and looking down the street saw a policeman running toward them. The policeman appeared to be armed only with his whistle and a billy club.

"Get down!" Matt shouted at the policeman. "Get down!"

For just a second Matt's adversary seemed indecisive, trying to make up his mind whether to shoot at the policeman or at Matt.

"Drop your gun!" Matt shouted.

That seemed to make up the shooter's mind for him, because he swung his pistol back toward Matt and fired. The bullet whizzed by Matt's ear, much closer than was comfortable, and Matt returned fire. He heard a grunt of pain, and the man fell.

Matt hurried over to him, his pistol at the ready, and he stood there, looking down at the man he had just shot as the policeman, still blowing his whistle, came running up to him.

"Drop that gun, mister," the policeman said when he approached.

Matt, seeing that his first appraisal had been correct, that the policeman was unarmed, laughed.

"I'll give you this, officer," he said. "You are either one of the bravest men I've ever seen or one of the dumbest. What do you mean running up on two armed men, carrying nothing but that stick?"

The policeman stopped, looked at the stick he was holding, then smiled sheepishly.

"Offhand," he said in a voice that was amazingly calm considering the circumstances, "I'd say I might be the dumbest."

Matt laughed again and lowered his gun so that the barrel was pointing toward the street.

"You want to tell me what this was all about?" the officer asked.

"These two men tried to kill me," Matt said.

"Two? Where is the other one?"

Matt pointed to the open window on the second floor of the hotel. "He is up there in my room."

"Is he dead?"

"That was my intention when I shot him," Matt said.

Matt went back into the hotel where some of the hotel guests, awakened, frightened, and curious by the gunfire, were standing in the lobby, most barefoot, many in robes, some still in their sleeping gowns.

"What happened?" the night clerk asked, seeing Matt and the policeman heading toward the stairs. "What's going on?"

"It's all over now, and everything is under control," the policeman said. Then, turning toward the assembled onlookers he added, "Please, all of you, go back to your rooms."

CHAPTER ELEVEN

"Do you think that attempt on your life might have had something to do with me?" Gillespie asked over breakfast the next morning.

"It could have, I suppose," Matt said. "But I doubt it. The kind of life I've led has caused me to make a lot of enemies. I've had people try and kill me long before I ever agreed to come to work for you."

Matt could have told Gillespie about the attempts on his life just within the past four weeks but decided not to. There was no need to increase the man's worry.

"Drew has about gotten all the arrangements for the trip completed," Gillespie said. "And I'm looking forward to it, not only because of the trip itself, but because I think that, once we are on the train, there will be a decreased likelihood that anyone will try and kill me again."

"I hope that's true," Matt said.

"I'm sure it is. I think that Drew and Mr. Emerson are worried over nothing. But that doesn't mean I don't want you to come with us. I think Mary Beth and I will enjoy your company, and to be honest, I guess I would feel a little better knowing you are there. If not for me, then certainly for Mary Beth."

"I think you are doing the smart thing to take a bodyguard with you," Matt replied. "You know the old saying, 'Better safe than sorry.'"

"Yes, indeed," John said. "Better safe than sorry."

When Lucas Conroy learned that morning that McNair and Shardeen had failed, he was surprised. He had given them a key to the room; how hard would it have been to sneak into Jensen's room and kill him while he was sleeping? They not only didn't kill him, they got themselves killed.

"Mr. Conroy?" Beebe said, stepping into Conroy's office. "I have Frank Posey here to see you."

"Thank you, Michael. Show him in."

Frank Posey was at one time a deputy U.S. Marshal. Unlike McNair and Shardeen, who Conroy considered to be no more than saddle bums, Posey, Beebe had assured him, was a man of resourcefulness and intelligence.

"Beebe said you had a job for me," Posey said when he came into the room. Posey was a tall man with broad shoulders and a sweeping moustache. He lost his job as a deputy U.S. Marshal when he stole fifteen hundred dollars he was supposed to be guarding. This resulted in two years in prison, which changed him forever.

"I want you to leave tomorrow, and go to Reno, Nevada. Wait there until the first of September. On that day, a train will leave for Cheyenne at six thirty in the morning. If that train has a private car attached, I want you to board it, and when you do, show this to the conductor."

Posey was given an ace of spades playing card.

"What for?"

"Just show it to him. He will tell you when it is clear for you to go into the private car."

"What do I do when I get to the private car?"

"You will find a man and a woman there. I want you to kill them. Both of them."

"You said *if* the train has a private car attached. What if there is no private car?"

"If the car isn't attached, you won't be needed. You can continue on or take the next train back, as you choose."

"Will I still get paid?"

"If the car isn't attached, that will mean that someone else has already done the job, and I won't need you."

"Wait a minute. What do you mean, someone else will have done the job? Am I supposed to do all this, just on the chance of a job?"

"Yes, but I will pay you one hundred dollars now, and you may keep that money even if you won't be needed."

"Why are you hiring someone else, if you are also hiring me?"

"I am a man who likes to plan for every contingency."

"All right, I understand that. I don't like it, but I understand it."

"And you understand the arrangement? One hundred dollars now and four hundred more after the job is done. Look at it this way, Mr. Posey. The very worst that can happen to you is that you will get one hundred dollars for doing nothing at all."

Posey thought for a moment, then he smiled and stuck out his hand. "Yes, that's right, isn't it? All right, give me the one hundred dollars," he said. "You've just hired yourself an assassin."

"By the way, I notice you aren't wearing a gun."

Posey pulled a bowie knife from the scabbard on his belt and held it up. "I've learned that I don't really need a gun," he said.

On the night before they were due to depart, Drew Jessup invited Matt, John, and Mary Beth over to his house for a going-away dinner.

"I have to say that I'm more than a little concerned about your safety during this trip," Drew said. "And, Mr. Jensen, I'm glad that you have agreed to accompany them." Drew put his hand on John's shoulder. "We've been close friends since we were classmates back at the University of Pennsylvania."

"Not always that close, Drew. I do seem to remember that you once put a snake in my boot."

"Well, it was just a black snake. It couldn't have hurt you."

"It did scare the bejeezus out of me, though."

Drew laughed. "You have to admit that it was funny, the way you yelled and jumped around."

"Funny for you, perhaps. But I jumped so that I strained my ankle and had to hobble around for nearly a month."

"Yeah, well, it did help me beat you in the

steeplechase," Drew said.

"That was the only way you could win. As I recall you were so slow that sometimes the meet was over and everyone had gone home before you even crossed the finish line," John said, laughing.

"Shall we go into the library?" Drew invited. "I've got a fine bottle of brandy I've been holding back for a special occasion."

The four went into the library, where Drew removed a bottle of brandy, then held it up for the others to see. "This bottle comes from a brandy that was distilled especially for Napoleon Bonaparte."

Drew set the bottle on the windowsill.

"Now, where is that corkscrew?" he asked, as he returned to the liquor cabinet.

Suddenly there was a crash of glass as a bullet came through the window. The bullet struck the bottle, sending up a little fountain of brandy.

"Oh!" Mary Beth cried out in alarm.

"Everyone get down!" Matt shouted.

Two more bullets came crashing through the window.

"Get over there, behind the sofa," Matt said, and drawing his pistol, he started toward the door.

"Where are you going?" Drew asked. "Don't go out there, you'll be shot! What are you doing?"

"I'm doing my job," Matt said.

Matt hurried out of the library and started toward the front door, then he stopped. Whoever was out there would probably be looking for someone to come through the front door. Instead, he hurried over to the side of the parlor, raised the window, then climbed out onto the side of the house.

The night was dark and foggy, but the lights shining through the windows of the house enabled Matt to find a long hedgerow. Sticking close to the hedgerow, he followed it to the side of the estate from where the shots would have had to come.

Another shot was fired, and Matt was able to locate the shooter by the light of the muzzle flash. He moved toward the sound of the gun. Then, he saw a man, kneeling on one knee, pointing his rifle toward the house.

"Drop it!" Matt called.

"Where the hell did you come from?" the man asked.

"Never mind that. Just drop the rifle."

Instead of dropping the rifle, the man swung it toward Matt. Matt shot before the man was able to get off a round, and the rifle shooter went down.

Matt hurried over to him. "Who hired

you?" Matt asked.

"It wasn't . . . it wasn't supposed to be like this," the man said, gasping the words out.

"Who hired you?" Matt asked again, but the shooter breathed his last before he could answer Matt's question.

When Matt turned back toward the house, he saw what an ideal target they had been. Despite the darkness and the fog, the gaslit interior caused the house to be brightly lit.

"Is he gone?" John asked when Matt returned.

"He's dead."

"Dead?" Jessup gasped. "You mean you killed him?"

"He was about to shoot me, and it seemed to be the thing to do," Matt replied.

"Yes, of course it would be. I meant no criticism."

"None taken. You should probably send for the police. I don't imagine you would want his body lying out there all night."

"No, I don't. Yes, I'll send one of the servants for the police. Did he say anything?"

"Yes, he said something just before he died, but it didn't make sense."

"What do you mean?" Mary Beth asked. "What did he say?"

"He said, 'It wasn't supposed to be like this.' Like I say, it doesn't make much sense."

"Maybe he meant he didn't expect to be killed," John suggested.

"Yes, I suppose that's it," Matt said.

"Drew, here we've been worrying about me, but it is obvious, now, that you are a target as well."

"Yes," Drew replied. "It would seem so, wouldn't it? You know what that tells me?"

"What?"

"It tells me that it isn't just you they are after. It's the company. Somehow, we have done something as a company that has angered someone."

"I told Jeff Emerson that I thought it might be a disgruntled employee some-where. Or perhaps some business competi-tor," John said. "But now, I think it is more than that."

"I think you're right. If it was just a disgruntled employee, I think it would have ended with the carriage accident."

"Do me a favor, will you, Drew? Come with me tomorrow to see Mr. Emerson. I don't want to make this trip, all the while worrying about your safety."

"All right," Drew said. "This was a little too close for comfort. And" — he added with a smile — "it destroyed a very expensive bottle of brandy."

"I think, after this close call, that a drink is in order," John said. "And it doesn't have to be expensive."

Drew laughed. "Come back into the library, I have just the thing."

In another part of town, Conroy was just finishing a meeting with someone.

"You will be on the train for the entire trip?" Conroy asked.

"Yes."

"You do understand, don't you, that I am not asking you to actually do anything. All I shall require from you is your cooperation and your . . . let us say, facilitating the actions of those men I have hired."

"How will I know who those men are?"

Conroy showed his visitor a playing card, the ace of spades.

"This is how they will identify themselves to you," he said.

CHAPTER TWELVE

In another part of the city, Jonas Butrum sat at a table in the Waterfront Café, nursing a cup of coffee. He would rather be eating, but he had only enough money for coffee.

"Darlin', I want you to know that that was one fine supper," a man said, stepping up to the counter to pay for his meal.

"I'm glad you enjoyed it, sir," an attractive young woman replied.

"Oh, yes ma'am, I did." The man pulled out a fat roll of bills, then peeled one off the top.

When the man left the café, Butrum followed him. The streetlamps had been lit, but the light they produced was so weakened by the evening mist that the familiar yellow patches beneath each lamppost were missing. Then the man turned up a side street that had no lights at all, and it was even darker. Within a moment, the man

Butrum was following was swallowed up by the night and the fog. Butrum moved back into the paralleling alley and ran several yards ahead, then slipped into the gap between two buildings. He returned to the main street, then waited for his mark to appear.

Butrum looked back up in the same direction from which he had just come, but it was much too dark for him to be able to see anything. He could, however, hear the hollow footsteps echoing in the night. He waited until the man was actually close enough to be seen, then he stepped out in front of him.

"Who are you? What do you want?" the man gasped, startled by the sudden appearance.

Butrum didn't answer. Instead, without a word, he stuck the barrel of his pistol into the man's stomach and pulled the trigger.

The gunshot seemed exceptionally loud in the still of the night, and from the residential section, a little farther up the street, a dog barked.

"Who's there?" a frightened voice called.

"That sounded like a gunshot!" another shouted.

In the distance, Butrum could hear the bleat of a policeman's whistle, but he knew he was protected by the darkness, and the whistle was far enough away that he didn't feel at all rushed. He searched the man's pockets until he found the roll of money. Then, going back through the gap between the buildings, he used the alley to make his escape.

The next day, Matt accompanied John and Drew in John's personal carriage, a new one to replace the one that had been destroyed, to a building on Mission Street. A sign on the front of the building read:

Jefferson Emerson
PRIVATE INVESTIGATIVE SERVICES

"Mr. Gillespie," Emerson said, when the three men entered his office. He looked at the other two. "Is everything all right?"

"We need some more of your services," John said.

"Oh?"

John told Emerson of the shooting that had taken place at Drew's house last night. "It's not just me, now. Whoever it is, is after Drew, too," he added when the story was told.

"What happened to the shooter?" Emerson asked.

"I killed him," Matt replied. It was the first time he had spoken since the three men entered the office.

Emerson nodded, then turned back to Drew. "Mr. Jessup, are you sure you are the one he was shooting at?" he asked. "We already know that Mr. Gillespie has been a target. Could they have been shooting at him?"

"That's a good question," Drew answered. "Now that I think of it, they may have been shooting at John."

"Nonsense," John replied. "How could they have been shooting at me? This happened at your house, remember? Who would have even known I was there?"

"I guess that's right," Drew said. "I don't think there is any way anyone could have known that you would be there. That makes it fairly obvious that I was the target."

"Any reason why you would be the target?" Emerson asked.

"Well, sir, John and I have discussed that, and we're sure it is business related."

"But you don't have any idea who it might be?"

"No," Drew replied. "But believe me, I'm going to do everything I can to find out."

"In the meantime, Jeff, I would like for you to arrange for someone to protect Drew.

141

I'm not so worried about Mary Beth and me, not as long as Matt is with us. But I do worry about Drew."

Emerson nodded. "Yes, I think you have every right to worry. All right, I'll find someone to watch over him."

"Good," John said, standing and extending his hand. "That makes me feel a lot better."

With the money from last night's murder and robbery in his pocket, Jonas Butrum decided to have his lunch in a restaurant that was considerably nicer than the places he normally frequented.

By the expression on the face of the man who met him, the maître d' also realized that Butrum was out of place here.

"Sir," the maître d' said, in his most cultured voice. "You do realize, don't you, that there are no low-priced items on the *carte de menu* of this establishment? Perhaps you would be more comfortable somewhere else."

Butrum took a dollar bill from his pocket. "You just find me a good table, sonny," he said, handing the bill to the haughty gentlemen.

The maître d' smiled and took the bill. "Yes, sir, right this way, sir."

Butrum was halfway through a good cut of steak when someone approached his table.

"Hello, Butrum."

Butrum was startled by the greeting. "Well, if it ain't Merlin Bates. How come you ain't in jail?"

"I'm too smart to ever get put in jail."

Butrum laughed. "I've heard you called lots of things, Bates, but smart ain't never been one of 'em."

"I'm smart enough to have found you."

"Yeah, how did you find me, anyway?" Butrum looked around the dining room, then smiled. "This ain't exactly like the kind of place I normally come to."

"I seen you outside, 'n I followed you in here."

"Why?"

"I've got a way for you to make some money."

"I've got money," Butrum said.

"How much?"

"What do you need to know how much for?"

"I don't need to know. Could be that you've got enough money so's that you aren't interested in where a thousand dollars can be had. Actually, five hunnert apiece, but like I say, if you've got money, maybe you ain't interested."

"Wait a minute. Five hunnert dollars? Just where would that five hunnert dollars be?"

"I'll tell you, soon as we finish eatin'," Bates said.

"What do you mean, we? I don't see you eatin'."

"I will, soon as you buy it."

"Why should I buy your dinner?"

"You don't have to. I can find someone else who wants to make five hunnert dollars."

"All right, but eat quick. I want to see what this is all about."

Bates called the waiter over. "I'll have what he's havin'," he said, pointing to Butrum's steak.

"Now, tell me what this is all about."

"You ever heard of a man by the name of Michael Beebe?"

"No, can't say as I have. Who is he?"

"He's the one who come to tell me 'bout the job."

"The one that's goin' to pay us a thousand dollars?"

"Yeah, well, it ain't him who's goin' to pay the money. It's the feller he works for."

"Who does he work for?"

"He works for a man named Lucas Conroy. You ever heard of him?"

"No. You know this Conroy feller, do you?"

"I've never met him, but I have heard of him. From what I've heard, he . . . arranges things . . . for rich folks. 'N that's made him rich, too. Right now, according to Beebe, this feller Conrad is wantin' us to do a special job for him."

"A special job? What kind of special job?"

Bates grinned across the table. "The kind of job that only people like you 'n me can do."

"Do you know how to get ahold of this feller?"

"Yeah, Beebe told me where he lives," Bates said, just as the waiter arrived with his steak.

After they finished their meal, Bates, as promised, took Butrum to see the man who would be the source of their money.

"I thought you said this here Conroy was rich," Butrum said.

"He is rich."

"Then if he's rich, how come he lives in a hotel like this? Seems to me like he'd live in a house somewhere."

Bates laughed. "This is a house."

"Are you a-tellin' me that this ain't no hotel? This is a house?"

"That's exactly what I'm tellin' you," Bates replied.

"I'll be damned."

The two men climbed the steps to the porch, then Bates pulled on the bell cord. From inside, they could hear the resonant sound of a ringing bell.

A moment later an elegantly dressed man answered the door. He turned his nose up at the sight of the two raggedly dressed and very dirty men.

"I don't know what you want, but you have come to the wrong place," the man said.

"Ain't this where Conroy lives?" Bates asked.

"It is."

"Go get 'im. We want to talk to 'im."

"I most certainly will not," the butler replied haughtily. He started to close the door, but Bates stuck his foot in the doorjamb. Then, with his left hand, he grabbed the butler's shirt collar. With his right, he drew his pistol and pushed it up under the butler's chin.

"Never mind. I'll just kill you, 'n then me 'n my friend will go find him our ownselves," Butrum said.

The butler's eyes grew wide in terror. "No, sir, please!" he said.

146

"It's all right, Mr. Watts, I know these gentlemen," Beebe said, then stepping out into the foyer. "Put your gun away," he said to Butrum.

"What if I don't?" Butrum asked.

"Oh, I think you will," Beebe replied with a small smile. He looked to the right and left of the foyer. "All right, gentlemen, you can come in now. I believe the danger has passed."

Four men stepped out into the foyer, two from each side. All four men were carrying pistols.

"I know your name," Beebe said to Bates. "But who is this with you?"

"My name is Butrum. Is what Bates said true? Does this here Conroy feller have a job for us?"

"I do indeed," Conroy said, coming into the foyer then. "Let's step outside, shall we? Some business deals are best discussed with the minimum number of participants."

"Mister, I don't have no idea in hell what you just said," Butrum said.

"Let's go outside," Conroy repeated. "Mr. Beebe, you won't be needed for this discussion."

"Yes, sir," Beebe said.

The three went outside. "Shall we discuss our business in the gazebo?" Conroy asked.

147

"In the what?"

Conroy pointed to a small, lattice-worked structure. "There," he said.

The three men walked over to the gazebo, then, at Conroy's invitation, they all took a seat.

"Now, Mr. Bates, what exactly did Mr. Beebe tell you?" Conroy asked.

"He told me that there was some folks that was goin' to Chicago on a train . . . 'n you didn't want 'em to get there," Bates replied.

"You do understand, don't you, that there is more to it than that; I don't just don't want them to not get there. I don't want them to get anywhere."

"You mean, you want 'em dead."

Conroy smiled. "You are a most astute man, Mr. Bates. That is exactly what I want."

"We're the ones that can do it for you. How much will you pay?"

"I am willing to be . . . quite generous," Conroy said. "Five hundred dollars, after the job is done."

"Five hundred each?" Butrum asked.

Conroy shook his head. "No, five hundred for the two of you."

"I thought Beebe said that it was s'posed

to be five hunnert dollars apiece," Bates said.

"Five hundred dollars would be two hundred and fifty dollars for each of you. When is the last time either of you ever had that much money, all at the same time?"

"Hell, I ain't never had that much money," Butrum said.

"If you don't think that is enough money, you don't have to take the job."

"All right, but we want the money now," Bates said.

"After the job is done. You aren't the only ones working on this project."

"Why would you hire other people to do the job, if you've got us?"

"Because I want the job done."

"You don't need nobody but us," Butrum said.

Conroy studied the two men before him for a long moment.

"All right, I will give you one hundred dollars now, and I will also give you the first opportunity. As soon as you are successful, I will give you the rest of the money."

"All right, it's a deal. Give us the hunnert dollars," Bates said.

"Not here. Meet me at the depot tomorrow afternoon. I'll give you the money there."

CHAPTER THIRTEEN

The next afternoon, Lucas Conroy was at the depot with Merlin Bates and Jonas Butrum. If everything worked out right, he could have his special job completed before Gillespie even got underway. It was to his advantage to accomplish his goal earlier, because the sooner the successful conclusion, the less money he would be out. And, by arrangement with the consortium, the fifty thousand dollars was his to work with, and the less money he would actually have to spend, the more he would be able to keep.

"The people that I need you to deal with are a man named John Gillespie and his daughter, Mary Beth," Conroy said.

"Gillespie? I've heard of him," Bates said. "He's some real rich man, isn't he?"

"Yes."

"Why do you want to kill him?"

"What difference does that make to you?"

"I guess you're right. As long as you pay

for it, it don't matter none why you want it done. But you want his daughter kilt, too?"

Conroy sighed. "Perhaps I should get someone else for the job," he said. "Someone who won't ask so many questions."

"No, no, you don't need nobody else. We'll do it."

"Then either do it, or don't do it so I can hire someone else. But quit asking all your foolish questions."

"All right, I won't ask no more."

"Good."

The two men were walking through the track yard, and Conroy held out his hand to stop them. "There it is," he said. "That's Gillespie's private car. They'll be making the trip in that car."

"They won't be goin' very far," Bates promised. "Me 'n Butrum will take care of it."

"That's what I'm paying you for," Conroy said.

"How do you want us to do it?" Bates asked.

"How? I don't care how you do it. I just want it done, and the sooner you do it, the better."

"What about the money?"

"I told you, I'll pay you as soon as you complete the job."

"No, I'm talkin' about the hunnert dollars that you said we'd get right away."

"Yes," Conroy said. "All right, here's the one hundred dollars."

"You wouldn't try 'n pull no fast one on us now, would you, Conroy? I mean, you will give us the rest of the money after we do this."

"Mr. Bates, I have worked with a great many people over the last few years. My very livelihood depends upon me treating both my clients and my employees honestly. If I had been in the habit of not keeping my end of the bargain, word would get out, and I assure you, I would be out of business." Conroy smiled. "And believe me, considering some of the people I have worked with in the past, when I say I would be out of business . . . I mean permanently. I'm no fool. If you accomplish the job I have assigned you . . . you will be paid."

On the day they were to leave, Drew Jessup came down to the depot with John, Mary Beth, and Matt to see them off.

"Drew is absolutely my right arm," John explained. "I don't know if I could get along without him."

Drew laughed. "You're going to give me a big head here, John. But everyone knows that you are the one who had the intelligence and the wherewithal to put this company together. I'm a very rich man, and I owe it all to you. You've made me the number two man in your organization, and I wouldn't trade it for any other job in the entire United States."

"Well, you have certainly earned your position. Now, Drew, I believe you wanted to show off a little bit?"

"Yes," Drew said. "I'll have you know that you aren't just going to be taking a train ride to Chicago. The Union Pacific has agreed to put on a very special engine for you, and I would like you to see it."

The four of them walked up the track until they were standing alongside a beautiful engine, painted green with gold filigree. The number 502 was painted under the cab window and on the tender. The name *Conqueror* was under the numbers on both the engine and the tender.

"Mr. Kirkpatrick, I believe you will be the engineer for the first leg of the trip to Chicago, won't you?" Drew asked a man who was standing alongside the engine. Kirkpatrick was a big, round-faced, red-nosed man, wearing striped, bibbed overalls.

"Yes, sir," he said.

"Tell us about this engine," Drew invited.

"She's a beaut, isn't she?" Kirkpatrick asked.

"Oh, yes," Mary Beth said. "Why, I believe it is the most beautiful engine I've ever seen."

"Well, she's a lot more 'n just bein' pretty. This is a special engine, a new type from the Rogers Locomotive Works. It is a four-six-four and it burns coal, not wood," Kirkpatrick explained, pointing out the details of the engine. "Coal provides for a much more efficient combustion than wood, and it will give you more range. The boiler is capable of handling superheated steam, which allows for a significant increase in pounds per square inch at the cylinder head. The twenty- by twenty-four-inch cylinders and the sixty-nine-inch drivers will give this engine more speed than anything else on the tracks today. Why, flat out, and on a smooth track, she could do seventy miles to the hour. Of course, there aren't that many places where you could run that fast, and we won't ever be going anywhere near that speed. But that's just to show you what this engine is capable of doing."

"Do you mind if we step up into the engine cab to have a look around?" Drew asked.

"Sure, I don't see why not. Watch your

step going up."

The four followed the engineer up into the cabin, and he had begun pointing out the various features when Drew held up his hand.

"Hold it, wait a minute, what's this?" Drew asked. He pointed to the coal tender.

Matt moved to the object Drew had pointed to, then pulled it from the coal. It was a stick of dynamite.

"What the hell?" the engineer asked. Then seeing Mary Beth, he covered his mouth. "Sorry, ma'am."

"That's all right," Mary Beth replied quietly. "But, I don't understand. That's a stick of dynamite, isn't it?"

"Yes, darlin', it certainly is," Drew said. "The question is, what is it doing in the coal tender?"

"It would appear that someone was trying to sabotage the train," Matt said. "Mr. Kirkpatrick, what would have happened if that stick of dynamite had been introduced into the furnace? Is the steel strong enough to withstand the blast?"

Kirkpatrick shook his head. "If it was just the dynamite, it might. But the blast would more than likely compromise the boiler, and with the steam under pressure, the engine would have been blown to pieces," Mr.

Kirkpatrick said. "Cooper and I would have both been killed."

"But wouldn't the fireman have seen it when he was shoveling the coal?" John asked.

Kirkpatrick shook his head. "Not necessarily. When Cooper is shoveling the coal into the furnace, he does it in a rhythm. Even if he had seen it, it probably wouldn't have been until just before he tossed it into the flames, and by then it would have been too late."

"Yes, that would have been tragic, especially if you two were killed in a blast that was meant for me. Doesn't seem like a very efficient way to get to me, though."

"Oh, but that's where you are wrong, sir," Kirkpatrick said. "I understand that your car will be just behind the tender. That being the case, your car would have derailed, and at the speed we'll be running, it would be totally wrecked. The chances are that anyone in that car would be killed, along with me 'n Cooper."

"But I don't understand. Won't my car be the last car on the train?"

"No," Drew said. "I've arranged for you to keep this same engine for the entire trip. You'll be changing trains at Ogden and again at Cheyenne. But because you will

156

keep this same engine, your special car will be just behind the tender. That way, each time you change trains, you won't even have to leave your car unless you want to, because the engine, tender, and your car will leave one consist and pick up another."

"That's very convenient," John said. "I thank you for arranging that, Drew."

"Yes, I thought you might appreciate that."

"Convenient, yes," Kirkpatrick said. "But with your car being there, you can see that if the engine were to explode, your car couldn't help but be jerked off the track. And if that was to happen, I don't think anyone in the car would survive."

John looked at Drew. "So, you not only arranged the trip for my convenience, you have also saved my life. I owe you a huge thank-you for noticing that stick of dynamite before it was able to do any damage."

"Oh, don't get me wrong, John. It's not that I care that much about you. I was just looking out for my job. If something happened to you, what would happen to the business?" Drew laughed out loud at his joke.

"Then, you'll just have to keep me alive, won't you?"

Drew held up his hands. "Not me. I'm afraid that from this point on, keeping you alive is Mr. Jensen's job. Mr. Jensen, don't let us down now. I'm not the only one whose job is at stake. You have no idea how many people there are who depend on John Gillespie for their livelihood."

"I'll do my best," Matt said.

"What time will we be getting underway?" John asked.

"At eight thirty this evening," Kirkpatrick replied.

San Francisco, Monday, August 31, 1885
After having dinner with the others in the depot dining room, Matt excused himself, then walked out into the car shed and passed along the head of all the tracks until he came to track number six, where their train stood. The consist was six cars, including John's private car, the baggage car, a Pullman car, the dining car, and two day cars.

As Matt walked along the brick platform, looking over the train, he saw two men squatting down between the tender and the private car. At first, he thought they were workers, making some last-minute repair or modification. But he thought he should confront them, just in case.

"What are you men doing?" he called.

Matt's unexpected challenge caused the

158

two men to run off. They ran toward the train on the adjacent track, then disappeared between the two cars, and Matt started after them. He had gone no more than half-a-dozen steps, however, when one of them leaned back around the end of the car and fired at him.

He drew his own pistol and fired back, but because there were people on the other train, he purposely shot low and saw the sparks of his bullet striking the rear truck of the car, which shielded the two men. The bullet then ricocheted under and between the train cars, coming close enough to the two to cause them to dash off to the other side.

The engineer, Mr. Kirkpatrick, and some yard workers, drawn by the shooting, hurried up the track toward Matt.

"What is it, Mr. Jensen?" Kirkpatrick called. "What's going on? What's all the shooting?"

"Stay back!" Matt warned, lifting his left hand to hold them in place. Kirkpatrick and the others did as Matt instructed.

Matt hopped over the coupling, where he saw the two men disappearing behind a freight that was being made up. Matt ran after them, but before he could reach them the freight moved between him and the men he was chasing. By the time the freight passed, the two men were gone.

Frustrated that they got away and puzzled as to why they were here, Matt returned to the siding where the special train stood. He saw the engineer and two of the workers looking at the car where the men had been.

"Did you get them?" the engineer asked, as Matt returned.

"No," Matt admitted. "I'm afraid they gave me the slip."

"Too bad," the engineer said. He pointed to the rubber hose that was a part of the coupling. "They were trying to sabotage us all right. They were cutting into the airbrake hose."

"They were being real smart about it, too," one of the workers said. "They didn't cut far enough into the hose for it to separate yet. But after a hundred miles or so, what with the swaying and the strain between the cars and all, that line would have come apart . . . maybe just on the other side of some high pass. And likely as not, when that happened, it would've caused a wreck."

"You'd better get the damaged lines replaced," Matt suggested.

"Yes, sir, we'll do that right away."

■ ■ ■

"Me 'n Butrum was discovered," Bates said.

"Did you get the hoses cut?" Conroy asked.

"Well, yeah, but that don't mean nothin'. Seein' as we was discovered, they'll more'n likely get 'em fixed before they leave."

"All right, that train doesn't leave until eight thirty, and that's another hour. I want you two to take the eastbound to Carson City, it leaves in about fifteen minutes. But I don't want you to go all the way. Gillespie's train will stop for water between Kingsbury and Carson City. You get off there and wait. It'll be the middle of the night by the time Gillespie's train gets to the water tank, and when it stops, you get on."

"You mean just get on board? How are we goin' to do that?"

"Here are two tickets. Show them to the conductor."

"Are you tellin' us that the conductor is just goin' to let us on in the middle of nowhere?"

"If you show him these tickets, yes, he will let you on."

"All right. What do we do once we are on

161

the train?"

"As I said, it will be the middle of the night. Most of the people will be asleep, so you shouldn't have any trouble passing through the train. Go into Gillespie's private car and kill him and his daughter. It will only be a few more miles until the train stops in Reno. When it does, get off and take the next train back here. Because it is the middle of the night, you'll be halfway back to San Francisco before anyone discovers the two dead bodies, and you will be in the clear."

Bates and Butrum, each of them fifty dollars richer than they had been when they woke up that morning, boarded the train for Carson City. If everything went as planned, they would be another two hundred dollars richer before another full day had passed.

CHAPTER FOURTEEN

By a quarter till eight, the brake hoses had been changed, the fire was stoked, and the steam pressure built up. As the *Conqueror* sat waiting on the track, the engine relief valves were opening and closing rhythmically so that the locomotive almost took on a life of its own. The heaving sighs of escaping steam seemed to match that of those who were waiting anxiously for the train to depart.

Once they were aboard, John went into the Pullman car with Matt to introduce him to the conductor, Dan Kelly, and the porter, Julius Calhoun.

"Mr. Kelly, Mr. Calhoun, this gentleman is Matt Jensen," John said. "He is one of my employees. There will be times when he will be visiting me in my car, which, as you both know, is just forward of the baggage car. Because of that, I want you to make certain that his passage back and forth through the baggage car is unimpeded. May I have that assurance from the two of you?"

"Yes, of course," Kelly replied.

"Mr. Calhoun?" John asked.

"Yes, sir," Calhoun said.

"Very good."

"Mr. Jensen, will you be sleeping in the private car, or here in the Pullman car?" Calhoun asked.

"Here," Matt replied.

"Very good sir. I'll let you have this front sleeper unit, and I'll make certain that you are undisturbed."

"I expect he'll spend most of the time in my car," John said. He pulled a watch from his vest pocket and examined it. "Speaking of which, we'll be getting underway in just a couple of minutes, so, Mr. Jensen, would you like to come to the car now? You may as well be with us as we depart."

"Oh, I intend to stay in the car with you until it's time to go to bed tonight," Matt said.

John smiled and nodded. "I thought you might." He looked at the conductor and the porter. "We'll just pass through the baggage car, if you don't mind."

They had been underway for over an hour, and the train, clear of the city and surrounding smaller towns, was flashing across the valley at a very rapid speed. John had been entertaining Matt and Mary Beth with stories of famous people he had met.

"I was once presented to Queen Victoria," John said. "I helped some British businessmen, and she wanted to knight me for that. I told her I couldn't accept it, being American and all, and she offered to make me a British citizen on the spot."

Mary Beth giggled. "I told Papa he should have taken the queen up on it. Then he could have bought a suit of shining silver armor and ridden all over San Francisco on a white horse."

"I told President Arthur about the offer of knighthood, and he got a big kick out of it," John said.

"Did you go to Europe as well?" Matt asked Mary Beth.

"Oh, yes. It was fascinating, though I must confess that I got a little seasick on the ship on the way over and on the way back."

"A *little* seasick," John said. "Didn't you tell me once to just throw you into the sea and go on without you?"

"No, Papa, I didn't ask you to do that, you threatened to do it," Mary Beth replied with a laugh.

"Oh, yes, as I recall now, it was your

mother who talked me out of tossing you overboard."

Mary Beth laughed again, then glanced out through the window. "Oh, my, we seem to be going very fast. I wonder how fast we are going."

"Would you like me to tell you?" Matt asked.

"Wait a minute. Are you saying you can tell me how fast we are going?"

"Yes."

"How?"

"Mr. Gillespie, do you have a watch with a second hand?"

"I do indeed," John said, pulling a gold-chained watch from a vest pocket.

"Say the word 'start,' time me for twenty seconds, then say 'stop,' " Matt instructed.

"All right. I have no idea what you have in mind, but I will do as you ask."

John held the watch in his right hand and held his left hand up as he examined the watch face.

"Start," he said, bringing his left hand down sharply. There was silence in the car until John said, "Stop."

"We are traveling at forty-seven miles per hour," Matt said.

John laughed. "Good joke. We all sit here for twenty seconds, then you declare that we are going forty-seven miles per hour."

"It's no joke, we are going exactly forty-seven miles per hour."

"How could you possibly know that?" John asked.

"Yes, how did you do that?" Mary Beth asked.

"There's really nothing to it," Matt said. "I have done some detective work for the railroads, and this is a trick that was taught to me by one conductor and verified by several others."

"Oh, do tell me how it is done," Mary Beth pleaded.

"All right. Listen, do you hear the clicks the wheels make as they roll across the rail joints?"

"Yes."

"Count those clicks for twenty seconds," he said. "The number of clicks you hear in twenty seconds' time is how fast you are going in miles per hour."

"Oh, what a fascinating thing to know!"

At that moment there was a knock on the door, and quickly, Matt drew his pistol. He held out his hand to stop John from answering the door.

"I'm sure it's just the porter," John said. "I arranged to have some ice cream delivered to our car tonight. You do like ice

167

cream, don't you?"

"I do," Matt said. "But I still think I should answer the door."

John was right. It was Mr. Calhoun, and he was bringing ice cream.

After the ice cream, Matt sat up with them talking, then Mary Beth began yawning.

"It's nearly eleven o'clock," Matt said, "and I'm getting sleepy."

Mary Beth chuckled. "Are you really getting sleepy? Or are you just covering for me?"

"Let's just say that I'm glad you are tired, too," Matt said. "That way I won't feel bad about leaving you and going to bed myself." He yawned again and stretched. "So, if you good folks will excuse me, I think I will go back to the Pullman car and turn in."

When their train stopped for water, Bates and Butrum slipped down from the platform between two of the cars, doing so on the opposite side from the water tower so they wouldn't be seen. They walked out into some scrub brush and waited until the train pulled out.

"What do we do now?" Butrum asked.

"We wait."

"Two hunnert fifty dollars apiece, that's what he said, isn't it?" Butrum asked. "Two hunnert 'n fifty dollars?"

"Yes, two hunnert 'n fifty dollars apiece. You heard him same as I did," Bates said.

"It's like I told that Conroy feller, I ain't never had that much money at one time in my whole life. Have you?"

Bates thought for a moment. "No, I can't say as I have."

"What are you goin' to spend your money on?" Butrum asked.

"I'm goin' to get me a new shirt 'n a new hat. And, I'm goin' to get me a silver band to go around my hat," Bates replied.

Butrum laughed. "You're goin' to waste your money on a shirt 'n a hat? Hell, I ain't. Women 'n whiskey. That's what I plan to do."

"I'll be savin' some for women and whiskey."

"How are we goin' to do it?"

"When the train stops here for water, we'll get on board."

"No, I mean, how are we supposed to kill Gillespie and his daughter?"

"They will more'n likely be asleep, so we'll sneak into the car. I say we get a pillow or somethin' and hold it over the girl's face. That way we can keep her quiet while we smother her. Then, I'm thinkin', the best way to kill Gillespie is with a knife, if we catch him sleepin'. But we'll shoot 'im if we have to."

Matt slept restfully, but lightly, so when the train stopped, it awakened him. He had no idea what time it was, but looking through the window, he could see that it was pitch black. He heard bumps and noises from the tender, which told him that they were taking on water. He lay back down and closed his eyes, intending to drift back to sleep.

He had just about dozed off again when he heard voices just outside his car.

"You think they're asleep?"

"Hell, yes, they're asleep. What else would they be doin' this time of night? You don't see no light comin' from the car, do you?"

"Just 'cause there's no light, don't mean nothin'. It's a private car, and they don't hardly have no winders."

Matt had decided to sleep in his trousers, just in case he would have to get up in the middle of the night. And this was just such a case.

With pistol in hand he moved quickly through the baggage car, reaching the front end just as he saw two men climbing up into the vestibule of the private car.

"More than likely those folks are asleep," Matt said. "Why do you want to go waking them up?"

"What the hell?" one of the men shouted. Both men swung toward Matt with guns blazing. Two bullets ricocheted off the door frame. Matt returned fire, and both men went down.

With the smoking gun in his hand, Matt approached the two men, both of whom now lay in the vestibule. It took but a quick glance to ascertain that both were dead.

The door to the private car opened, and John stood there in his nightgown.

"What happened?" he asked.

"You were about to have some unwelcome visitors," Matt said. He leaned down for a closer look at the two men he had just killed. He recognized them as the men he had chased through the track yard back in San Francisco.

"These are the same two men who were trying to cut the brake hose before we left."

John breathed a sigh of relief. "That means it's over then, doesn't it?"

"What makes you say that?"

"Well, if these are the same two who cut the brake hose, they are more than likely the same ones who cut the tongue pin on my carriage. And now that they are dead, I think the danger is over."

"Have you forgotten the man who tried to

kill Mr. Jessup?"

"No, but, I don't see the connection. Whoever that was, he tried to kill Drew. These men tried to kill me."

"I think it might all be connected," Matt said. "It's obvious that there's more than one, or even a few people involved here. And since they tried to kill Mr. Jessup as well, then they are after your company, not you as an individual."

"Yes," John replied. "Yes, I hadn't thought about that. You might be right."

"And if I am right, then these two — and the man who tried to kill Mr. Jessup — were working for someone else. That means that whoever hired these men still wants you dead. And since these men failed, more than likely, he'll try again."

At that moment the train started up.

"Oh, we're getting underway. What . . . ?" John pointed at the two dead bodies, but it wasn't necessary for him to complete the question.

"Don't worry about them. I'll put them in the baggage car, and we can take care of them when we reach the next stop."

CHAPTER FIFTEEN

Though the other passengers eventually showed up for their breakfast, either in the dining car, or in the case of John and Mary Beth, in the private car, Matt did not. Instead, he chose to eat a biscuit and bacon sandwich with the engineer and fireman up in the cab of the engine. He had dropped in on them just before dawn, crawling across the tender and climbing down onto the platform.

Mike Kirkpatrick was the engineer at the throttle; his fireman was Billy Cooper. In the little mirror that hung on the front wall of the engine, Matt could see Mike's face and the small chin whiskers that stuck forward, waving like a little flag as the engineer chewed his breakfast. Kirkpatrick's arm was laid along the base of the window, showing the tattoo of an American eagle.

Cooper closed the fire door, then checked the gauge. It was holding at exactly 210 pounds of pressure per square inch. The fire was roaring, the steam was hissing, and the rolling wheels were pounding out a thunder of steel on steel.

"Is it true we got two dead men lyin' back in the baggage car?" Cooper asked.

"Yes."

"You shot 'em, did you?"

"I did."

A broad smile spread across Cooper's face. "I thought you did. I heard the shootin', but I didn't see it. Damn, it must be mighty fine to be so good with a gun."

"It has its advantages and its drawbacks," Matt said.

Cooper held his hand in the form of a pistol, then made a "rapid draw" from the imaginary holster at his side.

"If I was real good with a gun, I'd give up bein' a fireman, 'n just go around the West shootin' bad guys."

"How would you make a livin'?" Kirkpatrick asked.

"Hell, that wouldn't be no problem," Cooper said. "I'd do the same thing Mr. Jensen is doin'. I'd sell my gun to people that needed it."

"There's a problem with that," Matt said. "You don't always know if someone is buying your gun for good or for evil. And the people who want to use your gun for evil purposes are always willing to pay a lot more than the people who want it for good reasons."

"Yeah," Cooper said. "Yeah, I hadn't thought about that." He laughed. "Only, it don't make no nevermind, on account of I ain't good with a gun in the first place."

"How long before we get to Carson City?" Matt asked.

"Oh, I would say no more than half an hour or so."

Matt returned to the private car where John was reading a newspaper, and Mary Beth was looking through the window.

"There you are," she said. "You missed a wonderful breakfast."

"I ate in the engine cab with Mr. Kirkpatrick and Mr. Cooper," Matt replied. "We'll be in Carson City in about another half hour."

"I'm sure I won't have time to connect the teleprinter, but I do need to send a telegram to Drew," John said. "I hope we have time for me to step into the depot to send it."

"I'm sure we will."

Carson City, September 1, 8 a.m.
"Yes, sir, I will see that the two bodies are

175

taken care of," the stationmaster at Carson City said when Matt and John approached him. The two bodies had been discreetly removed from the train, and were now lying on a baggage cart under a tarpaulin. None of the passengers, either boarding or departing, had even noticed them.

"Here," John said, handing the stationmaster fifty dollars. "I don't want the undertaker to be out the cost of their burial."

"Thank you, sir, he will appreciate that, as will the county."

"Now I would like to send a telegram, if you think I have time," John said.

The stationmaster pulled his watch from his pocket, opened the cover, and examined it.

"Yes, sir, you have exactly twenty-two minutes and forty seconds left before the train leaves," he said, authoritatively. "Western Union is right inside the building and over to the left."

"Good, thank you," John replied, following the directions.

Once inside the depot, he stepped over to the Western Union office and wrote out the message to Drew Jessup.

ANOTHER ATTEMPT MADE ON

MY LIFE STOP JENSEN HANDLED
IT STOP WILL KEEP IN TOUCH
FOR ENTIRE TRIP

After sending the telegram, John returned
to the private car where Matt and Mary
Beth were already waiting.

"I got it sent," he said. "Matt, do you
really think that someone else may try to
kill me?"

"Yes, I do," Matt replied. "Those men
weren't trying to kill you because of some
personal reason. They were paid to kill you."

"How do you know they were paid to kill
me?"

Matt stuck his hand down in his pocket,
then pulled out two fifty-dollar bills, then
handed them to John.

"I found this money in their pockets. How
likely do you think it would be these men
would have fifty dollars apiece? And, in a
single bill?"

John shook his head. "It doesn't seem to
me as if it would be all that likely," he said.

"No, I wouldn't think so either. The
danger is not yet over, so, if you've no objection, I plan to keep a close watch on both of
you until we reach Chicago."

"You'll get no objection from me," John
said.

"And you certainly won't get any objection from me," Mary Beth added, flashing a flirtatious smile toward Matt. "What young woman wouldn't appreciate the attention of a handsome man?"

"Mary Beth, for crying out loud," John said. "What would your mother think?"

Mary Beth laughed. "Why, I'm sure she would also think Matt is handsome."

John shook his head. "I apologize, Matt. She is impossible."

As Matt, John, and Mary Beth waited in the Gillespie car for the train to get underway again, one of the others who had been on the train sent a cryptic telegraph message to Lucas Conroy:

JOB IS STILL OPEN STOP ARE THERE OTHER APPLICANTS

The sender of the telegram waited for the answer.

MORE JOB APPLICANTS ARE IN THE QUEUE

Reno, Nevada
It was eight thirty in the morning, and Frank Posey, who had already bought his

178

ticket to Cheyenne, was waiting in the Reno depot. He had spent the night in the depot, because he didn't want to take a chance on missing the train. Conroy had told Posey that if the private car was not attached, that would mean the job had already been done, and his services wouldn't be needed.

He did have the one hundred dollars Conroy had given him, so he decided he would go on to Cheyenne whether the private car was attached to the train or not.

Posey was standing on the platform waiting as the train came rolling into the station. The sun danced from the deep green color of the engine and glistened off the brass trim.

"Whoowee, ain't that a pretty engine?" someone asked, and several others agreed with him.

"Look at that! It's pullin' a private car!" another said. "There must be some awful important person ridin' on this train."

Posey smiled. Whoever Conroy selected to do the job before him hadn't done it. That meant the money was his for the taking.

And he did intend to take it.

The train came to a stop, and after a moment, a few of the passengers stepped down. The conductor waited until the last passenger had detrained, then he pulled out his watch and examined it.

"All aboard!" he shouted, and Posey and the others waiting on the depot platform boarded. Shortly after he took a seat in one of the two day cars the train got underway, and soon after that, the conductor came through collecting the tickets. When he reached Posey's seat, Posey gave him his ticket and showed him the ace of spades.

"Does this mean anything to you?" he asked.

"Yes," the conductor said quietly.

"What does it mean?"

The conductor looked around the car, took the card, and slipped it into his pocket.

"Wait until I contact you," he said, speaking just as quietly as before.

Matt was in the private car with John and Mary Beth, and at the moment, he was peeling an orange.

"Have you ever tasted an orange ripe from the tree?" Mary Beth asked.

"Isn't this orange ripe?" Matt replied, holding it out.

Mary Beth shook her head. "No. You can eat an orange at almost any stage of its development, but when you take one ripe, straight from the tree, they are delicious."

"Well, why don't they wait until they are

ripe before they ship them out to be sold?"

"Because they would go bad too quickly."

"Hmm. Well, I'd like to taste one ripe from the tree someday."

"Go down into Southern California," Mary Beth suggested.

Matt finished his orange, then stood up.

"I think I'll take a walk through the train," he said. "If there is more to this threat than these men, then it is likely that there is someone else on the train now."

"How will you know?" John asked.

"I'm not sure that I will know," Matt replied. "But I often have sort of a feeling about things like this. Anyway, I think I'll check it out."

"I won't question you, Matt. One of the things I learned a long time ago is to hire people who are experts in fields where I am lacking and then depend on them. So, I am depending, absolutely, on you."

"You will be back for lunch, though, won't you?" Mary Beth asked.

Matt smiled. "I'm never late for lunch," he said.

Letting himself out of the private car, he walked through the baggage car, the Pullman car, and then the dining car. Between the dining car and the two day cars, he stopped in the vestibule and looked out over the countryside. They were running through wide-open space now and going very fast. A couple of times he had gauged their speed using his "counting-the-joint-clicks" method, and for a while they were going faster than fifty miles per hour.

He went into the day car and walked down the aisle, looking at everyone, and making eye contact with several, then he went into the last car.

In the day car Matt had just left, the conductor stepped up to Posey's seat.

"Come with me," he said, quietly.

Posey got up and followed the conductor through the diner and into the Pullman car.

"There are two more cars," the conductor said. "Go on through the baggage car. The private car is between the baggage car and the tender."

"How many are in the private car?"

"Now, only Gillespie and his daughter. Wait until I am no longer in this car, then move quickly. Once you have completed your task, then return to where you were, and take your regular seat. Get off at the next town, which will be twenty-two minutes from now."

"All right."

Posey waited until the conductor left, then

he walked through the baggage car. Not until then did he pull his knife.

Chapter Sixteen

Maybe John Gillespie had been right. It could be that there were no more threats against them. Matt had passed through the entire train and nobody triggered any suspicion. There was one man, in the first day car, who almost caused him to take a second look. But there was nothing concrete about it.

Matt smiled. He couldn't suspect someone just on a hunch. He would give the man a closer look when he passed back through the car.

But the man wasn't there. Matt took a quick look into the gentlemen's restroom, but it was also empty.

It could be that the man had gone to the dining car, but that didn't seem very likely. Matt knew that the car was not serving now. It was too late for breakfast, and it was too early for lunch.

He darted forward, walking very quickly

through the train.

"Mr. Jensen, can I help you?" the conductor asked, stepping in front of him.

"No, thanks."

Matt tried to move around him, but the conductor moved again, putting himself in the way, almost as if purposely impeding Matt's progress.

"Please, excuse me," Matt said, pushing the conductor to one side so he could resume his rapid walk to the front of the train.

Matt hurried through the empty dining car, moved even more quickly through the Pullman car, then literally ran through the baggage car. Exiting the front end of the baggage car, he stepped through the vestibule, then jerked open the door to the Gillespie car. He wasn't surprised by what he saw. John and Mary Beth were standing to one side of the car, their faces reflecting their fear, their only protection being the table that was between them and the man who had aroused Matt's suspicion. The man was holding a knife, and his mouth was stretched into a sneering smile.

"John, you didn't tell me you had invited a guest for lunch," Matt said.

The fear on John's face was replaced with a relieved smile.

"You might say that he dropped in unexpectedly," John replied.

Shocked by Matt's entry, Posey looked toward him for a second, then turned and ran out the other end of the car. Matt pulled his gun, then handed it to John.

"Do you know how to use this?"

"I'm not very proficient, I'm afraid."

"You and Mary Beth get into your bedroom compartment and close the door. I want both of you to get into the same room, and shoot anybody but me who might come in. You don't have to be good, that compartment is so small, whoever is after you will be so close that all you'll have to do is point and shoot."

"All right," John agreed.

Matt was shouting the last as he was heading toward the front door. Opening it, he looked around, then up, and saw the heel of the assailant's boot, just as he reached the top of the car.

Matt followed him up, climbing onto the top just as the would-be assassin leaped across to the baggage car. Matt followed him, leaping from car to car until both wound up on top of the first of the two day cars.

"You're going to run out of train soon, and what are you going to do then?" Matt yelled at him.

Posey stopped, then turned to face Matt. He was in a crouched position, and the knife was in his right hand, low, with the blade turned sideways.

"I'll tell you what I'm going to do," he said. "I'm going to gut you like a fish."

Matt reached for where his pistol should be, but the holster was empty, and he remembered that he had given the gun to John.

"Ha, you ain't got your gun, have you?" Posey challenged. "You ain't got a gun, so what are you going to do now?

"I don't have a gun, but I do have this," Matt said, pulling a knife from its sheath.

"I'll just bet you've never fought anyone with that knife," Posey challenged. He held his knife up. "I'm goin' to spill your innards onto the top of this car, sonny boy."

"You mean you're going to try," Matt said.

"Oh, I'm goin' to do it all right," Posey replied as he turned to face down his adversary. He began advancing toward Matt.

The train went around the curve and Matt had to adjust his feet to maintain his balance.

From below, the passengers saw the shadows of the two men cast beside the train, moving along the ground at fifty miles per hour.

"Oh, my God!" one woman passenger shouted. "Look! Look out there!"

At first nobody quite realized what they were seeing . . . other than the shadows of two men, standing erect on top of the car. Then someone saw the arm of one of the shadows make a move toward the other, and when he drew back, she realized that that there was a knife in his hand. She screamed.

"They're trying to kill each other!"

"They won't have to try," another passenger said. "The way them two fools is standin' on top of the car like that, goin' this fast, they'll both more'n likely fall off 'n kill themselves!"

Back on top of the train Matt and Posey were either unaware, or unconcerned, that they were, by their shadows, providing a show for the passengers down inside.

"I once cut out a man's liver while I was in prison," Posey said in a sibilant hiss. And like the head of a snake, he moved the knife blade from side to side. "I cut it out 'n I ate it, just like I'm plannin' on eatin' yours." Posey concluded his comment with a demonic chuckle.

Posey made yet another wide slashing mo-

188

tion with his knife, but as he had done before, Matt bent forward and pulled his stomach back so that the knife just missed him. Matt replied with a counterthrust, and Posey pivoted to one side, so that Matt's riposte missed as well.

"Ha! You can't stick me if I'm not there now, can you?" Posey challenged.

Matt jumped back, and for another moment the two men were poised atop the speeding train, knives held low.

"As long as we're having this little conversation," Matt said, "suppose you tell me why you want to kill Mr. Gillespie and his daughter?"

"I'm getting paid to do it. I didn't know the girl would be so good lookin' though. It'll be a shame to kill her. Maybe I won't kill her till after."

Another slash of Posey's knife left a slicing wound in Matt's left arm. Blood began flowing down from the cut.

"Oh, now I bet that hurt, didn't it?" Posey mocked.

"Who's paying you?"

"You don't need to know that. Besides, what good will that information be to a dead man?" Posey asked. Stepping in quickly, he made another wide, arcing, slashing motion, but missed.

Matt counterthrust, and catching Posey's left hand, sliced off his ring and little fingers. Blood began to gush from the two wounds.

"You son of a bitch!"

"Drop your knife, and we'll get that looked at," Matt suggested.

"The hell I will!" Posey made a long, slicing motion with his own knife but missed.

"Who's paying you to kill John Gillespie?"

"What difference does it make to a dead man?"

The blood was now flowing rather profusely from Posey's traumatically amputated fingers.

"If I'm about to be killed, I'd at least like to die with my curiosity satisfied," Matt said, countering Posey's swipe with one of his own.

"Nah! I want you to die curious."

Posey made another thrust, doing so just as the car passed over a rough section of the track. Because of that, it threw Matt slightly off balance, and while reaching down to keep from falling, he dropped his knife. He made a desperate grab for it but missed, and the knife went over the edge of the car.

Seeing his advantage, Posey rushed toward him, this time with his knife raised over his

190

head in position to make a downward stab-bing motion. Standing quickly, Matt reached up to grab Posey's knife hand by the wrist, and for a moment, the two men stood there, their shadows projecting a *tab-leau vivant* on the ground beside the train.

Posey managed to change hands with his own knife, and with his blade now in his bloody left hand, he opened up another slice across Matt's arm. Blood from the wound joined the blood from the earlier wound, and Matt released his grip on Posey's wrist.

Posey immediately seized the opportunity to break contact, and he leaped back.

"Must be kind of hard for you, being in a knife fight without a knife," Posey mocked.

He rushed toward Matt again, this time with his knife held low. But to Posey's surprise, Matt dropped onto his back, then raised his legs to put his feet into Posey's stomach. Using Posey's own momentum, Matt swung his legs around and Posey, with a scream of terror, went over the side of the speeding train.

Getting up quickly, Matt looked over the edge and saw Posey's twisted and still body lying along the track, rapidly receding in the distance as the train sped along its way.

Matt returned to the Gillespie car the same way he had left it, by running along the top of the train and leaping from car to car.

When he opened the door to step back inside, he saw that John and Mary Beth must have taken his advice and gone into one of the bedroom compartments.

"John, it's me," Matt called.

The compartment door opened, and John relaxed visibly when he saw that it was Matt. But when they both saw all the blood, Mary Beth cried out.

"Matt! You're hurt!"

"It looks a lot worse than it is," Matt said. "I got a couple of cuts on the arm, but I don't think they are very deep. Most of this blood is his."

"You must let me tend to it," Mary Beth said.

"Here," John said, returning Matt's pistol. "I'm glad I didn't have to use this."

A few minutes later Matt was sitting at the table with Mary Beth bathing his arm. The bleeding had stopped, and Matt had been correct in his assessment. The cuts were not very deep.

"John, had you ever seen that man before?" Matt asked.

"No, I haven't. Have you, Mary Beth?"

"No," Mary Beth replied.

"Did you find out who he was?" John asked.

Matt shook his head. "He said he had been in prison, so I didn't really think it was very likely that either of you would have known him. He did say someone had paid him to kill you, though."

"Did he say who it was?"

"No. I was hoping that you might have some idea."

"I've been thinking about that, and last night I looked over some of the notes that Drew gave me before we left. At first, I didn't pay much attention to them, because I thought the attempt to kill me had been an isolated event. But now I'm beginning to have second thoughts. He gave me three names who might be possible suspects."

"Are the names people that you know?" Matt asked.

"Yes, I know all three of them. The names Drew gave me are Fred Keaton, Donald Mitchell, and Raymond Morris."

"Who are they?"

"Keaton, Mitchell, and Morris are people who once owned businesses that went bankrupt. I took over all three of the businesses, saved the jobs of their employees, and kept them on as managers. But as I told you before, there is bound to be some resentment there. I mean when you think about it, being an employee of the very business you used to own has to be difficult for a person's pride."

"Did any one name seem more likely than any of the other names?" Matt asked.

John shook his head.

"No, none have. Actually, I don't think I would have suspected any of them if Drew hadn't suggested the names. But, as I have thought about them, I'm afraid he could be right. It could be any one of them."

There was a light knock at the door and Mary Beth started toward it, but Matt stopped her. With his pistol in hand, he stepped up to the door, then jerked it open.

"Oh!" Kelly, the conductor, said, jumping back in surprise and throwing his hands up in fear.

Matt lowered his pistol.

"Sorry if I frightened you," he said.

"What can I do for you, Mr. Kelly?" John asked.

"Some of the passengers reported seeing . . . uh . . . I know this may sound absurd, but they reported seeing shadows on the ground of two men on top of the train. I was just wondering if you might know anything about it."

"I was one of the men," Matt said.

"Oh? And what happened to the other man?"

"He got off."

"He got off? But how could he? The train hasn't stopped since we left Reno."

"I guess he was just impatient."

"Mr. Jensen is being quite modest," John said. "Another attempt was made on our lives. Thanks to Mr. Jensen, it was unsuccessful."

It wasn't until then that the conductor noticed the blood on Matt's clothes.

"Oh! Were you hurt?"

"Only slightly," Matt replied.

CHAPTER SEVENTEEN

Elko, Nevada, September 2, 1885, 6:15 p.m.
The train was stopped in Elko long enough for the teleprinter to be connected to a Western Union wire. Mary Beth tapped out the message that John wanted sent.

THE ATTEMPT ON OUR LIVES IN SAN FRANCISCO WAS NOT ISO-LATED. THERE HAVE BEEN TWO MORE ATTEMPTS SINCE WE LEFT. I AM THEREFORE BEGIN-NING TO THINK THAT ONE OF THE NAMES YOU SUGGESTED KEATON MITCHELL OR MORRIS MAY INDEED BE THE GUILTY PARTY. WHO AMONG THESE WOULD YOU THINK MOST LIKELY? HAVE YOU ANY OTHER SUGGESTIONS? WE ARE CUR-RENTLY IN ELKO NEVADA AND WILL BE HERE FOR TWO MORE

HOURS. PLEASE REPLY WITHIN
THAT PERIOD IF POSSIBLE.

Because there was a teleprinter in the
home office, the exchange of messages
between John and Drew was almost instan-
taneous.

GLAD YOU HAVE SURVIVED ALL
ATTEMPTS ON YOUR LIFE SO FAR
STOP PLEASE BE CAREFUL STOP
AM GRATIFIED YOU ARE TAKING
SERIOUSLY MY SUGGESTION
THAT IT MIGHT BE KEATON
MITCHELL OR MORRIS STOP I
THINK IT MAY MORE LIKELY BE
MORRIS STOP PLEASE KEEP IN
CONTACT THROUGHOUT YOUR
TRIP STOP I WANT TO KNOW
THAT YOU ARE SAFE

John read the message tape, then glanced
toward Matt. "I think Drew is correct. Morris probably is the most likely suspect."

"Tell me about Morris," Matt said.

"Raymond Morris owned a coal mine in
Assumption, Illinois. Ten years ago, he had
an explosion in his mine that killed forty
men."

The mine explosion had devastated the town, not only because of the loss of life, but also because it was the financial backbone of the town. With the mine badly damaged and all production stopped, the money stopped as well.

Raymond Morris tried to convince the miners to work for a delayed income in order to get the mine reopened.

"If we work together to get the mine reopened, it will pay off for all of us in the long run."

"You mean it'll pay off for you, don't you Morris?" Muley Sullivan asked. Sullivan was the president of the Mine Workers Union, and it was he who organized the strike and the demonstrations against the mine.

"Not just me, Sullivan. Can't you see that if we don't get this mine reopened, there will be work for nobody? I'll have no option but to close the mine and all the miners will lose their jobs. And it won't just be we, of the mine, who will be hurt. The merchants in town will suffer as well. They'll have no choice but to close up their businesses and go somewhere else. If that happens, the town will dry up and die."

"Mr. Morris may be right, Sullivan," one

of the mine workers said. "I can't afford to lose my job. I got me a wife and kids to feed. If the mine closes down like Mr. Morris says, what will I do?"

"Hold your ground, Pittman," Sullivan ordered. "If we all stand solid, we'll win this fight. You can count on that."

When John stepped down from the train, he could feel the tension in the air, and when he approached the mine, he could see it. There were at least a hundred men standing outside the mine office shouting.

"We must be paid!"

"No pay, no work!"

John made his way through the picket line, then went into the mine headquarters.

There was only one man in the building, and he was sitting behind a desk drinking whiskey from a bottle.

John pointed to the whiskey. "I'm afraid you won't find the solution to your problem from that bottle."

"Yeah? How the hell do you know?"

"I've seen many try, I have yet to see one succeed."

"What do you want?" he asked

"I take it that you are Raymond Morris?"

"Yeah, I am. What of it?"

John pointed toward the window. "You

seem to have a lot of upset men outside."

"Oh? Are there people outside?" Morris took another drink of whiskey straight from the bottle, then he wiped his mouth with the back of his hand. "I hadn't noticed," he added with a burp. "What do you want?"

"I want to clean the mine up and get it open again," John said.

"Yeah? Well, mister, that's what we all want. Only thing is, they want to be paid before the mine starts making money again, and I'm not able to do that. Especially since it is going to cost so much to replace lost equipment, shoring, and everything else."

"I might have a solution for you. If you are interested."

Morris took another swallow of his whiskey before he replied. "And what would that be?"

"I'll buy all the new equipment that might be needed, and I'll pay the men to clean up the mine and get it reopened."

"And just why would you do that? What I mean is, why would you be so generous?"

"Believe me, it isn't as much a matter of generosity as it is a matter of business. I'll do this, you see, because I want to buy the mine."

"You want to buy the mine? You mean as it is now?"

"Exactly as it is now."

"As it is now, it will take several thousand dollars to get it opened and operating again. To say nothing of the salaries and back salaries of the men. And they have let it be known that they won't work again until all their back pay is brought up-to-date."

"Yes, I'm quite aware of that."

"And you are prepared to spend that much money?"

"Yes."

"Who the hell are you, mister?"

"My name is John Bartmess Gillespie."

Morris was about to take another drink, but upon hearing the name he put the bottle down and stared at John.

"Are you lyin' to me, mister? Is that really who you are?"

"It is.

"This was a very productive mine, one of the most productive mines in the country. What makes you think I'd be willing to sell it?"

"I know that you can't get any more financing on it. And I know that if you don't get the mine reopened, the loans you do have are going to come due, and you'll lose the mine. If that happens, I could leave you completely out of it and just buy the mine from the lien holders. But I don't want to do that."

"And why don't you want to do that?"

"Because I will need those men out here to work the mine, and I will need someone to manage the mine. I would hope that would be you."

"Let me get this straight. You expect me to work for the same mine that I now own?"

"Yes."

"You said you were willing to buy me out. How much are you prepared to pay me for the mine?"

"Oh, Mr. Morris, I won't pay you anything," John said.

"What? Well now, that's a hell of a thing. You expect me to give the mine to you?"

"Mr. Morris, I will pay off every lien holder there is. Some of the liens I know are personal in nature, but I will pay them as well. And I will hire you to work as the manager. You will probably make more money than you were making when you owned this place, and you will be relieved of the worry of having to keep the mine afloat."

"It's more than a question of money," Morris said.

"What more is there?"

"I'm a man who likes to run things," Morris said. "If I see a decision that needs to be made, I want to be the one to make it. I don't want to have to wait on instructions from somebody who lives way off somewhere."

"Oh, but Mr. Morris, the reason I would want to keep you in control is for exactly what you just stated. I want someone who is self-motivated, someone who can make a decision on his own, whenever a decision has to be made.

"No, sir, Mr. Morris, I want to buy this mine as an investment. I have no intention of trying to run it myself."

Morris stared at John with a questioning expression on his face. "Are you saying that if you buy this mine, and you hire me to run it . . . that I'll have free hand?"

"That's exactly what I'm saying."

Morris extended his hand. "You've just bought yourself a mine."

On board the Gillespie car
Instead of leaving the train, they ate in the private car that evening. The dining table was set for dinner, and little flashes of light bounced off the shining silverware, the sparkling china, and the softly gleaming stemware. Julius Calhoun, the porter, brought the meal to them on a pushcart. The menu was leg of lamb, buttered noo-

dles, minted green peas, and rolls.

"Please don't tell any of my cattlemen friends how much I enjoyed lamb, but this was a fine meal," Matt agreed.

"I won't," John replied with a chuckle.

"So, Morris took you up on the offer to take over the mine," Matt said as he took a sip of wine. "Excellent wine," he said.

"I'm glad you like it. It's from a winery that I own in the Napa Valley. I think the day will come when California is as well known for its wines as France. Yes, he took the offer, and I was right about the results, too. Since I bought the mine, Morris has wound up making much more money as the manager than he ever made while he was still the owner."

"Then, I don't understand. Why do you think he might have enough resentment to be trying to kill you?"

"I don't know that he does have that much resentment against me," John replied. "But the mine is making money now, a lot more money than it was ever making while he owned it. And I suppose there is always the possibility that, deep down inside, he wishes he had never sold out."

"But didn't you say he had no choice? That he was going to lose the mine anyway?"

"Yes, but that requires reason," John said. "It has been my observation that when men are involved in high-stakes business, much like in high-stakes poker, reason often becomes one of the first casualties."

Matt smiled. "Mr. Gillespie, it is absolutely no wonder that you are successful. You are a very smart man."

"Well thank you, Matt. Coming from you, that is indeed a huge compliment."

Salt Lake City, Utah, September 3, 2 a.m.
Kelly had come to the realization that the job of getting Gillespie and his daughter killed wasn't going to be accomplished as long as Matt Jensen was around. It was time, therefore, to stop trying to kill the Gillespies and concentrate instead on getting rid of the bodyguard.

But how was he to do that?

As he stood out on the depot platform at two o'clock in the morning, he saw a couple of sheriff's deputies who had come down to meet the train. That gave him an idea, and he walked over to talk to them.

Matt was standing on the platform alongside the private car, keeping an eye on both the front and rear entrances. John and Mary Beth were both inside, and he was sure that, at this hour, they were asleep. He didn't want to disturb them, but he knew that whenever the train was stopped for any length of time the danger was greater.

Two men came toward him, and he became instantly alert until he saw their badges glinting in the light of the platform lamps. He relaxed.

"Mr. Jensen?" one of them said.

"Yes, I'm Matt Jensen."

"Would you come with us please, Mr. Jensen?"

"I'd rather not."

Both deputies drew their pistols. Matt didn't expect it, so he made no attempt to reply. Even now, if he had wanted to, he knew that he could draw and shoot both of them before they could react. But if they actually were officers of the law, he didn't want to do that.

"We're not going to ask you again," one of the two men said.

Matt wasn't sure what he should do. On one hand, he didn't want to leave the train and leave John and Mary Beth unprotected. On the other hand, he didn't want to defy the law.

"How long is this going to take?" Matt asked. "I can't leave the train."

"It will take as long as it takes."

Matt sighed, then went with them. They took his gun from him, then they took him to the sheriff's office.

"Would you please tell me what this is for?" Matt asked.

"We received word that you murdered someone on the train yesterday between here and Reno."

"Who told you that?"

"Never mind who told us. We know that there were several witnesses."

"I did kill someone on the train, but it was in self-defense," Matt said. "And we were standing on top of the train, so there couldn't have been any witnesses."

"That's where you're wrong. There were many witnesses. They saw your shadow on the ground."

"And they are telling you they can identify me by my shadow?"

"They don't have to identify you, Mr. Jensen. You have already confessed to it," one of the deputies said.

CHAPTER EIGHTEEN

Kelly had watched, from afar, the confrontation between Matt Jensen and the sheriff's deputies. He felt a sense of accomplishment in getting Jensen out of the way, and he would have to let Conroy know that he was ultimately responsible for the success of the job.

He thought for a moment that it might be a good idea for him to hire some men here . . . but he wouldn't know who to hire, and he wasn't sure that Conroy would reimburse him for the cost of hiring. He would just wait for Conroy's next step, which, because Jensen had been removed, was bound to be successful.

"All aboard!" he called, and the passengers, some of them new and some of them passengers who had taken advantage of the brief stop, climbed onto the train.

When the last passenger was boarded, Kelly raised his lantern to signal the engineer. Then, with a blast of the whistle, the train began to roll out of the station. Kelly climbed onto the step, collected the tickets from the new passengers, then went to the front of the train, passing through the baggage car until he was standing in the vestibule between the baggage car and the private car.

It was the middle of the night, and he knew that Gillespie and his daughter would both be asleep. Now would be the perfect time to do it.

But how? He had no weapon.

Wait, he had seen a hammer in the baggage car. He could kill them in their sleep by bludgeoning them to death.

Yes, that's exactly what he would do.

Kelly stepped back into the baggage car, retrieved the hammer, then returned to the private car. He took a deep breath, then reached down to turn the doorknob.

It was locked!

Damn!

With a sigh of frustration, Kelly turned and walked back through the baggage car. When he stepped into the Pullman car, he saw that Matt Jensen's berth was empty. He decided to take a little nap. And why not? He asked himself. Jensen won't be needing it anymore.

Back at the sheriff's office, Matt heard the train whistle.

"Look, you're making a mistake," Matt said. "I have to be on that train, and it is leaving without me."

"Looks like you ain't goin' to make it, don't it?" one of the deputies asked in a cruel tease.

In a move that was so quick that neither of the deputies expected it, Matt snatched a pistol from the holster of one of the two men.

"What the hell?" the two deputies called out in shock and fear. Both of them put their hands up.

"You got a judge in this town?" Matt asked.

"Yes, of course we do."

He pointed to the deputy whose pistol he had taken. "Go get him."

"Are you serious? It's three o'clock in the morning! I'm not going to wake the judge up in the middle of the night."

"I think you will," Matt said, cocking the pistol and pointing it at the other deputy.

"Mason, for God's sake, go get him!" the deputy said in a frightened tone of voice.

■ ■ ■ ■

According to the Regulator clock that was standing against the wall in the sheriff's office, twenty minutes had passed since Deputy Mason left on his errand.

"How far does he have to go to find the judge?" Matt asked.

"Not far. The judge lives on the street behind us," the deputy answered nervously.

Less than five minutes later, Mason returned with a sleepy and grumpy-looking white-haired man.

"What do you want with me, young man?" the judge asked. "The deputy woke me in the middle of the night, so whatever it is, it had better be good."

"You are a judge?"

"That's who you sent for, isn't it? Yes, I'm Judge Craig. Now, what is it you want?"

Matt, who now had his own pistol, put it back in his holster.

"Thank you, young man. I find it easier to talk when someone isn't pointing a gun at me."

"I put it away to let you know that I'm not a threat to anyone," Matt said.

Out of the corner of his eye he saw the deputy who was still armed pull his pistol.

Matt let him get his gun all the way out before he reacted. He drew his pistol, pointed it at the deputy, and cocked it.

Chagrined, the deputy returned his pistol to its holster. Matt did the same thing, then resumed his conversation with the judge.

"Judge, when these two deputies pulled me from the train, they also pulled me away from the two people I have been hired to protect. And in doing so, they put Mr. John Gillespie and his daughter in grave danger."

"John Gillespie?" Judge Craig asked. "Are you talking about John Gillespie, the wealthy industrialist?"

"Yes, I am talking about that John Gillespie. There have been several attempts made against his life, and not only his life, but his daughter's life as well. The two of them are traveling to Chicago, and I have been hired to see that they get there safely. Right now, Mr. Gillespie and his daughter are in a private car that is attached to the train that left at least half an hour ago."

"Deputy Mason said that you killed a man on the train."

"I did, that is true. The man I killed had come to kill Mr. Gillespie. When I stopped him, he came after me with a knife. We fought on top of the car, and apparently we cast shadows onto the ground that were seen by several of the people on the train."

"How do I know you are telling the truth? How do I know you are guarding Mr. Gillespie?"

"You can send a telegram to the Emerson Private Detective Agency in San Francisco. Emerson will confirm what I have told you."

"All right, I'll do that first thing in the morning."

"No, sir, I need you to do it now," Matt said. "I can't afford to wait until tomorrow morning. I have to catch up with the train as quickly as I can."

"There's nobody who will be doing business at this hour of the night," Judge Craig said.

"I've worked with Emerson before," Matt said. "He keeps someone in his office twenty-four hours per day. You must do this."

The judge waited for a moment, staring pointedly at the pistol in Matt's holster.

"Is that a threat, Jensen? You have already demonstrated how fast you are with that gun."

"Your Honor, I could have killed both of these men and gotten away easily," Matt said. "But I've no wish to kill innocent men, and you've no reason to keep me here. Not when you can verify my story by a simple telegram."

"All right," Judge Craig said. "Let's go down to the depot and send the message."

Half an hour later they were standing at the Western Union desk waiting for the reply to the telegram Judge Craig had sent. The telegraph key started clacking, and the telegrapher began recording the message. When he was finished he handed the message to the judge.

MATT JENSEN PRESENCE ON TRAIN IS CRITICAL TO PROTECT INDUSTRIALIST JOHN GILLESPIE AND DAUGHTER STOP PLEASE DO NOTHING TO IMPEDE HIS MISSION
                    JEFFERSON EMERSON

Judge Craig showed the message to Matt, then to the two deputies.

"I apologize, Mr. Jensen," Deputy Mason said.

"I . . . don't know what we can do to undo the damage," Judge Craig said.

"Where is the train now?" Matt asked the telegrapher.

"It should be halfway between Evanston and Rock Springs by now," the telegrapher said. He made a few taps on the key, then waited. It took but a moment for the response.

"That's funny, it hasn't even reached Evanston yet. It should have been there before now."

"Do you suppose something has happened to it?" the judge asked.

"I don't know," the telegrapher said.

"Judge, I want you to order that a fast engine be put on the track so I can catch up with the train. I will pay the railroad for the engine."

The telegraph key began again, and as the telegrapher recorded the message, an expression of relief appeared on his face.

"It has a bad wheel on the tender," he said. "They can't fix it in Evanston, they are going to have to go on through to Rock Springs. It'll be running much slower than normal, so they're clearing the track ahead of it."

"Come, Mr. Jensen, let's get that engine for you," Judge Craig said.

Matt paid five hundred dollars to hire an engine and crew, and it raced down the track at more than fifty miles per hour. The sun came up, and the bright orb hung over the track right in front of them, impeding

215

their vision. But just under three hours after they left Salt Lake City, they saw the train on the track in front of them.

"I guess we'll just follow it on in to Rock Springs," the engineer said.

"No, I need to get on it now."

"How are you going to do that? We've got no way of telling them to stop."

"I'll climb out on front of the engine, then onto the last car of the train ahead."

"Have you ever done anything like that before?" the engineer asked.

"No, but how hard can it be?"

"Harder than you think. But if you are fool enough to want to do it, go right ahead," the engineer invited.

Matt had never done it before, but he knew what it would require. He would have to climb out onto the running board of the moving engine and pick his way alongside the boiler. It was simple enough when the engine was standing on a siding, but quite another matter when the train was running at full speed.

Actually, they weren't running nearly as fast now as they had been running, because the train ahead had been greatly slowed by the damaged wheel.

Grabbing the handhold outside the window, Matt climbed onto the board and clung there for one dizzying moment, trying not to fall onto the blur of ballast below or against the searing hot jacket of the boiler. Then he moved forward.

They were going down a little grade. It wasn't steep, but the rails swooped down and around a hill. The wheels pounded in his ears, screeching as they took the curve. Finally, he reached his position, then hung there as the wind was cutting his face and blowing his hair. He felt as if he were falling through space.

At that moment the engine rolled over a rough section of track bed. It gave a little twist and Matt was pitched back. He made a desperate grab for the guardrail, caught it, and hung there for a moment with his legs dangling but a foot away from the huge, rapidly spinning drive wheels. Finally, he pulled himself back up onto the running board. Once he was back on the running board, he paused for a moment to get reoriented, then he started moving forward until he reached the front of the engine. There he measured the distance between the engine and the trailing car of the train ahead of them. Looking back at the engineer he held up his hand, directing him to close the distance, providing him with as precise directions as he could.

Matt knew that if he tried to pass between this engine and the train in front of him and missed, that he would be ground into a pulp under the engine.

He looked down at the tracks between them and the car ahead and saw the cross ties whipping below him at blurring speed. When he gauged the distance to be correct, he held up his hand, palm open, which he hoped the engineer would take as a signal to hold it exactly where he was.

Matt climbed out onto the cowcatcher, then jumped across the gap to the back of the car ahead. He caught onto the railing that ran around the back car, climbed over it, then leaned out to wave at the engineer.

The engineer caught his signal, then slowed down enough to open up a considerable space between the two trains.

The first thing Matt noticed once he was back aboard the train he had missed this morning was how much slower it was going now than it had been.

He stepped into the car, which was a day car, surprising many who had not expected to see anyone come into the car from the back door. He nodded and smiled at a few of them, then passed on through the car as if there was nothing at all unusual about his entrance.

When he passed through the diner he saw Kelly sitting at the front table having his breakfast. Kelly dropped his fork in surprise.

"Hello, Mr. Kelly. Surprised to see me?"

"I . . . uh . . . yes. I haven't seen you since we left Salt Lake City. I thought, perhaps, you had gotten off the train."

"Now, why would I have done that? I'm committed to seeing the Gillespies safely through, all the way to Chicago."

"Well, yes, but I thought Mr. Gillespie said that the danger had passed, so when I didn't see you this morning, I gathered that you must have left the train in Salt Lake City and started back."

"No, I'm still here," Matt said, without providing any additional information. "Have you seen them this morning?"

"No, I didn't want to disturb them."

With a nod, Matt continued on through the train until he reached the private car. He knocked quietly.

"Who is it?" John called from the other side of the door.

"It's me, Matt."

The door was jerked open quickly.

"We thought you were gone," John said with an obvious sigh of relief.

"I was, for a while."

Matt told them the story of his being arrested and of subsequently hiring an engine and crew.

"It wasn't all that hard to catch up with you," he concluded. "This train has a bad wheel, and that has made it necessary for it to run a lot slower than it has been."

"I thought so!" Mary Beth said. "I used your formula to see how fast we were going. Why, we are only doing about fifteen miles to the hour."

"Yes, and I'm glad of it. I wouldn't have caught up with you had you been going as fast as we were in the beginning."

"Why were you arrested? I know you said it was for killing the man who tried to kill us. But who would have reported that?"

"According to the deputies, several people on the train saw the fight. Or at least they saw shadows of two men fighting."

"But if all they saw was shadows, how could they relate that to you?" Mary Beth asked.

"Good question," Matt replied with a broad smile. "How could they possibly know that I was one of the two men dumb enough to get into a knife fight on top of a fast-moving train?"

Chapter Nineteen

Rock Springs, Wyoming, September 3,
6 p.m.

Once the train reached Rock Springs it was shunted to a sidetrack because one of the wheels on the tender had gotten "out of round," and it was necessary that the wheel be replaced.

There was another eastbound through train due at two o'clock in the morning, but they were told that the wheel could be replaced in no more than six hours, which meant they would be able to be on their way again before having to transfer to the next available train.

"We'll get underway again at midnight," Kelly promised all who complained to him about the delay.

Mary Beth wanted to leave the train and look around the town. She had never been here before, and as she explained to Matt and John, "I like to see new places."

"I don't mind looking around either," John said. "There is a very productive coal mine here, producing coal for the railroads, and I would like to get a good look at it."

"Are you planning to buy it?" Matt asked.

"Ha, I wish I could. But the coal mine belongs to a couple of brothers, Archibald and Duncan Blair. They opened the mine at just the right time, when the Union Pacific Railroad arrived."

"Were they the first pioneers, Papa?"

"No, darlin', that would be Ben Holladay. He brought his Overland Stage Company through here because of something that was even more valuable than coal then, and perhaps even now. Rock Springs is a valuable source of water in the midst of the desert."

As Matt, John, and Mary Beth were walking around town, the conductor was standing at the Western Union counter inside the depot. He was waiting for a reply to the telegram he had just sent to Conroy in which he said simply and cryptically . . .

AT ROCK SPRINGS WYOMING STOP JOB REMAINS OPEN

When the telegraph key started clacking,

he looked toward the telegrapher.

"Yes, sir, Mr. Kelly, this is what you've been waiting on."

As the key continued its clatter, the telegrapher wrote the note on a piece of yellow paper, then he handed it to Kelly.

CONTACT ARNOLD HELLMAN AND FENTON LADUE WHO ARE LOCALS STOP MENTION MY NAME TO THEM STOP AM WIRING TWO HUNDRED DOLLARS FOR EXPENSES

The telegrapher filled out a form and handed it to Kelly. "Sign this receipt, and I'll give you the two hundred dollars."

"Thanks," Kelly said.

"Oh, I would like to go in here before they close," Mary Beth said as they passed by a dress shop. "I always like to see what the ladies are wearing in other towns."

"We'll come in with you," Matt said.

Mary Beth laughed, then tilted her head. "Matt, do you really want to come into a dress shop?"

Matt laughed as well. "No, not really. I just don't think I should let you out of my sight. I am responsible for your safety."

"What do think is going to happen to me in a dress shop? Look, there's a saloon just down the street. Why don't you and Papa go in there and have a beer? If anything happens, I'll scream loud enough for you to hear me, you don't have to worry about that. I'll scream loud enough for the whole town to hear me."

"She's right," John said. "I can't see anything happening to her in a dress shop. And I would like to have a beer."

"All right," Matt agreed. He smiled. "It's not really that hard to talk me into having a beer."

Matt and John watched Mary Beth go into the dress shop, then they headed toward the saloon. They were about halfway there when they heard someone's distressed voice coming from behind one of the buildings. It was a plea in broken English.

"No, please! You no hit no more!"

The plea was followed by a thumping sound.

"You damn Chinamen come over here and think you own the place. Well, we showed you last night, didn't we?"

Matt hurried between the two buildings and saw three men standing around an Asian man. The Asian's face was bruised so badly that one eye was swollen completely

224

shut. There was blood on his lip.

"That's enough," Matt said sharply.

"Stay the hell out of this, mister! This ain't none of your business," one of the three men said, angrily.

"I just made it my business."

Two of the men started toward Matt, but they stopped when he drew his pistol.

"You ain't got the guts to use that," one of them said.

Matt shot twice, the gunshots coming on top of each other. With shouts of pain, both men slapped their hand to their ear and blood slipped through their fingers.

"You son of a bitch! You shot off my ear!" one of the men said.

"No, just the earlobe. Now, I'm asking real nice for the three of you to leave."

The three men glared at him a moment longer, then they left.

"What is your name?" Matt asked.

"My name Ling."

"Mister Ling, you can go home now. They won't bother you again."

"I no have house now. White men burn my house. White miners burn all Chinaman houses." With that, Ling turned and walked away, going in a different direction from that taken by the three men who had been ac-costing him.

"What do you think that was all about?" John asked.

"I don't know. I gave up trying to understand evil a long time ago."

Once they ordered their beers, it didn't take long for them to learn what Ling was talking about when he had said that *"White miners burn all Chinaman houses."* It was the subject of half a dozen conversations, and from listening they gathered that there had been a near riot the night before, resulting in the death of many of the Chinese and the destruction of several houses.

"When them damn Chinamen come over here, they got to learn who is boss," one of the saloon patrons said. "They got no business comin' here in the first place. This here country is for Americans, it ain't for Chinamen."

"Well, yeah, I can see that, Karl, but I can't see no reason for killin' so many of 'em, 'n burning their houses down."

"It taught 'em a lesson though, didn't it?"*

* The Union Pacific Railroad employed 331 Chinese and 150 whites in their coal mine in Rock Springs, Wyoming. On September 2, 1885, Chinese and white miners, who were paid by the ton, had a dispute over who had the right to work in a particularly desirable area of the mine. White min-

■ ■ ■ ■

From a distance, Dan Kelly had watched Matt and John step into the Miners' Saloon. There were three saloons in town, and, because Dan Kelly had been through Rock Springs many times, he knew all three of them. The Miners' Saloon was the nicest of the three.

The names Conroy had mentioned in his telegram, Hellman and Ladue, were familiar to him, because he had heard about them from his previous visits to Rock Springs. Before he contacted them, though, he realized he was going to have to do something about Matt Jensen.

He had thought that the coups he pulled off yesterday would take care of the situation for him, yet somehow Jensen had talked his way out of the arrest. He had not only

---

ers, members of the Knights of Labor, beat two Chinese miners and walked off their jobs. That evening the white miners, armed with rifles, rioted and burned down the Chinese quarter. No whites were prosecuted for the murder of twenty-eight Chinese and $150,000 in property damage, even though the identities of those responsible were widely known.

done that . . . he had managed to get back to the train.

Kelly learned from some of the passengers in the last car what had happened. He had come in through the back door, and when a few of the more curious had checked, they saw that a detached engine had come up behind them in order to make the transfer.

Whatever else one might say about Matt Jensen, he was certainly resourceful.

Kelly went into the Pick Axe Saloon. If the Miners' Saloon was the nicest of the three, the Pick Axe was the worst. Here, the beer was green and the whiskey was foul. The bar girls who worked the Pick Axe were on the last run before they wound up in a crib in the alley. But it was those very characteristics that caused Kelly to choose this saloon, a saloon that he would have never chosen under ordinary circumstances. But these weren't ordinary circumstances; he was here for a particular reason.

He didn't go to the bar but chose a table in the back of the room. One of the bar girls came over to flirt with him, and this was exactly what he wanted. She smiled, but she shouldn't have; the smile showed two teeth missing on top and one on the bottom.

"I ain't never seen you in here before," the girl said.

"Would you like to sit and have a drink with me?" Kelly invited.

The girl's smile grew broader. "Yeah, sure," she said. "What will you have?"

"Which is better, the beer or the whiskey?" Kelly asked.

The girl looked around, nervously, before she answered. "There ain't neither one of 'em any good, but the beer is prob'ly easier to get down."

"What's your name?"

"Lil."

"All right, Lil, bring me a beer, and get somethin' for yourself."

Kelly gave her a dollar bill.

Lil returned to the table a moment later, carrying one beer and one small glass of what Kelly assumed to be tea. Though given Lil's appearance and the appearance of the other girls here, it could well have been whiskey.

Lil put the change on the table in front of Kelly.

"You can keep it," he said

"Gee, thanks, mister."

"How well do you know the people of this town?" Kelly asked.

"I don't know too many of 'em. Only the ones who come in here a lot."

"Who do you figure is the meanest of

them all?"

Lil got a look of apprehension on her face.

"Uh, they are all pretty nice," she said, her voice betraying her fear at being involved in such a conversation.

Kelly took two dollars from his pocket and held the bills on the table in Lil's plain view.

"I'm going to ask you again, who is the meanest person you know?"

"Well, it might be a man by the name of Runt Logan," Lil said.

"Runt Logan? That's his name?"

"Well, I don't think nobody knows what his real first name is. They call him Runt Logan 'cause he's pretty much of a runt. Only there don't nobody call him that to his face, on account of he's just real good with a gun, and he's got a real big temper. That's him over there."

She pointed to a relatively small man, but he was wearing his gun slung low, and a bad scar caused his lip to be deformed.

"What makes you think he's so bad?"

"Don't know if you've heard of it yet, but last night, a bunch of Chinamen was kilt. 'N folks is saying that Logan kilt three of 'em his own self."

"Thanks," Kelly said. He slid the two dollars across the table to the girl.

"Give this to Logan," he said, giving her

an additional two dollars. "And tell him I would like to talk to him."

"Oh, goodness, mister, you ain't one of them kind, are you? 'Cause if you are, 'n you're askin' Logan to come over here, why, he's likely to kick your teeth in."

"One of what kind?" Kelly asked, confused by the direction the conversation had taken.

"You know what kind. I mean one of them kind that likes men more 'n he likes women."

Kelly laughed.

"I'm not one of those kind," he said.

He watched as Lil walked over to the other table, handed the money to Logan, then pointed back toward Kelly. Logan took the money, listened for a moment, glanced over at Kelly, then approached his table.

"What do you want?" he asked. His voice sounded like he had gargled with broken glass.

"I want to offer you a job."

"What kind of job?"

"I want you to kill someone."

"Mister, are you crazy?" Logan asked. "What makes you think I'd take a job like that, anyhow?"

"From what I understand, you are pretty good at it. In fact, I hear you killed three men last night, and you weren't paid any-

231

thing for it."

"Yeah, well, it ain't like they was regular men. These here three was Chinamen."

"Well, the man I want you to kill is white. And I'll give you one hundred dollars to do the job."

The one hundred dollars got Logan's attention right away.

"A hunnert dollars?"

"Yes."

"And all I have to do is kill one man?"

"Yes."

"Where is this son of a bitch you want me to kill?"

"He is here, in town. He just got off the train."

"Where is he?"

"Right now, he is in the Miners' Saloon."

"What's he look like?"

"You go in first, I'll come in after you. I'll go over to say something to him, and you'll see me put my hand on his shoulder. That will show you who he is. But don't do anything until I have left the saloon."

"Why are you goin' to leave? Don't you want to see me do it?"

"I don't need to see you do it. If you do it, I'll know about it."

"They ain't no if about it. If I set out to kill somebody, I get the job done. Hell, you

can ask them three Chinamen I shot last
night." Logan laughed out loud. "No, come
to think of it, you can't ask 'em, can you?
You can't ask 'em, 'cause they're dead."

CHAPTER TWENTY

Kelly waited across the street until Logan went into the Miners' Saloon. Then, about a minute later, Kelly went in, too. He saw Jensen and Gillespie standing at the bar, and he walked over to them and put his hand on Matt's shoulder.

"Mr. Kelly," John said. "Won't you join us for a beer?"

"Thank you, no, I can't stay. I'm just going around town looking up all our passengers to remind them that the train will leave around midnight, and we would like ever'body to be aboard no later than eleven fifteen."

"All right, we'll be there," John promised.

"And you'll make sure your daughter is with you?"

"Yes, of course, I will."

During the entire conversation, Kelly had kept his hand on Matt's shoulder, and though Matt didn't say anything about it, the intimacy made him feel uneasy. When Kelly took his hand down, Matt hunched his shoulder, as if getting rid of the touch.

"I wonder why he thought it was necessary to tell us that," Matt said. "We were already told that before we left the train."

"Probably some railroad rule, just to make sure they don't run off and leave anyone," John said. "That would be bad for business," he added with a little laugh.

At his table in the back of the saloon, Logan had watched Kelly come in and touch the shoulder of one of the men at the bar. He didn't know who the man was, but it didn't matter. As far as Logan was concerned, the man could be called "One Hundred," because he was being paid one hundred dollars to kill him.

Of course, he couldn't just murder him. He would have to pick a fight with him but do so in a way that after he killed him, he could claim that it was a fair fight. It hadn't been necessary for him to be so cautious yesterday. Yesterday he had killed Chinamen, and the law didn't seem to care. But this was a white man.

Matt saw the man in the mirror sitting at a table on the far side of the room. The man seemed to be studying him, and Matt had, long ago, developed an intuition about such things. It was that intuition, almost as much as his prowess with a pistol, that had kept him alive through the years.

A couple of times Matt looked directly at the man's reflection, wanting to look him in the eyes, but the man cut his gaze away both times.

Finally, the man stood up and started toward Matt.

"Move away, John," Matt said quietly.

"What?"

"It's just a feeling I've got. Go down to the other end of the bar, now!"

Matt was insistent enough with his order that John didn't question him a second time.

"Mister, I want to know why is it that you're 'a starin' at me in the mirror?" the man who had just stood asked. He spoke the words loudly, and he put more reproach into the question than was required. It was, Matt realized, a direct provocation. It was also a dangerous one, because the man was much too small to be making any kind of a physical challenge.

Matt turned to face him.

"Was I staring?" Matt asked, the quiet calm of his voice in direct contrast to the feverish tone of the man's voice.

"Yeah, you was."

"Well, I'm sorry, about that. I don't mean to make you uncomfortable."

"Yeah? Well you are making me damn uncomfortable."

"I assure you, sir, any thought that I am staring at you is unfounded. I'll make certain not to do so in the future."

"What makes you think you're even goin' to have a future?" the man asked.

"Logan, that's enough!" the bartender said. "This man ain't done nothin' to you, and he apologized even though he didn't do nothin'."

Logan held a hand out toward the bartender, though he didn't take his eyes off Matt.

"This ain't none of your business, Tucker. 'N if you don't keep your mouth shut 'n stay out of this, I'll be takin' care of you, right after I take care of . . . hey, mister, what the hell is your name, anyway?"

"It's Jensen. Matt Jensen."

Logan smiled, a twisted smile without mirth.

"Reason I asked is, yesterday I kilt me three Chinamen, 'n I didn't know the name of a one of 'em."

"Oh? And tell me, Logan, is it?"

"Yeah. Logan's the name, all right. Heard of me, have you?"

237

"No, I can't say as I have. But tell me, Logan, why did you want to know my name? Are you planning on killing me?"

"It might come to that," Logan said. "If you don't apologize to me."

"Well, then, this disagreement needn't go any further, need it? I've already apologized to you."

"Not on your knees, you ain't," Logan said.

"Well now, Mr. Logan, while I did say I'm sorry if I have made you uncomfortable in any way, and I'm willing to say that again, I will not get down on my knees to apologize to you. So I guess this conversation is over."

Matt turned back toward the bar, and when he did so, Logan drew his pistol.

Because Matt had turned away, it put him at a disadvantage, and that allowed Logan to actually draw his gun and get one shot off. The bullet punched a hole in the bar just behind Matt. But Matt had his gun out just as fast, firing at almost the same time. And unlike Logan, Matt didn't miss.

Logan dropped his gun and grabbed his chest, then turned his hand out and looked down in surprise and disbelief as his palm began filling with his own blood. His eyes rolled back in his head, and he fell back, then lay motionless on the floor with open but sightless eyes staring toward the ceiling.

It all happened so quickly that the saloon patrons had been caught by surprise and had no chance to get out of danger. But now that the danger was over, they all began to edge toward the body.

Gun smoke from the two charges merged to form a large, acrid-bitter cloud that drifted slowly toward the door. Beams of light from the kerosene lamps hanging from a wagon wheel suspended from the ceiling became visible as they stabbed through the cloud. There were rapid and heavy footfalls on the wooden sidewalk outside as more people began coming in through the swinging doors.

Sheriff Barton Ames was one of the first ones to come in.

Seeing that the dead man was Logan, Sheriff Ames nodded grimly.

"I'll be damned. Someone finally got Logan."

"Yeah," the bartender said. He pointed to Logan's body. "And if there was ever anybody who needed killin' more than Runt Logan, I don't know who it would be."

"Hell, anybody that knew him knew this was bound to happen someday." The sheriff looked over at Matt, who had put his gun back in the holster and was now leaning casually against the bar.

"You the one that killed him?" the sheriff asked.

"I didn't have much choice, he drew on me." Matt pointed to the bullet hole in the bar. "Here is where his bullet went."

"Damndest thing I ever saw, Sheriff. Logan come over and started pickin' a fight. This fella tried to calm him down, but Logan wouldn't hear of it. This fella turned his back on Logan, 'n that's when Logan drew his gun."

"You're saying that Logan drew first, and this man still beat him?" Sheriff Ames asked, his voice expressing his surprise.

"Yes, sir, that is exactly what I'm a-sayin'."

"That's the way I seen it, too," another patron said.

"I tell you the truth, I've seen Runt Logan in action before, 'n I never thought anyone would be able to beat him," yet another said.

"Sheriff, if you need someone to give a statement 'bout what happened here, I mean as to who drew first 'n all that, why, I'll be more'n willin' to give you a statement," the bartender said.

"Me, too," yet another said.

Sheriff Ames smiled. "No need for any statements. I know how Logan was." He turned to Matt. "What's your name?" he asked.

"Jensen. Matt Jensen."

"Well, Mr. Jensen, I don't mind telling you that you did us all a favor. But then, I reckon you know who Logan was."

"Truth to tell, Sheriff, I'm just a passenger on the train and a stranger in town. I've never heard of Logan until right now."

"Really? You never heard of him, huh? It's too bad Logan didn't live long enough to hear that. He was about the most arrogant son of a bitch I've ever known."

Kelly learned quickly that Logan had failed in his attempt to kill Matt Jensen. And while he still believed that it would be easier if Matt Jensen were dead, as it was now, he had no alternative but to follow Conroy's instructions in locating Hellman and Ladue. As the discussion with Sheriff Ames was going on, Dan Kelly was meeting with the two men Conroy had suggested that he find. He returned to the Pick Axe Saloon, where he asked the bar girl, Lil, if she knew them.

"Yes, I know both of 'em. They work for Mr. Garner."

"Who is he?"

"He runs the stable."

A few minutes later, Kelly found the two men mucking out stalls. Their boots and the lower part of their trousers were covered with horse dung, but it didn't seem to matter to them.

"What do you want?" one of the two asked, when they saw Kelly staring at them.

"Are you Hellman and Ladue?"

"Yeah, I'm Hellman, he's Ladue. What of it?"

"Does the name Lucas Conroy mean anything to you?" Kelly asked.

"Yeah, it means something," Hellman said. "Does he have a job for us?"

"Yes."

"What does he want done?"

"What have you done for him before?"

"What do you mean?"

"Have you ever killed for him before?"

"Are you the law?"

"No. I'm working for Conroy. I have been instructed to pay you to take care of a job for him."

Hellman looked around to make certain there was no danger of their conversation being overheard.

"Who does he want killed?"

"There are three of them."

"Three of them? Two of us, and three of them?" Ladue asked.

"Yes, but only one of them is wearing a gun. And one of the three is a woman," Kelly said.

"Only one with a gun? All right, I can't see as it can be much of a problem to handle the job," Hellman said.

"How much are we getting for the job?" Ladue asked.

"You'll get fifty dollars apiece when the job is done," Kelly said. He had already decided to keep for himself half of the money Conroy had sent him and all of the money if they failed.

"Who is this two men and a woman he wants kilt?" Ladue asked.

"Their names aren't important."

"The hell the names ain't important. We got to know who it is, don't we?" Hellman asked.

"They are passengers on the train that's having to stay here for a while, because they are replacing a wheel on the tender. But you will need to do it soon, otherwise they'll be back on the train."

"How are we going to do this?" Ladue asked. "I mean, we can't just shoot them down in the street in front of the whole town. We'd get hung for murder."

"The three of them are riding in a private car, and it's down at the depot, setting off on a sidetrack way over by itself. There are some trees alongside the track, and I figure you two could wait in those trees until you see them coming back. That's where you can do the job, because there won't be anyone there to see you."

"All right," Hellman said.

While this discussion was going on in the Pick Axe, Logan's body was removed from the Miners' Saloon, and everything returned to normal. Matt and John were still there, but they had moved from the bar to a table.

"What do you think of my daughter?" John asked. The question had come out of the blue, and for a moment Matt wasn't sure how he should answer it.

"Why, I think Mary Beth is a beautiful and intelligent young woman," Matt replied.

"Don't you think most men would think the same thing?"

"Yes, I'm sure they would."

"Then I'd like you to tell me, if you can, Matt, why Mary Beth doesn't have any serious suitors? She's twenty-three years old with no husband, and beyond that, there is no husband in sight. I'm leaving her the entire company, and before I die I would like to think that she had a husband by her side to help her run it. Of course, she'll have

Drew to help her . . . but Drew is as old as I am, so he won't be around forever either. For crying out loud, I should be a grandfather by now."

"Give her time, Mr. Gillespie. There is no way I could ever see someone like Mary Beth Gillespie becoming an old maid."

"I wouldn't mind giving her time if she would ever show any interest in anyone."

"I think women have a feeling about this," Matt said. "You wouldn't want her to wind up with someone who was marrying her just for the money, would you?"

"No, of course not."

"Then let her make up her own mind. Like I said, most women can tell if the man is worth their attention, and from what I've learned about Mary Beth, I would say she would be better at it than most."

"You're probably right," John said. He glanced over at the grandfather clock that stood against the wall next to the piano. "Speaking of Mary Beth, I think she may be finished looking around at all the stores by now."

The two men finished their beers, then left the saloon.

By the time they stepped outside, it had grown dark.

"I should have been paying more attention," John said. "I hate for her to be out in the dark all alone."

Seeing that the dress shop was still well lit, Matt and John stepped inside, their entry marked by the tinkling of a bell attached to the door.

"Papa! We're back here!" Mary Beth called.

When the two went into the back of the store they saw Mary Beth sitting with two other women.

"This is Mrs. McCormack and her daughter, Susan," Mary Beth said. "They were nice enough to keep their shop open until you came for me."

"Darlin', I'm sorry I'm late. We got to talking and . . ."

Mary Beth laughed. "Heavens, Papa, you don't have to apologize. I know how men are."

"Mrs. McCormack, it was very nice of you to keep the store open for my daughter," John said.

"Well, what with all the trouble we had yesterday, the miners killing the Chinamen and all, I just didn't feel good about Miss Gillespie being out on the street by herself."

"I told her that you would buy me the most expensive shawl she had," Mary Beth said with a broad smile.

246

"A shawl?"

"Yes. Oh, and it is beautiful, Papa. Besides, I may need it in Chicago, because it will probably get quite cool there."

"I expect you're right. All right, Mrs. Mc-Cormack, where is this shawl?"

Mary Beth held up a package. "She's already wrapped it up for me."

"Pretty confident that I would buy it, weren't you?" John asked, smiling as he withdrew the money from his wallet.

"Of course," Mary Beth replied. Then to the shopkeepers, "Mrs. McCormack, Susan, thank you very much for being so nice to me."

"Oh, it was a pleasure, Mary Beth. And do have a safe trip to Chicago," Mrs. Mc-Cormack replied.

Leaving the dress shop, they had dinner in the Palace Café. They lingered over dinner for a while, then John looked at his watch.

"Oh, heavens, it's after nine o'clock. I think we should go back to the car," John said. "I asked the stationmaster to arrange to have the teleprinter connected so I could get in contact with Drew. And we may as well wait in the car until the repairs are made, and we can get underway again."

CHAPTER TWENTY-ONE

"I gotta take a leak," Ladue said.

"Well, hell, do it. It's dark enough so that no one will see you. Not that you've ever worried about that."

"What if they come while I'm pissin'?"

"How long you plannin' on pissin'?" Hellman asked.

"Till I'm through."

"If you had started doin' it when you started talkin' about it, you'd be done by now," Hellman said.

"Yeah. Yeah, you're right." Ladue began relieving himself.

The two men were waiting just inside a line of trees no more than one hundred feet from the private car.

"You 'bout finished?"

"Yeah."

"Good, 'cause here they come," Hellman said.

"You sure that's them?"

"There's two men and a woman, just like he said."

Hellman was able to point out the two men and a woman because there was a lamppost near the private car, and the three were passing through the patch of light.

"We goin' to shoot from here?" Ladue asked as he buttoned his trousers. "On account of it seems to me that this is pretty far away."

"We'll get a little closer, but we need to shoot 'em before they get out of the light. Shoot the one that's wearin' the gun first."

"Yeah, good idea," Ladue said.

Both men pulled their gun, and they heard the trill of a woman's laughter as the three approached.

"Now!" Hellman said, and both men fired.

Concurrent with the sound of the gunfire, Matt heard a bullet whiz by.

A second bullet kicked up dirt in the rail ballast very near him.

"Get down!" Matt shouted as he made a lightning-quick draw. He couldn't see the shooters because they were in the dark. However, he had seen the flame patterns made by the muzzle flash, and using that as his reference point he fired twice.

"Move quickly out of the light," Matt said, and John and Mary Beth did so.

Matt also moved out of the light, purposely going to the opposite side from John and Mary Beth, then, with gun in hand, and using the dark for cover, he moved, cautiously, toward the place where he believed the shooters to be.

When he got close enough, he saw two men lying on the ground, and approaching them, leaned over for a closer examination. Both were dead.

"It's all right," he called back. "There's no danger now."

He looked down at them for a moment, then walked back toward John and Mary Beth. John had his arms around his daughter.

"Are they dead?" John asked.

"Yes."

Not wanting to leave John and Mary Beth unprotected, he had them come with him when he reported the shooting to the sheriff.

"You again?" Sheriff Ames asked, when Matt reported having killed two men.

"He didn't have any choice, Sheriff," John said. "It was either Mr. Jensen kill them, or they would have killed us."

"Who are you, and why would they have wanted to kill you?" Sheriff Ames asked.

"My name is John Gillespie. You may have heard of me."

"Why should I have heard of you?" the sheriff asked. Then he frowned. "Wait a minute. *The* John Gillespie? Are you telling me that you are the industrialist John Gillespie?"

"Yes. This is not the first attempt on my life. There have been several over the last few days. I hired Mr. Jensen to escort my daughter and me safely to Chicago, and, fortunately, he has successfully turned back every previous attempt."

"Why is someone trying to kill you?"

"I can't answer that question. I know only that from the moment we started this trip that someone has been trying to kill me."

"Well, let me ask you this, Mr. Jensen," Sheriff Ames said. "Do you think the incident in the saloon, with Logan, was related in any way to this?"

"Yes, I do," Matt replied. "I think that someone figured out that if they could get rid of me, they would have an easier time of it with Mr. Gillespie."

"Where are the bodies of the two men you just killed?"

"Unless someone has moved them, they are still lying back at the rail yard, not too far from Mr. Gillespie's private car."

"All right. Let's go see them."

"Hell, these two men weren't trying to kill you," Sheriff Ames said.

"Then why did they shoot at us?" John asked.

"I didn't mean that the way it sounded," Sheriff Ames corrected himself. "They probably were trying to kill you, but I doubt it was because of any scheme. I know these two men. Their names are Hellman and Ladue, and I would bet a month's pay that they never even heard of you. Over the last few years, they've spent as much time in jail as out. It's more'n likely that they heard about someone riding in a fancy railroad car and thought a payday had just dropped into their laps. I would guess that they figured to kill you, then rob you."

"They shot first," John said. "They made no demands for cash."

"Cowards like these two are likely to do it that way," Sheriff Ames said. "I'll get the undertaker to move their carcasses out of here. I can't expect it would be too pleasant for you in your car, knowing they are still here."

"Thank you for that, Sheriff," Mary Beth said.

"Just common courtesy, ma'am," the sheriff replied.

"Sheriff, will you need Mr. Jensen to stay behind for any reason? I mean after the train leaves. Because if you do, let me know, and I'll arrange for my daughter and me to stay as well. I'll also hire an attorney if you think we need one."

"I see no need for Mr. Jensen, nor either of you, to have to stay behind," Sheriff Ames said. "It's as I told you, these two have been in trouble for as long as they have been in town. And based on what everyone in the saloon told me about your run-in with Runt Logan, I don't imagine this was much different. You're free to go on, when the train leaves."

He gave a low, grunting laugh. "In fact, I'll be more than glad when you are out of here. Ever since you've arrived, the body count seems to have piled up."

"Do you think that's what it was, Matt? Do you think they were just trying to rob us? Or was it another attempt to kill us?" Mary Beth asked as they walked back to the car.

"I don't know, the sheriff was probably right," Matt said. "It could be that they were trying to rob you. But I wouldn't count out the possibility that they also were working

253

for the same person who has been trying to kill you."

"But how could two strangers here in Rock Springs be involved?" John asked. "I mean, how did they know when we would be here?"

"I expect that whoever is behind trying to kill you has someone on the train who has been keeping him informed. And he may also have people set up waiting for you all along the route," Matt replied. "That's what I would have done, if I had been the one setting this up. I would have people stretched out between San Francisco and Chicago, just waiting for you."

"Yeah," John said. "Yeah, that would make sense, wouldn't it?"

When they reached the car, the lantern was burning low so that it was dimly lit. Mary Beth walked over to turn it up, causing the car to be well illuminated.

"Good," John said. "I see that the wire has been connected. I'm going to send Drew another message."

WE ARE DELAYED IN ROCK SPRINGS FOR A FEW HOURS FOR REPAIR TO THE ENGINE TENDER. EXPECT TO BE UNDERWAY

WITHIN ANOTHER TWO HOURS.
WILL CONTINUE WITH REPORTS.

"It will probably be tomorrow morning before Drew gets the message, but I may as well keep him up on what's going on with us," John said.

At Matt's suggestion, John had said nothing about the attempt made by Hellman and Ladue.

"You know, Matt . . . so many have been killed because of me," John said after the three of them settled into the overstuffed chairs that made up the parlor area of the private car. "I can't help but feel guilty about that."

"Would you rather it be you?" Matt replied. "Or Mary Beth?"

"No, of course not."

"Then, if you will excuse me for being blunt, feeling bad because people who are trying to kill you, are themselves killed, is stupid."

"I . . . I guess it is. You've done this before, haven't you? I mean, you've had to kill before."

"So do soldiers in war," Matt replied.

"I suppose that's right."

"My mother, father, and sister were all three killed when I was quite young," Matt said. "I was partly raised in an orphanage but mostly by a man named Smoke Jensen, who became my teacher and my friend. And he once told me that I should never kill because I can, I should kill only if I must. I paid very close attention to those words, and I have followed them for my entire life."

"Jensen? You are related?"

"No. My birth name is Cavanaugh. But I took the name Jensen out of respect for the man who taught me so much."

"I must say, he taught you well," John said.

A light knock on the door interrupted their conversation. Mary Beth started toward the door, but Matt held out his hand.

"I'll get it."

It was the conductor.

"Yes, Mr. Kelly?" Matt said.

"I wanted to ask Mr. Gillespie if he was ready for his telegraph machine to be disconnected. If so, I have some people here who will do it now."

"Yes, Mr. Kelly, I'm through with it, thanks," John called.

"Go ahead, take it down," Kelly said to someone down on the ground. He turned back to Matt. "I'm told you had some trouble earlier this evening."

"Who told you?"

"I . . . I'm not sure. Maybe whoever it was, was wrong."

"Someone tried to rob us," John said.

"Oh. Well, I'm glad they didn't succeed. By the way, the repairs have been completed, and the engine will be here to pick up this car soon. Then you will be connected to the rest of the train, and we'll be on our way."

"Thank you," John said. "It will be good to get going again. What will be our next major stop?"

"That would be Cheyenne," Kelly said. "We'll be there at nine thirty tomorrow morning."

"How long will we be there?"

"No more than half an hour. I had better get back to the train."

After Kelly left, Matt came back in and sat down again. He had a very pensive look on his face.

"What is it, Matt?" Mary Beth asked.

"What do you mean?"

"You look worried about something."

Matt pointed to the front door. "I'm not sure I trust that guy."

"Mr. Kelly?" John said, surprised by Matt's comment. "What do you mean? Why not?"

"It's nothing I can put my finger on. It's

just a feeling I have."

John nodded. "I know about your feelings. I got a vivid demonstration of them in town. *It's just a feeling I've got. Go down to the other end of the bar, now!*"

"What?" Mary Beth asked. "Papa, what are you talking about?"

"You remember when the sheriff commented about the encounter Matt had with a man named Logan?"

"Yes, Runt Logan." Mary Beth laughed. "I remember because I thought that was such a very strange name."

"Matt knew it was going to happen even before. He said he had a *feeling,* and he moved me down to the other end of the bar to be out of the way when the shooting started."

"You had a feeling?" Mary Beth asked.

"Yes."

"And you have that feeling now? Good heavens, you don't think Mr. Kelly is going to try and shoot us, do you?" Mary Beth asked.

"No, I don't think he'll try anything like that. But I just can't shake the idea that, somehow, he's involved. I think we would do well to be cautious around him."

"Well, we won't have to worry about him much longer," John said. "The entire train crew will change before we get to Chicago."

Damn! Kelly thought as he walked away from the Gillespie car. Does that son of a bitch have nine lives?

Kelly walked back to the depot, then went up to the Western Union desk. The night operator was sitting in a chair that was tipped back against the wall. His arms were folded across his chest, and his eyes were closed.

Kelly slapped his hand on the counter, and when he did so it startled the telegrapher so that the chair came forward, the legs making a loud pop when they hit the floor.

"Uh, yes, sir! Can I help you?"

"I need to send a telegram."

"All right. Write it out, and I'll send it for you."

The telegrapher read the message. "That'll be a dollar and a nickel. Will you be expecting a reply tonight?" he asked.

"No."

"All right, I'll send it." He sat down at the desk, then began working the key.

MONEY POORLY SPENT. JOB REMAINS UNDONE.

KELLY

Kelly remained in the depot until the train was reassembled, then, after all the passengers were boarded, he boarded himself.

CHAPTER TWENTY-TWO

Cheyenne, Wyoming

Fred Keaton was the Keaton part of the McKnight-Keaton Wholesale Grocery Company. There was no McKnight, and truthfully, there was no Keaton either, except as the manager of the company that bore his name. At one time, Keaton and his brother-in-law, Phil McKnight, owned the company.

Four years ago Phil McKnight had insisted that they buy all new wagons and enlarge the warehouse. Keaton had been against it, but McKnight was not only the senior partner, he was also family, so Keaton didn't fight him. The timing had been terrible, because two new railroad spurs came into existence at the same time. The expansion proved to be disastrous.

McKnight bailed out, leaving Fred Keaton with all the financial obligations of the failing company. The company was on the verge of bankruptcy when Gillespie Enterprises came in to buy McKnight and Keaton out. John had done some preliminary investigation into the company, and not only knew that McKnight was the cause of the company's financial difficulty, but he also knew that McKnight had run off, leaving everything in Fred Keaton's hands. Just as he had done with the Assumption mine, John offered Keaton the opportunity to stay on as manager, and Keaton accepted the offer.

"We'll keep the name of the company," John told him. "You've built up a familiarity for the name, and it would be a shame to lose that recognition."

Keaton was being adequately compensated for his role as manager, but he couldn't help but feel a sense of loss. There was a time when he had high hopes and great ambition for the company. He had imagined passing it on to his son and having a comfortable income for his old age.

None of that was possible now, and he sometimes wondered if perhaps he and McKnight shouldn't have held on to the business. He was sure that if they had drawn everything in, they would have been able to weather the hard times. And the success of the company since Gillespie bought it validated that belief, because as it turned out, the railroads proved to be good for business. The long distance freighting ended, but the railroads increased the amount of freight, and the wagons of McKnight-Keaton provided the short-run connections.

Keaton's musings were interrupted when a boy from Western Union walked into the Wholesale Grocery Company carrying a telegram.

"What can I do for you, boy?" Fred Keaton asked.

"I've a telegram for Mr. Roy Slade," the boy replied.

"Slade? You'll find him in back." Keaton jerked his thumb toward a door that led out into the warehouse.

The boy stepped into the back and saw several wagons backed up to a dock. Half a dozen or more men were loading the wagons.

"Mr. Slade?" the boy called.

"Yeah, that's me." The man who answered was carrying a box.

"You have a telegram, sir."

Slade put the box onto the wagon, then came over to retrieve the telegram.

The boy stood there for a moment.

"What are you still here for?" Slade asked

after he took the message.

"Hell, Slade, give the boy a nickel," one of the other men on the dock said.

"What for?"

"It's common courtesy. When someone brings you a telegram, you give them a tip."

Slade looked at the boy, who was waiting with an expectant smile.

"Get out of here," he growled. "I ain't got a nickel."

The smile left the boy's face, then he turned and hurried away.

"What's the telegram say, Slade?" the man who had suggested the nickel tip asked.

"It ain't nobody's business but mine."

FIFTY DOLLARS WIRED TO YOU AND JONES AVAILABLE AT THE WESTERN UNION OFFICE STOP BOARD THE LINCOLN BOUND TRAIN AT TEN OCLOCK THIS MORNING STOP WAIT UNTIL IT LEAVES THE STATION THEN SHOW THE CONDUCTOR THE AGREED UPON SIGNAL STOP CONDUCTOR WILL PROVIDE FURTHER INSTRUCTIONS

LC

With the telegram in hand, Roy Slade

walked out into the wagon yard, where Marcus Jones was packing grease into the hub of a wagon wheel.

"You remember that letter we got?" Slade asked. "The one that said we could make some money by doing a special job?"

"Yeah, I remember."

"Well, we just got a money transfer of fifty dollars apiece and a telegram."

Jones began wiping the grease from his hands. "What does the telegram say?"

Slade read the telegram.

"I thought we was supposed to get two hundred and fifty dollars apiece."

"Yeah, but you remember, the letter said we'd get the rest of the money after the job is done."

"Ten o'clock, huh? You think Mr. Keaton will give us the morning off?"

A twisted smile spread across Slade's face.

"Yeah, he'll give us the morning off."

Half an hour later, Slade and Jones were waiting at the depot for the eastbound train. It was supposed to have arrived at four o'clock this morning, and a lot of the departing passengers were complaining about the delay. Those who were here to meet arriving passengers were just as upset. It made no difference to Slade and Jones that the train was late. They hadn't even known they would be meeting it until they received the telegram.

As the heavy engine rolled by, the red-hot coals dripping from the firebox left a glowing path between the tracks. There was a screech of steel on steel as the train finally came to a stop, and the great drive wheels were wreathed in steam.

The two men watched until the arriving passengers disembarked from the train, then Slade and Jones joined the ten or so who were boarding at this stop. They took a seat in the last car and waited until the conductor came through checking the tickets.

Slade and Jones showed the conductor their ticket, then Slade showed him the ace of spades playing card.

The conductor took the card, then nodded.

"Wait until I tell you," he said.

"Wait until you tell us what?" Slade asked.

"Wait until I tell you what I'm going to tell you," Kelly said.

At the front of the train at that moment Matt had climbed over the tender, then dropped down onto the engine deck. When he first dropped down, neither the engineer nor the fireman saw him, as both were looking forward. They were engaged in conversation.

"Hey, Prouty, have you ever pulled a private car, like that'n we're a-pullin' now, before?"

"I've pulled private cars before. I don't know as I've ever pulled one quite like this. I bet it's a purty thing inside."

"Oh, believe me, it is," Matt said.

Matt's sudden and totally unexpected appearance startled both men so that they jumped.

"Who are you? Is this a holdup?" the engineer asked.

"No, no, I'm sorry, I didn't mean to startle you," Matt apologized, holding out both hands.

"Then who are you, mister? And what are you doin' here?" the engineer asked. "There ain't no one allowed on the engine deck 'ceptin' me and the fireman."

"My name is Matt Jensen, and I've been hired by the railroad to look out for the passengers of the private car you two were talking about."

Back in the train itself, Kelly left the rear day car, and smiling and greeting several of the passengers, he was every bit the gracious host that a conductor was supposed to be. As he passed through the dining car, he could smell the food being prepared for lunch. From the dining car, he stepped into the Pullman car. Here the occupants were generally wealthier than the passengers in the day cars. They were considerably better dressed, and they projected their elevated status with a haughtiness about them as they rested in their more comfortable seats and stared through the windows, rather than meet the gaze of a mere railroad employee, albeit he was the conductor.

From the Pullman car Kelly walked through the baggage car, then stepped into the rear vestibule of John Gillespie's car. The conductor tapped on the door of the private car and Mary Beth opened it. That surprised him. On every previous visit to the private car, the door had been opened by Matt Jensen.

"Hello, Mr. Kelly," Mary Beth said, greeting him with a smile.

"Miss Gillespie," Kelly replied.

"Won't you come in?"

Kelly stepped into the car and saw John sitting in one of the comfortable armchairs reading a book. John looked up.

"Something I can help you with, Mr. Kelly?"

"No, I just wanted to check with you to

make certain everything is all right. Do you need anything?"

"No, we're getting along just fine, but I thank you for your concern."

Kelly touched the bill of his cap as if in a salute.

"Well, since everything is going well here, I'd better get back to work. Just send the porter for me if you need anything."

"We will, thanks."

Kelly left the car and passed back through the baggage car and the Pullman car. He had noticed when he came through a moment earlier that Matt Jensen wasn't in his seat, nor had he seen him in the private car.

Could it be that he had left the train, thinking the danger to Gillespie was passed? Kelly didn't see him get off in Cheyenne, but that didn't mean that he didn't leave. If Jensen had left the train — and since Kelly hadn't seen him in a while, he was convinced that he probably had — now would be a good time for the two men to take care of business. And with Jensen finally out of the way, the job had suddenly gotten much easier.

The thought that this business was about to be over pleased Kelly, and as he walked back through the cars of the speeding train he thought back to his own business arrangement.

"I'm not asking you to do anything except facilitate the operation," Conroy had told him. "From time to time you may be approached by individuals who are working for me. In every case, they will identify themselves by showing you a playing card, the ace of spades. I ask only that you do nothing to impede their task. To ensure your loyalty, I will give you two hundred and fifty dollars now. If Mr. Gillespie and his daughter are dead by the time the train reaches its destination, you will be paid an additional seven hundred and fifty dollars."

"I am a person of some importance," Kelly replied. "Because of that, I will be taking a considerable risk in helping you with your scheme. I want the entire thousand dollars now."

"No. It is not my policy to pay the entire amount before the job is done."

After some discussion, Kelly had agreed to take five hundred dollars, to be paid in full, in advance. He was taking less money than the original offer, but he received the money up front, and it wasn't dependent upon the final outcome, which, after all, was beyond his control. And, he had increased his share by the one hundred and fifty dollars he kept from the failure of Hellman and Ladue to do the job.

Kelly wished now, though, that he had taken the original deal. With Jensen out of the picture, he was convinced that the job would be done.

He got an idea. He would ask for the money anyway, but he would do so in such a way that Conroy would think it would be in his best interest if he paid up. Otherwise . . . there might be some suspicions raised as to Conroy's participation in the whole affair.

But upon further thought, he put that idea aside. That was blackmail, and though this was the first business he had ever done with Conroy, he had quickly learned what a dangerous man Conroy was. He was much too dangerous to blackmail.

When Kelly reached the day car where Slade and Jones were, he worked his way back to them, speaking to everyone in the car.

"And how is that young man doing? Is he enjoying the train ride?" he asked a woman with a little boy.

"Oh, yes, I think he is," the woman replied with a smile.

He carried on small talk with everyone

until he reached Slade and Jones.

The two men, who were sitting in the last seat on the left side of the car, were only slightly less disreputable looking than Hellman and Ladue had been. They were certainly not the kind of people Kelly would ever engage in any social conversation with, but he realized that these were exactly the type of men that would be needed to carry out the job that Lucas Conroy wanted done.

"Are you gentlemen doing all right?" he asked.

"Uh, yeah," Slade replied.

"Oh, let me check the latch on that window."

When Kelly leaned toward the window, he spoke very quietly. "Wait until I leave the car, then go forward. You'll have to pass through the baggage car to reach the private car."

"What do we do when we get into the private car?" Slade asked.

"Haven't you been told?"

"I want to hear it from you," Slade said. "I need to know that we can trust you."

"You are to kill Gillespie and his daughter."

Slade smiled and nodded. "Yeah, like I said, I just wanted to hear it from you."

"What do we do after, uh, the job is

done?" Jones asked.

"The car is private and separated from the rest of the train by the baggage car, so nobody will have any idea what has taken place. When you are finished, just leave them there and come on back here. You can get off the train at the next stop."

"What about the rest of the money?" Slade asked.

"That's between you and Conroy."

"I thought maybe you was supposed to give it to us."

"I don't have the money, that's between you and Conroy," Kelly repeated. "There!" he said, loudly enough for others in the car to hear him. He raised the window. "That should take care of it. I'm sorry if this window was giving you any trouble."

"Thanks," Slade said.

CHAPTER TWENTY-THREE

The reason Kelly hadn't seen Matt was because he was still in the engine cab speaking with Mr. Prouty, the engineer, and Mr. Hastings, the fireman. The two men had relieved Kirkpatrick and Cooper back in Cheyenne, and unlike Kirkpatrick and Cooper, were unaware of the attempts already made on the lives of John and his daughter. Matt was filling them in on the situation.

"Be especially alert," Matt said. "From the time this train left San Francisco, someone has been trying to kill Mr. Gillespie and his daughter. I wouldn't put it past them to do something to sabotage the train, like pull up a rail or block off a bridge."

"Yes, sir, we'll be on the lookout, I can promise you that," Prouty said.

"Mr. Hastings, I think I should tell you that just before we left San Francisco we found a stick of dynamite in the coal tender."

"Damn!" Hastings said. "That's not good. I get to shovelin' so fast that most of the time I don't even look at what I'm shovelin', and I just throw it into the furnace."

"Yes, that's the way it was explained to me as well. That's why I'm warning you."

"I guess I had better start lookin' just real close at ever' shovel I take," Hastings said.

"I'd say that would be a good idea," Matt replied.

Matt nodded at the engine crew, then climbed over the tender to return to the private car. Just as he opened the front door, he saw two men with drawn pistols coming in through the opposite end of the car.

"What are you doing here?" Matt demanded.

Both men swung their guns toward Matt, but Matt drew and fired before either of them could get off a shot. Jones went down, and Slade turned and ran back outside.

Matt holstered his own pistol and caught up with him out in the vestibule, just as Slade was trying to open the door to the baggage car. Slade whirled around with gun in hand, but Matt knocked the pistol away with a sweep of his hand.

Slade swung at Matt but missed. Matt

swung back connecting with a straight punch to the chin, knocking Slade back against the front door of the baggage car. At that same moment, the train started out onto a trestle over a deep gorge.

The two men struggled for a moment longer. Slade had done physical labor for most of his life, and he was a very strong man, strong enough to resist Matt's attempt to gain leverage over him. Slade was stronger, but Matt was much more agile, and that evened the odds.

Then Slade saw something that he thought might give him the advantage. Attached to the front of the baggage car was an ax, to be used to break into a car in the event of an accident. Pushing away from Matt, Slade grabbed the ax, then lifted it over his head.

"Say good-bye, you son of a bitch!" Slade shouted.

From behind him, Matt heard a gunshot. Slade, with a shocked expression on his face, dropped the ax and grabbed his stomach. He took a couple of steps toward Matt, reaching out toward him, his hands bloodied by the wound in his stomach. Then he fell off the train and over the trestle, tumbling down toward the bottom of the gorge, two hundred feet below.

"Ayiiieeee!" he screamed, the shout growing dimmer as he plummeted down.

Matt stepped the edge of the vestibule, then leaned over and looked down and back. He saw his would-be assailant hit the side of the trestle, then bounce away to fall, the body perfectly still now, the rest of the way to the bottom.

"Good-bye," Matt said quietly.

Matt turned back toward the open door of the private car and saw Mary Beth standing there, holding a smoking gun in her hand. She was trembling, and there was an expression of horror on her face.

"I . . . I . . ." Mary Beth said, her bottom lip quivering. She dropped the pistol and covered her face with her hands.

Matt stepped up to her, and wrapping his arms around her, pulled her to him. Once, as a child, he had held a wounded bird in his hand and had felt its heart beating rapidly and in fear. He recalled that moment now as he held this frightened young woman.

"Let's go back inside," he said, leading her back into the car.

He sat her down on one of the chairs, and John appeared beside them, holding a glass of brandy.

"I think you need this," John said.

Mary Beth took the glass with a shaking

277

hand, then drank the brandy without turning the glass down. Tears were streaming down her cheeks, but she wasn't crying out loud.

"Until we started on this trip, I had never seen a dead man," she said. "Now I've seen four, and one of them I killed."

"Don't look at it as killing," John said. "Look at it as saving Matt's life. And probably ours as well."

"Oh, Papa, we should have never come on this trip. It is accursed."

"It isn't the trip, Mary Beth," Matt said. "Whoever is behind this would be after you in San Francisco as well as on this train. And to be honest, you are probably safer on the train, because it is easier for me to watch over you."

At that moment there was a light knock on the door. Matt pulled his pistol, then jerked it open.

It was Julius Calhoun, the porter.

The porter threw his hands up and jumped back.

Matt holstered his pistol. "What is it, Mr. Calhoun?" he asked.

"Mrs. Sappenfield was in the baggage car getting a book from her trunk, and she said she heard shots."

"Yes," Matt said. "We had a couple of

unwanted visitors." He pointed to the body on the floor.

"Oh, Lord almighty!" Calhoun said. "Is he dead?"

"Yes."

"Mr. Calhoun," John said. "I wonder if you would be so kind as to help us put Jones's body in the baggage car? I'm sure you can understand that I don't want him in here."

"Yes, sir," Calhoun said. "Yes sir, we can do that."

"Grab his feet," Matt said. "I'll get his arms."

"You called him by name," Matt said, when he returned to the car a moment later.

"Yes, that was Marcus Jones. The other man was Roy Slade. I may have been wrong in suspecting Raymond Morris. I am now convinced that the man who is trying to kill me is Fred Keaton. These men worked for him. The next stop where I will have enough time to do so, I intend to send a telegram back to Drew. According to the schedule, that will be North Platte, and we'll reach there at about three thirty this afternoon."

"How long will we be in North Platte?" Mary Beth asked.

"We are supposed to be there for about

279

half an hour," John said. "But, that was before the long delay back in Rock Springs, so I may have to wait until we reach Lincoln before I can send the telegram."

"How long will we be in Lincoln?"

"I think we will be there for at least two hours. It is the longest scheduled wait time we have anywhere between San Francisco and Chicago, though the wait should not be as long as the wait was in Rock Springs. The reason our wait will be so long in Lincoln is because our car, and the *Conqueror,* will be disconnected there and reconnected to another train that will be headed for Chicago. This train will be going on to St. Louis."

Matt excused himself, then walked back through the train until he found the conductor.

"What happened?" Kelly asked when he saw Matt. "Are Gillespie and his daughter both dead?"

"What?" Matt replied, stunned by the question. "Mr. Kelly, why on earth would you ask such a thing?"

"Mrs. Sappenfield reported that she heard shots coming from Mr. Gillespie's car."

"No, they are not dead."

"Good, good," the conductor said. "It's just that when I saw you coming back here,

I got a little worried is all. So, they are both fine?"

"Miss Gillespie is a little shaken, but she's recovering nicely."

"You can understand, I hope, why I would be worried about such a thing," Kelly said. "After all, I'm the conductor, and that makes me responsible for the safety of everyone on my train."

"I suppose it does. But only until Lincoln," Matt said.

"Why only until Lincoln?" Kelly asked.

"It's my understanding that we'll be changing trains there, I guess I just figured we would get a new train crew."

"You'll be changing trains, but not railroads. I intend to stay aboard and see this thing through to the finish. It's as I said, Mr. Jensen. I feel a sense of obligation toward Mr. Gillespie and his daughter."

"Well, I appreciate that, Mr. Kelly, and I'm sure that the Gillespies do as well."

When they stopped in North Platte, they learned that the stop would be only long enough for the engine to take on water. The through passengers were asked not to leave the train, but arrangements were made to remove Marcus Jones's body. John Gillespie provided written statements from Matt, himself, and his daughter as to the circum-

281

stances surrounding Jones's death. He also gave the sheriff enough money for Jones's body to be returned to Cheyenne.

They barely had time to conclude their business with the sheriff before the train left the station.

It was nearly ten o'clock that night when the train pulled into Lincoln, and upon arrival, they learned that because their long delay in Rock Springs had upset the schedule all up and down the line, they were going to be held over until ten o'clock the next morning.

"I know there has to be a good hotel in this town," John said. "And while this car is quite comfortable, I don't particularly want to spend the night in a railroad yard. Let's find one and get us some rooms before they are all sold out for the night.

"That will also give me an opportunity to have this car thoroughly cleaned."

"Will they clean the carpet as well?" Mary Beth asked, glancing toward the spots on the floor.

"Yes, I'll make certain that they do."

"Thank you, Papa," Mary Beth said. "And I would appreciate staying in a hotel tonight."

Before finding a hotel, though, John

stopped by the Western Union office in the train station to send another telegram.

IN LINCOLN NEBRASKA NOW STOP WILL BE HERE UNTIL TEN OCLOCK TOMORROW MORNING STOP THERE WAS A TRY IN CHEYENNE ON MARY BETH AND ME STOP ASSAILANTS WERE ROY SLADE AND MARCUS JONES STOP BOTH WORKED FOR KEATON SO SUSPICION NOW SWINGS TO HIM

JG

"Do you wish to wait for a reply, sir?" the telegrapher asked.

"No, I'm quite sure I won't hear back from him tonight. But I will check in with you before the train gets underway again tomorrow."

"Are we going to the hotel now, Papa?" Mary Beth asked.

"Indeed we are, darlin'," John replied. "And, Matt, I expect you would like a room as well, wouldn't you? A hotel room has to be better than that cramped berth in the Pullman car."

"Yes, sir, I would appreciate that," Matt said. "To say nothing of the fact that I don't intend to let either you, or your daughter,

283

get too far away from me."

"Well, good. Then I shall get us three adjacent rooms for the night."

Matt had already seen that the attacks on John and his daughter were not limited to attempts on the train only, and he was sure that whoever was behind these endeavors would take advantage of any situation to accomplish their mission. He was determined that if they were going to kill John and his daughter, they were going to have to come through him. He hoped that, by now, word had gotten back to whoever was behind all this and that dealing with him wasn't going to be all that easy.

They checked in to the Marshal Hotel in the Haymarket District of Lincoln. John was able to get three adjacent rooms. John's room was 207, Mary Beth was room 205, and Matt was in 203.

Supper in the hotel dining room was Welsh rarebit and a red wine that Mary Beth pointed out, which came from the Gillespie wineries. Mary Beth was in a talkative mood, and Matt knew that she wanted to talk, needed to talk, to put behind her the trauma of having shot Slade.

"Have you ever read *Ivanhoe*?" Mary Beth asked.

"*Ivanhoe*? No, I don't think I have. What

is *Ivanhoe?*"

Mary Beth laughed, the lilting sound of her laughter good to hear.

"It isn't a what, silly. Ivanhoe is a 'who.' He is a knight, in shining armor, who rescues damsels in distress. It's a novel by Sir Walter Scott. *'Now fitted the halter, now traversed the cart, and often took leave, but seemed loath to depart.'* "

Now it was Matt's time to laugh. "I don't have the slightest idea what that means."

"I don't either," Mary Beth said with a giggle. "But it's written on the title page of the book."

"Why did you ask me if I had ever read it?"

"You should read it, because you, Sir Matt Jensen, are every bit as much a knight as is Ivanhoe. Even more so, because I have only read of Ivanhoe, but you, I have but to reach across the table to touch.

Mary Beth put her hand on Matt's arm. "Are you sure you don't have a suit of shining armor somewhere?"

"I can tell you without hesitation, m'lady, that I do not," Matt replied.

"M'lady. Oh, I like that," Mary Beth said.

"I'm glad you are feeling better now, my dear," John said.

"I do feel better, Papa. You know, yourself,

that I have never been a weak sister, and I don't intend to start now. I guess I did what had to be done."

She smiled at Matt. "Besides, how often does m'lady get to rescue a knight in distress?"

After supper, all three went directly to their rooms. It had been four days now since Matt had had a bath, and he was feeling a little scruffy. He decided to go down to the desk clerk and make arrangements to have a bathtub and hot water delivered to his room.

"Why, there's no need to bring a tub up to your room, sir," the desk clerk said. "I am proud to say that we have the finest bathing rooms of any hotel in Lincoln, yes, and in the state as well. There are two of them down at the end of the hall on each of the four floors. All you have to do is light the gas under the water heater, give it a few minutes to heat up, then turn the spigot. Before you know it, you'll have a whole tub full of hot water."

"Thanks."

Matt walked back upstairs, but before he returned to his room he went down to the end of the hall and found that neither of the bathing rooms were occupied. Going into one of them, he started a fire in the water heater, then he returned to his room while he gave the water time to warm up. It wasn't as nice as his room had been at the Royal Hotel back in San Francisco, but then he had seldom seen any room as nice as that one. But John was right, when he suggested that Matt would be more comfortable here than he would have been in the berth on the Pullman car. And he would certainly be more comfortable here than he was on the frequent nights he spent out on the trail.

Matt walked over to look out the window. From here he had a good view of the main street. The street, scarred with wagon ruts and dotted with horse droppings, formed an X with the track.

On this side of the track the buildings were substantial, many of them false-fronted and most of them well-painted. Right across the street from the hotel was a mercantile store, quiet and dark at this time of night. Below him and next door to the hotel, was the Farmer's Saloon.

Because the saloon was under him, he couldn't actually see it from his window, but he could see the bright splash of light it threw into the street, and he could hear laughter and piano music. He would like to have gone into the saloon to have a beer before turning in for the night, but he didn't think it would be a good idea to leave John and Mary Beth alone.

The railroad station was halfway down the street, and he saw that a train, heading west, was just now pulling away. After the train left he could see the Gillespie car on a sidetrack, gleaming under the glow of the gas lamppost. In contrast to the shining varnish of the car, he saw, on the far side of the track, a scattering of small structures, obviously homes for the less-affluent residents.

That single car, he realized, probably cost more than every one of those buildings combined, and yet, to meet John and Mary Beth, you would never realize they were so wealthy. They were two of the nicest people he had ever encountered, and he couldn't understand why they had become targets. From what Matt knew of John, he had treated fairly and generously everyone with whom he did business. Why would anyone want him dead? What did they stand to gain from it? More curiously, why would anyone want Mary Beth dead? What did she have to do with the business?

Whoever it was, they were certainly persistent. There had already been several attempts made, and even though John was convinced that the danger was over now because he had identified the last two attackers as employees of Keaton, Matt wasn't so sure. There was no way he was going to let his guard down.

Deciding that the water was probably well heated by now, he left the room and walked down to the end of the hall to take his bath.

Mary Beth was just getting into the tub when Matt opened the door. She stood there for a moment, so surprised by his unexpected appearance that she made no effort to cover herself. She was totally nude and Matt breathed in a quick gasp of appreciation for her beauty. He had known from the moment he first met her that she was a woman of great pulchritude, but this unexpected feast for his eyes left him somewhat stunned. So stunned that he just stood there for a long moment, unable to look away.

"Matt, I'm sure that you can readily see that this room is occupied," Mary Beth said. Her voice was calm, not shrill, and the expression on her face was one that was more of amusement than it was fear or anger.

Matt smiled. "Yes, ma'am, I can surely see that," he replied. "I'm sorry, I had built the fire for my own bath, but I see you beat me to it." He continued to stare pointedly at Mary Beth's nudity and, as if realizing for the first time that she was naked, Mary Beth took in a sharp breath, then sat down in the water so quickly that she raised a splash.

"You are the one who heated the water?" she asked.

"Yes."

Mary Beth, who was now holding her arms crossed over her breasts, shook her head.

"I'm sorry. I thought that the hotel had heated it for the convenience of the guests. It never dawned on me that I would have to heat my own water."

"It's no problem, I can always heat more water," Matt said. "I'm sorry I walked in on you like this. I had no idea the bathing room would be occupied. Bu, really, you should have locked the door."

"I thought I did."

"No harm done," Matt said. "As I said, there's another bathing room next door. I'll use it."

"Yes, thank you, I believe that would be most appropriate."

With another smile and a nod of his head, Matt pointed to the key in the door.

"You should probably come over here and

lock it after I leave. The next person to come in here may not be as much of a gentleman as I have been."

"Oh, you!" Mary Beth said with a laugh, as she raised her arm to throw the wet sponge at him. She hadn't realized that in so doing she would, once more, expose her breasts to him. Matt laughed again, then stepped outside. He waited in the hall until he heard the key click, then he went next door to heat the water up again.

CHAPTER TWENTY-FOUR

San Francisco

Lucas Conroy studied the telegram. It told him two things: Gillespie and his daughter were still alive despite all his best efforts, and the train would be spending the night in Lincoln, Nebraska.

Conroy was beginning to think that he should have charged the consortium more than fifty thousand dollars. He had already spent more money than he had planned, but he knew that there was more than just money involved. He had a reputation to uphold. He couldn't afford to fail on this job, whether he made less money than he had thought, broke even, or even lost money. By now it had become an issue of necessity. He must succeed at all costs, for if he failed, he may as well give up the business altogether.

He had been told from the beginning that the biggest problem might well be Matt

Jensen, and as Conroy examined all the failures, except for the one when the cut tongue pin hadn't done the job, they were all directly attributable to interference from Matt Jensen.

Conroy had invested some time and money into researching Matt Jensen, and he recalled now some of the things he had learned about him.

"It is said that he killed his first man when he was nine years old," the private detective told him.

"Nine years old?" Conroy replied, surprised at the statement.

"Yes. A band of outlaws slaughtered his family, and he killed them all, killing the first one right there where it happened."

"So what did he do? Strap on a pistol and become a gunman, right away?"

"No. He spent some time in an orphanage, ran away, and was rescued by Smoke Jensen."

"Smoke Jensen? *The* Smoke Jensen?"

"One and the same. It is said that Smoke Jensen taught the kid everything he ever knew, and now there are many who think that Matt Jensen may even be faster than Smoke."

"So now he sells his gun to the highest bidder, does he?"

"Yes, in a manner of speaking."

"How much is he being paid to guard Gillespie and his daughter?"

"Five thousand dollars."

Conroy whistled quietly. "That's a lot of money. If he sells his gun to the highest bidder, do you think I could buy him for seventy-five hundred dollars?"

"No."

"Suppose I double the amount he is being paid to guard the Gillespies?"

The private detective shook his head. "I don't know what you want him for, but if you ask him to do something that he doesn't think is right, you couldn't buy him for two hundred thousand dollars."

"Yeah, that's what I thought. All right, Mr. Pollard, I thank you for the information."

As Conroy recalled that conversation, he drummed his fingers on the table for a moment or two while he contemplated the situation. Then, he pulled out a piece of paper and began making notes.

1. It is highly unlikely that I will be able to find anyone who can go face-to-face with Matt Jensen and beat him in a gunfight.
2. He is superior in gun handling to anyone I have ever heard of, so

good that he has bested multiple gunfighters in the same confrontation.

3. The only way I'm going to be able to take care of this situation is to find someone who isn't in it to make a name for himself by killing Jensen in a fair fight, but someone who is more interested in money than the notoriety.

After studying the notes he had made, Conroy took a ledger from the middle drawer of his desk. Here, he kept a list of people that he had worked with before, people he could buy favors from in exchange, not only for a little money, but also the promise of reciprocating a future service.

The man he could depend on in Lincoln, Nebraska, for such a favor was Vernon Spence. He sent Spence a telegram and within half an hour had a reply.

WILL LOCATE JENSEN AND DEAL WITH PROBLEM STOP PAY TO BE IN ACCORDANCE WITH YOUR SATISFACTION

When Conroy went to bed that night, he slept easily. Vernon Spence had the reputation of getting the job done. And that is exactly what Conroy needed now. He needed someone who would not let him down.

Lincoln, Nebraska

Matt was sound asleep when he was awakened by a woman's scream. And it wasn't just any woman's scream, it was Mary Beth's scream.

Grabbing his pistol from the holster he leaped out of bed, and without regard to the fact that he was wearing only his underwear, he opened the door to his room, just as he saw a man coming from Mary Beth's room.

"Mary Beth!"

"I'm all right!" Mary Beth called back.

Matt chased the man to the top of the stairs.

"Stop!" Matt shouted, running toward him.

A door opened right at the head of the stairs, and one of the hotel guests, an older woman who had been made curious by the noise, stuck her head out to see what was going on.

"No, get back in your room!" Matt called, but it was too late.

The intruder grabbed the old woman and pulled her in front of him. He held a knife against the old woman's throat.

"Put your gun down!" the intruder said.

Matt hesitated for a moment.

"Now! Put your gun now, or I will cut this woman's throat!"

"Please!" the old woman begged. "Please, do what he says!"

Reluctantly, Matt put his pistol on the floor.

"All right, the gun is down," he said. Matt stepped closer.

"Stay where you are!" the man with the knife shouted angrily.

Matt saw someone sneaking up very quietly behind the man with the knife. The stalker was carrying a water vase in his hand, so Matt began talking to keep the knife-wielder distracted.

"Why don't you let the lady go?" Matt said. "You know she's not the one you came to kill. I'm the one you want, aren't I?"

"I don't know what you're talking about."

"Sure you do. I'm the one you want."

"What if you are?"

"Well, you can see that I've put my gun down. You have a knife, I'm unarmed. You'll never get a better chance than now." Matt held both his hands out to show that he was unarmed.

The man with the knife smiled.

"Yeah," he said. He shoved the woman aside. "Yeah, I'll never . . ."

That was as far as he got before the man brought the water vase crashing down on the knife-wielder's head. The vase shattered and water came pouring down as the knife-wielder stumbled back, then flipped over the railing and fell to the lobby below. Matt ran to the railing and looked down. The assailant was lying still and in a distorted position on the floor, and Matt could tell that he was dead.

By then doors were open all up and down the hallway, and Matt, realizing that he was standing there totally exposed in his underwear, retrieved his pistol, then hurried back to his room. He saw that both Mary Beth and John were peering out through partially open doors.

"Are you all right, Matt?" John asked.

"Yes, except for being a little embarrassed for standing out here in my long johns," Matt replied.

"Ha. What have *you* got to be embarrassed about?" Mary Beth asked, as she shared a secret smile with Matt.

Matt realized at once what she was talking about, but he didn't say anything.

"I'd better get dressed and go downstairs," he said. "I expect they'll have a few policemen here soon, and they'll be wanting to talk to someone."

"What are you going to tell them?" John asked.

"I'm going to tell them that as far as I know, he was nothing but a prowler."

By the time Matt got dressed and hurried downstairs, there was a policeman in the lobby, wearing a blue uniform and a high-crowned custodian helmet. In addition to the policeman, there was the desk clerk, a couple of bellboys, half a dozen hotel guests, the woman who for a moment had been held hostage, and the man who had ended the crisis with a full water vase.

"That's him," the man said, pointing to Matt. "He was the other one in the hall."

"Thank you, Mr. Rodenberger," the policeman said.

The policeman turned to Matt. "May I ask your name, sir?"

"Jensen. Matt Jensen."

"And, Mr. Jensen, if you don't mind telling me, what was the reason for the altercation between you and Spence?"

"Spence?"

The policeman pointed to the body. "That is Vernon Spence."

"The reason Spence and I were confronting each other is because I heard the lady in the room next to me scream, and when I got out of bed to see what it was, I saw Spence with a knife. I imagine he had gone in there to see what he could steal."

"Was the lady hurt?"

"No. Apparently you know this man?"

"I know of him," the policeman said. "He's sort of a shady figure, but he's not a thief. He always seems to have money, but the money doesn't come from any known source. He's been tried twice for murder, but he beat both charges. Some of the other police officers and I have always thought that he might be a . . ." the policeman stopped in midsentence. "Ah, never mind, it was probably just us talking."

"Thought what?" Matt asked.

"Well, given that he always seemed to have money, and nobody knew where it came from, we've sort of thought that he might be someone who kills for money. The two murder trials I mentioned? One of the victims was a banker and the other was a lawyer. Neither one of them were very popular, and I don't mind telling you that there weren't that many people who were sorry to see them killed.

"That's when we got the idea that someone may have paid Spence to do it. But like I said, he beat both charges."

"Officer, you aren't going to charge me with anything, are you?" Rodenberger asked. "I mean, I didn't intend to kill 'im, I was just tryin' to make him drop the knife, so he wouldn't hurt Mrs. Kern. I didn't know he was going to fall over the bannister."

"Mr. Rodenberger is telling the truth," Matt said. "He probably saved the lady's life and mine as well."

"Yes, that's what Mrs. Kern said. No, Mr. Rodenberger, there will be no charges."

"That's good to know. Don't know how the missus back in Kansas City would take it if I told her I was being held for murder."

By then two men arrived carrying a stretcher.

"Can we move the body now, officer?"

"Yes," the policeman said. He turned to the rather substantial group of people who had gathered in the lobby. "Folks, you can break it up now. There's nothin' left here for you to see. Go on back to your rooms."

"Mr. Rodenberger, I thank you again, sir," Matt said.

A wide smile spread across Rodenberger's face. "Whoowee, this is something for a salesman to get involved in. I can't wait to get home to tell my wife what happened. Why, it's almost like I'm a hero, isn't it?"

"Indeed you are, sir," Matt agreed.

"Probably not to Grace. Besides which, I'm not even sure she'll believe me."

When Matt returned to his room, he thought about what the policeman had told him about Spence always having money but without any known source of his income. The officer had also said that he and his fellow policemen were speculating as to whether or not Spence could have been a paid killer.

Matt could have told him that their speculation was correct. From the moment he heard Mary Beth scream, he was certain that it was another attempt on the life of Mary Beth and her father.

The next morning, Matt was awakened by a totally different concert of sound than that which he had heard last night. Gone was the laughter, the boisterous conversation, and the piano music.

In its place were the sounds of a town at commerce, the ringing of a smithy shaping iron at his forge, the scratching sound of a shopkeeper sweeping his front porch, a carpenter sawing wood, and the squeaking wheel of a freight wagon rolling down the street.

As he washed his face and hands, he

looked at the pitcher that held the water. This was exactly like the pitcher that Rodenberger had used on Vernon Spence during the middle of the night, and hefting it, he could see how, especially filled with water as it was, it would be able to do the job.

Matt was hungry, and for a moment he considered going down to breakfast now, rather than waiting for John and Mary Beth to awaken. He put that thought aside quickly, though. It would not be wise to leave them unguarded, even for no longer than it would take to have breakfast. Last night had proven that.

As it turned out, though, he didn't have to wait long at all, because as he was drying his hands, he heard a knock at his door.

"Matt, are you up yet? Papa and I want to go have breakfast."

Smiling, Matt crossed the room in a few quick steps, then he jerked the door open.

"Good idea," he said.

When they reached the dining room, Matt saw the salesman, Rodenberger, sitting at the table with Mrs. Kern.

"I've someone I want you to meet," he said, leading John and Mary Beth over to the table.

"Mr. Gillespie, Miss Gillespie, this is Mr. Rodenbeger and Mrs. Kern."

Rodenberger started to stand, but Matt put his hand out.

"No need for you to stand," he said. "John, this gentleman saved my life last night."

"And mine too," Mrs. Kern said.

"Well, I thank you very much for that, Mr. Rodenberger," John said. "Matt is a very good friend of mine. And if you will allow me, I would like to pay for breakfast for you and Mrs. Kern and pay for your rooms as well."

"Mister, you don't have to do that," Rodenberger said. "I wouldn't want to have to put you out that money."

"Let him do it, Mr. Rodenberger," Mary Beth said. She lay her hand on his shoulder and smiled at him. "It will make him feel good."

Rodenberger returned the smile. "Well then, yes, sir, by all means. I mean, if it'll make you feel good."

CHAPTER TWENTY-FIVE

After they had breakfast, John checked with Western Union to see if he had received a reply from Drew.

"Yes, sir, Mr. Gillespie, I've got it right here for you," the telegrapher said.

BELIEVE YOU MAY BE RIGHT ABOUT KEATON STOP WILL INFORM SHERIFF IN CHEYENNE TO INVESTIGATE STOP THINK YOU MIGHT NOW BE OUT OF DANGER

"I don't think you are out of danger yet," Matt said when John showed him the telegram.

"You mean because of the thief who tried to sneak into Mary Beth's room?" John asked.

"He wasn't just a thief." Matt told them what he had learned from the policeman about Vernon Spence.

"So, what you are suggesting is that whoever it is that's wanting me killed paid this man to do it?"

"Yes."

"But how would they know we were staying in the hotel? For that matter, how would they even know that the train spent the night here?"

"I told you before that I thought there might be someone traveling with us whose sole purpose is to keep an eye on you and to report back. Now, I'm sure of it."

"Who would that be, do you think? Do you have any ideas?"

"Yes, I have an idea. I think it might be the conductor."

"Mr. Kelly?"

"Yes."

"Well then, let's go to the railroad and have him replaced. I'm sure I have enough influence to get that done," John suggested.

"No, not yet," Matt replied. "Let's leave him where he is. Better the devil you know, than the one you don't know. I intend to stay alert until we reach Chicago."

"Oh, I appreciate that, believe me I do," John said, "especially as the attempt last night started with my daughter."

"That's another thing I've been wondering about," Matt said. "I can see where you might have made some enemies in all your business dealings. But why would they want to kill Mary Beth? What has she done to make her a target?"

"I don't know that they have specifically included her," John replied. "I think it's just that she has been with me every time an attempt has been made."

"Perhaps that is so," Matt replied. "But at any rate, I do intend to stay with you all the way to Chicago and back."

"Have you ever been to Chicago, Matt?" Mary Beth asked.

"Yes. I once helped a friend of mine deliver some horses to Chicago."*

"Good, then you know how much fun Chicago can be. Papa, perhaps Matt and I can attend the theater while we are there."

"Well, that would be up to Matt, wouldn't it?" John asked.

Matt chuckled. "I can't think of anything that would give me more pleasure than to

---

* In the book *Snake River Slaughter*, Matt helped Kitty Wellington deliver five hundred horses to the U.S. Army at Fort Sheridan near Chicago. He felt a particular attachment to Kitty, because he had known her in the Soda Creek Home for Wayward Boys and Girls, the orphanage where they both were residents.

go to the theater with a beautiful young woman."

"Then that's what we will do. And afterward we can have a very expensive dinner, all on Papa's money."

John laughed out loud.

"You can find more ways to spend my money than anyone could possibly imagine."

"Well, what difference does it make, Papa, whether I spend it now, or I spend it later? It will all be mine someday anyway. You told me so yourself."

"So I did, darlin', so I did," John said. "Matt, I do hope you enjoy your time in Chicago with my daughter."

"I'm sure I will."

It will all be mine someday, anyway. Matt didn't say anything about Mary Beth's remark, but he did make a mental note of it.

"Mr. Kelly, I have a telegram for you. It just arrived about fifteen minutes ago," the Western Union operator said when he saw Kelly walking through the depot.

USING HOTEL INFORMATION SUPPLIED BY YOU STOP I HIRED SOMEONE LAST NIGHT STOP WAS

"Have you seen Mr. Gillespie this morning?" Kelly asked the telegrapher.

"Yes, sir, he stopped in to pick up a telegraph message no more than half an hour ago."

"What did the message say?"

"Well now, Mr. Kelly, you know I can't tell you what a private telegram says."

Kelly gave the telegrapher a five-dollar bill, and after looking around to make certain he wasn't being watched, the telegrapher gave Kelly the pad on which he took the original message.

Believe you may be right about Keaton stop Will inform sheriff in Cheyenne to investigate stop Think you might be out of danger now stop

Kelly had no idea who the telegram was from, but he was pleased that Gillespie might think the danger is over. He thought about the telegram he had just received from Conroy. Was there another attempt made on Gillespie last night? If so, the attempt failed, and in so doing may have also alerted Gillespie to the fact that he was still in danger.

Kelly picked up a pen and wrote a quick note.

SAW OUR FRIEND THIS MORNING STOP WHAT NOW QUERY

"Send this," he said, sliding the note across the counter. "I have some business to attend to. I'll check back later to see if there is any reply."

"Very good, sir."

After he left the Western Union desk, Kelly sought out the conductor who would be taking the train from Lincoln.

"Take a few days off, Andy," Kelly said. "Enjoy some time with your family. I'll take the trip on in to Chicago."

"Are you sure, Dan? I mean, you've made the run all the way from San Francisco. You have to be tired."

"I've slept. And I had a good sleep last night. I'm not too tired, I'll take it on in from here."

"Yeah, well, here's the thing," Andy said. "I admit, I would like the time off, but I'm not anxious to give up the money. The trip to Chicago and back will pay twenty-five dollars.

"I'll give you the twenty-five dollars now,"

Kelly said. "I'll get the money back when I collect for the trip."

"Are you sure? I mean, I don't understand why you would be interested in even doing something like that. Especially since by giving me the money, you would wind up doing it for free."

"All right, I confess, I do have a reason for going to Chicago."

"What reason?"

"Andy, really. Some things should be kept secret between a man and his lady friend, don't you agree?" Kelly asked with an exaggerated wink.

"Ahhh, you dog you," Andy said, though the huge smile spreading across his face ameliorated the words. "All right, take the trip. And you enjoy your dalliance."

Kelly held up his finger. "You must promise me, though, that you'll say nothing about this to anyone."

"Oh, not a word, not a word," Andy replied. "You can trust me on this."

"Which track are they using to make up the train?"

"Track two," Andy replied. "Where is the private car?"

"Why do you care?"

"I'd just like to see it, is all."

"You can see it if you'd like, but right now

it's all the way over on track eight. You'd have to walk through the entire marshaling yard."

"Yeah, you're right, it's not worth the effort. If you've seen one private car you've seen 'em all."

"That's my way of thinking. Truth is, I'm a little tired of those folks, anyway. They're always complaining about one thing or another," Kelly lied.

"Yeah, that's the way it is with rich folks sometimes. All right, if you're sure you want to do this, I think I'll just head on back home," Andy said. He held up the two bills, the twenty and the five. "And, thanks a lot."

"Oh, no, I thank you," Kelly said.

San Francisco
Lucas Conroy was very discriminating in taking on contracts. He was not in the business of killing cheating spouses or even vengeance killing. The contracts he took on were much more significant than that. In addition to arranging the assassination of a Russian prince, Conroy had arranged the assassinations of John Slough, Chief Justice of the New Mexico Supreme Court; Louis Cardis, Congressman from Texas; and Edward Holbrook, a delegate from Idaho to the United States Congress.

He had also arranged the murders of some very important businessmen but none more important than John Gillespie. The problem was, Gillespie was more than halfway to Chicago, and he was still alive. Conroy was certain that Spence would have been able to do the job. But, if the telegram he had just received was to be believed — and he was sure that it was true — Spence had failed.

The window was open on this warm September morning. Through it, the cry of seagulls competed with the clanging bells of channel marker buoys and the rattling sound of rigging and stays slapping against mast and arms on the oceangoing ships that were drawn up alongside the piers. Over it all could be heard conversations carried on in the dozen different languages of the foreign seamen on the docks. The breeze coming through the open windows carried on its breath the aroma of the sea with an under note of fish.

With a frustrated sigh over how difficult this job was turning out to be, Conroy sat down at his desk and wrote a telegraph to be sent to Dan Kelly. Because of his careful, prior planning, he had men waiting in Lincoln, as well as other cities along the route. And he had shared his plans with

313

Dan Kelly. He would just activate the next phase of the operation.

Lincoln, Nebraska

When Kelly returned to the Western Union desk, the telegrapher came over to see him.

"Here is a telegram for you, Mr. Kelly," the telegrapher said, handing him a folded, yellow sheet of paper. "It arrived about ten minutes ago."

"Thank you," Kelly said, taking the message.

MEET ASSOCIATES AS ORIGINALLY PLANNED

LC

With the message in hand, Kelly walked across the street to the Railroad Saloon. This had all been planned out prior to leaving San Francisco. If, when the train reached Lincoln, the job still hadn't been done, he was to meet three men who would be waiting for him in the Railroad Saloon on this day. Kelly had never met any of the men, but he knew what to look for. All three would be wearing red feathers in their hatbands.

As soon as he stepped into the saloon, he saw three such men sitting at a table near the stove in the back of the saloon. Because it was warm on this early fall day, the stove was cold, but there hung about it the ghost of smoke and burned wood from its last use.

Kelly walked over to the table, and the three men looked up at him.

"We don't want no company," one of them said.

"Oh, I think you'll want me. Would you three men be Koop, Jackson, and Stevens?" he asked.

"Yeah," one of them replied. "Are you Kelly?"

"I am."

"What's this about? We were told to wait here until you came and that you would tell us how we could make some money. And how come you're late? We thought you would be here yesterday."

"We had some problem with the train," Kelly explained. "Do you mean to say that you haven't been told what is expected of you?"

"No. The only thing we was told was to wait here until you showed up," the same man replied. He, it appeared, would be the spokesman for the three. "I figured you would know what we was supposed to do."

"Which one are you?" Kelly asked.

"I'm Jackson, this is Koop, and this is

Stevens."

"I, uh, don't know anything about you men," Kelly said. "But I assume that you are good for the job, or you wouldn't have been selected."

"What is the job?"

"You are to . . ." Kelly stopped and looked around the saloon to make certain there was no one close enough to overhear him. "Kill someone," he said.

Jackson laughed. "Is that all?"

"Is that all? My word, isn't that enough?"

"It ain't like we ain't none of us never done it before," Jackson said. "Who are we supposed to kill?"

"A man and his daughter."

"A man and his daughter? That don't sound too hard," Koop said.

"It may be more difficult than you think," Kelly said.

"Why's that?"

"There is a bodyguard watching over them."

"A bodyguard? You mean one body-guard?" Jackson asked.

"Yes."

Jackson laughed. "One bodyguard. Well, don't you worry none about it, Kelly. There are three of us. I expect we can get through one bodyguard all right. Don't you fellers think so?"

The other two men laughed.

"Yeah," Stevens said. "Don't you worry none about there bein' a bodyguard."

"What's the name of the people we're supposed to kill?"

"Mr. John Gillespie. And, as I said, his daughter as well."

"John Gillespie? Seems to me like I've heard that name before," Stevens said.

"That's quite possible. Gillespie is an extremely wealthy industrialist."

"Industrialist? What's that mean?" Koop asked.

"It just means that he's very rich."

"Where do we find this man Gillespie, his daughter, and the one bodyguard?" Jackson asked.

"He is traveling in a private car, which at the moment is waiting to be attached to the *Chicago Limited.* I just saw him in the depot, but I've no doubt he will return to the car before it is attached. I suggest that you be there to meet them. Right now, it's sitting on track number six."

"Track six? That's way the hell over there, ain't it?" Koop asked.

"Would you rather do this job in front of a lot of people?" Kelly asked.

"No. I guess you're right. Best to be away

from everyone," Koop agreed.

"I have to get back to the depot. If you are going to do this job, you need to get over there as well."

CHAPTER TWENTY-SIX

"Darlin', I'm a little tired," John said to his daughter. "I think I would like to return to the car. Do you mind?"

"Papa, you're getting old," Mary Beth teased. "That's all right, I guess it's a daughter's job to take care of her father when he gets old. All right, we'll go back."

Matt started out with them.

"Matt, you don't have to come with us if you don't want to. Why don't you stay here and look around a bit. You can join us when the train is ready to go. That way you won't have to walk as far," John said.

Matt shook his head. "No, sir, I'm being paid to see you safely to Chicago, and I intend to do just that."

"Oh, I'm sure that the danger is all over now. Seeing Slade and Jones has convinced me that Fred Keaton is the one who has been behind these attempts on my life all along, and Drew is contacting the sheriff to take care of that. I don't expect we'll have any more trouble."

"Are you forgetting about Spence?"

"No, I haven't forgotten him. I mean, how can I? He broke into my daughter's room last night. But I think if he was a would-be assassin, and not merely a thief in the night, then he, too, was probably sent by Keaton. So, I think we need have no further fear of any of Keaton's hired men."

Leaving the depot building, the three walked out under the high roof of the car shed. Here, they could smell burning coal and wood as the smoke and steam swirled around them. Trains were arriving and departing, and they could feel in their stomachs the heavy rumble of locomotives rolling by.

"There's the car," John said. "What do you say we relax, and even though it's midmorning, have a glass of wine?"

"Sounds good to me," Matt said.

Matt helped Mary Beth onto the step, then stood back as John climbed up. It seemed like the courteous and gentlemanly thing to do, but a few seconds later, he regretted his action, because when he stepped into the car behind them, he saw that both John and Mary Beth were holding their hands up. There had been three armed men waiting in the car for them.

"Who are you men?" John asked.

"What do you think, Jackson? Think we should tell 'im who we are?"

"Stevens, you dumb son of a bitch! What do you mean, usin' my name?"

"You just used my name," Stevens replied. "Anyhow, what difference does it make? They're all three goin' to be dead soon."

"We don't have your name," Matt said, pointing to the one who had not yet been identified."

"The name is Koop. Lon Koop, not that it matters to you. Like Tim just told you, you're goin' to be dead soon."

"Who sent you?" Matt asked. "Who wants Mr. Gillespie dead?"

"We want him dead," Jackson said. "Enough talkin'."

"Damn, Jackson," Stevens said. "Look at that woman! We wasn't told nothin' about how purty she would be. You think maybe we could save her to last, so's we could have a little fun with 'er?"

"Yeah," Koop said. "What do you say, Jackson? That seems like a purty good idea to me."

"I'd rather be dead," Mary Beth said defiantly.

"Oh, don't worry, girlie, you will be, right after we're finished with you."

Matt had been following the conversation, but more important, he had been watching the eyes of the three men. Mary Beth was proving to be the perfect distraction, because all three were looking at her with lust-filled eyes.

Matt knew that the moment was right, and he drew his pistol and fired three quick gunshots, shooting so quickly that all three of the assailants died before they even realized that they were in trouble.

Mary Beth screamed and jumped, but the scream died in her throat when she saw that all three gunmen had collapsed in front of her. Matt fired only three times, because that was all it took. Not one of the three would-be assassins managed to get off a single shot.

"My God!" John said, even as the gun smoke from the three discharges hung before them and burned their eyes and noses. "I've never seen anything like that in my life!"

"Are both of you all right?" Matt asked.

"Yes," Mary Beth said. "At least I am now."

"Yeah, I'm fine," John said.

"Do you know any of these men, Mr.

Gillespie?"

John looked closely at the three men who were now lying on the floor of his private car.

"No, I don't. I've never seen any of them before."

"You think they might have been working for Keaton?"

John shook his head. "No, I don't see how. By now I expect Keaton is either in jail, or is, at least, trying to explain to the sheriff why he sent three men to kill me. Four if you count the man last night, but now I'm not so sure that we should count him or these three. I think it must be someone else, someone other than Keaton."

"Who were the men you said you suspected? Morris, Keaton, and who was the third one?"

"Mitchell. Donald Mitchell."

"Tell me about Mitchell."

"At one time Donald Mitchell owned the Nebraska Stockyards in Omaha."

"Omaha? How far is Omaha from here?"

"It isn't too far at all," John said. "We'll be there in less than two hours."

"You listed three men as possible suspects, and Mitchell was one of them. Tell me about him."

John began telling the story.

Donald Mitchell was sitting at his desk, and he looked up hopefully and expectantly when his assistant came into the office.

"What do the sales numbers look like?" Mitchell asked.

"They look like nothing," Mitchell's assistant told him.

"Nothing? What do you mean, nothing?"

"I mean the packing plants all want Herefords. Nobody wants longhorns anymore."

"Somebody has to want them!" Mitchell shouted in alarm. "Carter, I have ten thousand head here, ready to be shipped out to the meat packers."

"Oh, we can sell them. But nobody has agreed to pay more than five dollars a head for them."

"Five dollars a head? That's less than we paid for them!"

"I told them that, and they laughed and said we paid too much."

"What are they paying for Herefords?"

"Thirty-five dollars a head."

"Damn," Mitchell said. "We paid seven dollars and fifty cents per head for the longhorns. We stand to lose twenty-five thousand dollars if we sell."

"If we don't sell, we'll lose everything,"

Carter said. "We can't afford to just keep them here. We have neither the space nor the food. We'll have to destroy the herd."

"We had to do that two years ago when we got in some cows with Texas fever, remember?" Mitchell replied. "We haven't even fully recovered from that yet."

"Then the only thing we can do is sell the herd at five dollars a head," Carter said.

"No, I won't do that. There has to be some other way."

Two days later, John Gillespie came to visit Mitchell. "I will pay you seven dollars and fifty cents a head for every animal you have, and I'll make up the loss you suffered from Texas fever two years ago," John said.

"Why would you do that?"

"I want to buy your company."

"How much will you pay me for it?"

"Like I said, I'll take these cattle off your hands, and I'll cover the loss from two years ago. And I'll keep you on as manager."

"That's it? You don't intend to pay me anything for the company?"

"No."

"I'm not interested."

"I'll be in the Morning Star Hotel, if you change your mind."

"I gather Mr. Mitchell changed his mind," Matt said.

"Yes, that same night."

"You paid him everything you agreed upon. What makes you think he might be the one who wants you dead?"

"Since I bought the company, we have been dealing with Herefords and Black Angus exclusively. And now the company is making a great deal of money, more than it has ever made in the past."

"Is Mitchell making money?"

"Yes, he's making a lot of money, a lot more than he was ever making when he owned the company."

"But you think he might resent that?"

"Well, I didn't think he resented it, because as I say, it has worked out very well for him. But I also felt the same way about Morris and Keaton. It was Drew Jessup who suggested it could be one of those three."

"Why would he suspect them, if you don't?"

"I think Drew is in a position to hear things happening within the company that I might not hear."

"Why is that? If you own the company, don't you know everything that's going on?"

"No, and it is precisely because I do own

326

the company that I don't hear as much as Drew. You see, even though Drew occupies a very high position within the business, when you come right down to it, he is still an employee. And I think other employees may feel sort of a kinship with him, strong enough to enable them to speak freely to him."

"But he doesn't share that information with you?"

"No. At least not always."

"Why not?"

"I think that he tells me what he thinks I need to know in order to run the company, but he shields me from any unpleasant complaints that he doesn't think I need to hear."

The door to the car suddenly jerked open, and Matt swung his pistol toward the intruder.

"Oh!" Dan Kelly said, gasping.

"What do you want, Kelly?" Matt asked.

"I . . . was just coming over to say that the car would be connected to the *Chicago Limited* soon, when I heard gunshots. I thought I had better check on it."

"Did you now?"

Kelly looked at the three men lying on the floor of the car.

"Who are those men?" Kelly asked.

"I was hoping you could tell us," Matt said.

"I, tell you? How could that be?"

"Let me ask you something. What did you expect to find when you opened the door?" Matt asked. "Did you expect to see us dead?"

"I don't know, I guess I didn't give it a second thought."

"I would say not. If these men had succeeded, and you opened the door on them as you just did on us, don't you realize that you could have been killed?"

"No. Why would they kill me? You three are the ones they're after."

"Why indeed?" Matt replied.

"I'll, uh, get the police. I'm sure you won't want to have these men lying here once we get underway."

"Good idea," John said.

Two men from the Lincoln Police Department came to interview Matt, John, and Mary Beth about how the three men were killed. They spoke to them one at a time, and all three of the stories matched.

The police were inclined to believe them anyway, since all three men had records, and they still had their guns in their hands. Finally, the bodies were removed, and Matt

328

and the others were told they were no longer needed.

Fortunately, the investigation was over before the scheduled departure time of the train, so they remained in the car as the *Conqueror* pulled it over to track two and backed it up against the consist, which made up the train that, from this point on, would be known as the *Chicago Limited.*

CHAPTER TWENTY-SEVEN

Shortly after the train got underway, Matt decided to visit the new crew in the engine cab. He crawled across the tender and climbed down onto the platform.

"Who the hell are you?" the fireman asked.

"Matt Jensen. I'm a special detective for this trip."

"They told us about him in scheduling, Clay," the engineer said.

"Oh, yeah, I remember that." The fireman smiled and extended his hand. "I'm Clay Harris."

"I'm Spud Dawes," the engineer said.

The engineer was considerably older than the fireman, and Matt could see scars, like little pits around the base of his neck. Matt had seen such scars before, and while they might resemble pox scars, Matt knew that they were actually scars made by the red-hot sparks that over the many years and miles of being an engineer on the railroad, had flown down the back of his collar.

"What brings you up here?" Dawes asked.

"I'm sure you know about Mr. Gillespie," Matt said.

"Yeah, we know that his car is attached to the train."

"Yes, but it's more than that. Someone wants him dead, and there have already been several attempts to kill him since we left San Francisco."

"What? You mean on the train?" Dawes asked.

"In some cases, yes. So, I'll tell you the same thing I told the previous engine crew. Be on the lookout for such things as obstructions on the track, missing rails, or damaged trestles."

"Thanks for the warning," Dawes said. "When something like that happens, it's usually the cab crew who are the most hurt in an accident."

Harris had tossed in several shovels of coal while Matt was there, and he closed the fire door, then checked the gauge. It was holding at exactly 210 pounds. The fire was roaring, the steam was hissing, and the rolling wheels were pounding out a thunder of steel on steel. The speedometer needle was quivering at fifty miles per hour.

"Damn! What's that?" Dawes asked, pointing to the front of the engine.

Matt looked toward the front of the engine and saw something tied just below the smokestack.

"You have a pair of binoculars in here?" Matt asked.

"Yes," Harris said. He opened a tool box and, taking the binoculars out, handed them to Matt.

Matt leaned out the window, and enlarged by the binoculars, saw that what he was looking at were three sticks of dynamite tied together. He also saw a fuse running from the dynamite into the opening of the smokestack. All it would take would be a spark from the smokestack to light the fuse.

"Damn!" Matt said. "That's dynamite."

"What?" Dawes asked.

"There's dynamite tied to the smokestack! Stop this train! I've got to get it off of there before it blows," he said.

The engineer put on the brakes, and Matt held on as the train slid to a halt. The braking action threw him forward, and he knew that everyone back in the train must be tumbling all over the place.

Finally, the train came to a halt.

"You're goin' out there?" the engineer asked.

"Yeah."

"That's dangerous, ain't it? I mean what it if goes off while you're trying to get it free?"

"If it goes off, it won't make much difference whether I'm out there or in here, will it?"

"No, I guess you've got that right," the engineer agreed.

"Harris, don't throw any more coal into the firebox until I get back. If I get back."

"I would extinguish the fire," Harris said. "But soon as I throw water on it that will raise a lot of sparks."

"Yes, that's what I was thinking," Matt said. "Well, here I go."

"It's too late!" Spud Dawes shouted. "Look at that!"

Dawes pointed to the fuse that had been ignited in the smokestack. Now it was sending off sparks as it worked its way down toward the dynamite.

"I'm going to have to cut it," Matt said.

"You'll never get out there in time!" Spud Dawes said.

Matt drew his pistol and aimed toward the front of the train. "I'll cut it this way."

"Wait, if you miss the fuse and hit the dynamite, won't that make it blow?"

"Yeah, it will. But we don't have any other choice, do we?"

He took a long, careful aim, then pulled the trigger. The bullet cut the fuse, just before the sparks reached the dynamite.

"Son of a bitch! How did you do that?" Dawes asked in a disbelieving voice.

"I was scared to death," Harris said.

"Are you too afraid to climb out there and get it?" Dawes asked. "I don't want to think of that thing being there for the rest of the trip. Hell, a spark from the smokestack could still set it off."

"Yeah, you're right, maybe I had better get it," Harris said. He stepped out of the cab, then climbed up onto the board that stretched from the cab, along the side of the boiler, to the front of the engine.

Matt stepped back onto the deck between the tender and the engine, then leaned out, with his pistol still in his hand.

"Mr. Harris?" he called.

"Yes, sir?"

"When you get the dynamite clear of the stack, throw it out toward the trees, but throw it as high as you can."

"What for?" Harris asked, confused by the request.

"There's no sense in leaving unexploded dynamite around. It's too dangerous. I'm going to shoot it to set it off."

"All right," Harris said.

"You think you can do that?" Dawes asked, then he took his hat off and ran his hand through his hair. "Of course you can, if you can shoot the fuse in two from here, you can damn sure hit the dynamite."

Matt watched as Harris worked with the sticks of dynamite until he got them free. There were three of them bound together, and holding them, he looked back toward Matt.

"You ready?" Harris called.

"Yes, throw it as high and as far out as you can," Matt said.

Harris threw the sticks of dynamite, and Matt fired. The dynamite exploded in mid-air.

"Whoowee!" Harris said as he came climbing back into the cab. "I'll bet that sure gave the folks back in the cars a show."

"Think we can go on now?" Dawes asked.

"I don't see why not," Matt replied. "Oh, Mr. Harris, keep an eye open as you're shoveling the coal, too."

Matt told him about finding the dynamite in the coal tender back in San Francisco.

"I see what you mean about being on the lookout," Dawes said as he opened the throttle.

There was a gush of steam as the drive wheels caught, then, with the chain reaction of connectors taking up the slack, the train got underway once more.

When Matt returned to the car, both John and Mary Beth wanted to tell him about the explosion they saw.

"It went off right by the track. Fortunately, it wasn't close enough to do any damage," John said.

"Well, it was too close," Matt said. "But I had Mr. Harris throw it as far away from the track as he could."

"Mr. Harris?"

"He's the fireman." Matt told them about the dynamite taped to the smokestack of the train.

"Oh my, that could have gone off in Mr. Harris's hand!" Mary Beth said.

"No, it hadn't been lit yet. The reason it exploded is because I shot it. I didn't think it would be good to have live dynamite too close to the track."

"No, you are quite correct. You did the right thing," John said. He laughed. "But I told you, didn't I, Mary Beth, that I wouldn't be surprised if Matt didn't have something to do with the exploding dynamite?"

"Yes, you did tell me."

"You do realize, don't you, that if the

engineer hadn't seen the dynamite, and if it had gone off, the engine would have been destroyed, and Mr. Dawes, Mr. Harris, and I would have been killed? You two would have been killed as well, and probably a dozen or more who are farther back in the train," Matt said.

"Then that means someone is still after me, doesn't it?" John asked.

"I'm afraid it does."

Kelly had been in the last car of the train when the dynamite blew. He had expected it, thinking it would take out the engine and the first few cars. That meant that Gillespie would either be killed or badly enough injured that he could be killed easily. He was prepared for several others on the train to be killed or injured as well, but he was certain that he would be safe by remaining in the last car.

Any investigation would probably conclude that the boiler had burst from excessive steam pressure. That happened often enough to make it a very believable reason, and especially in this engine, since the *Chicago Limited* was designed to operate under higher pressure than the ordinary locomotives. But somehow, and he wasn't sure how, the dynamite exploded, not on the train, but alongside the track. He didn't know how it happened, but he was reasonably certain that Matt Jensen had something to do with it.

Suddenly there was a squeal of brakes as steel slid on steel, bringing the train to an abrupt halt. Kelly and all the other passengers in the car were thrown forward by the abruptness of it.

"What is it?" one of the passengers asked. "What's happening?"

"I have no idea, but I'll find out," Kelly said. He really didn't have any idea what this was about. If this was some part of Conroy's plan to kill Gillespie, he had not shared it with Kelly.

Matt was still in the private car with John and Mary Beth when the train slid to a halt. He jumped down from the car and started toward the front of the train to ask Dawes why the sudden stop. Though sitting still, the engine was alive with potential energy . . . spitting steam and percolating water as if protesting the indignity of having been forced to stop while running at full speed. Others were beginning to get off the train as well, and Matt could hear them calling out to each other in curiosity, wondering what was wrong and why the train had made such an abrupt stop.

Matt didn't have to inquire. He could see, quite clearly, a missing rail in front of the engine. He could also see that the engine was only a few feet short of the track separation.

"You see that?" Dawes called down from the window of the engine cab.

"I see it. You did a good job of getting stopped in time."

"I'm lucky at that. The track made a little curve back there, and I just happened to be lookin' in the right direction to catch it," Dawes answered. "If I hadn't of seen it when I did, we woulda run off the track 'n the first three or four cars woulda more'n likely turned over. Or maybe even worse, the cars coulda all telescoped into one another, and that woulda killed dozens of folks."

By now John had also left the car and was standing on the ground alongside Matt.

"What do we do now?" John asked.

"Well, we can put out torpedoes on the track on the other side to warn any train that might be coming this way," the engineer said. "Then we can back up to Lincoln and pick up a track crew."

"Would it speed things up if we sent them a telegraph message?" John asked.

"Well, yeah, but how are we going to do

that?" Dawes asked.

"I can send a message from my car."

Many of the passengers left the train while they waited on a track repair crew to arrive from Omaha, that being the closest place now. There was a professional photographer on board, and he did a brisk business taking pictures of the passengers as they posed alongside the train, or on the damaged track, or even by some of the wildflowers that grew at trackside.

"Did you know about this? I mean about the rail bein' took up like it was?" Calhoun asked. Like Kelly, the porter had agreed to continue the trip all the way to Chicago. And like Kelly, the porter had been hired to provide any assistance as might be needed in arranging the demise of John Gillespie and his daughter.

"No," Kelly replied. "I knew about the dynamite, and I told you about that. But I didn't know about this."

"Hell, this coulda kilt us, too. I mean, more'n likely the whole train woulda run off the track. 'N there was bound to be some of the cars telescopin'. How come we wasn't told?"

"I don't know. Maybe Conroy thought we were told. Anyhow, the train wasn't wrecked, and Jensen and the Gillespies are still alive. This might be a good time for you to take care of them."

"How am I goin' to do it? The whole damn train has been unloaded. There's no way I can get to them."

"You know the arrangement as well as I do," Kelly said. "The only way we get paid is if they don't get there alive."

"Well, this ain't the place to do it is all I'm sayin'. We got a ways before we get to Chicago. I expect we'll get us another chance at 'em."

Kelly had not been entirely truthful with Julius Calhoun. While it was true that the porter wouldn't be paid anything unless Gillespie and his daughter were killed, Kelly had managed to arrange payment for himself, no matter whether Gillespie was killed or not.

Omaha

All traffic on the line had been stopped due to the necessity of repairing the track, and that changed the schedule of every train. Because of that, the *Chicago Limited,* which normally would have gone on through Omaha with a stop of only a few minutes, would now have to spend at least two hours in the station while they waited for all the traffic ahead of them to clear.

John had not sent a message to Drew while they were waiting for the track to be repaired, but because of their extended stay in Omaha, he did arrange to have the teleprinter connected, and he sent a message to Drew directly from his car.

TWO MORE ATTEMPTS SINCE WE LEFT LINCOLN BUT AM HAPPY TO SAY THAT WE HAVE SURVIVED BOTH ATTEMPTS WITHOUT HARM. INTEND TO CALL ON MITCHELL WHILE HERE IN OMAHA.

Fifteen minutes after sending the message, the teleprinter began tapping, and a long strip of paper was extruded from the bell jar.

KEATON BEING QUESTIONED BY POLICE STOP IS IT WISE TO APPROACH MITCHELL QUERY THINK YOU SHOULD CONTACT POLICE THERE IN OMAHA

"I disagree," John said, after he read the message aloud. "We are going to be here long enough, I think it would be better if I went to see him in person."

"All right," Matt said. "But I'll be going with you."

CHAPTER TWENTY-EIGHT

Leaving the depot, the three walked toward the stockyard. In order to take advantage of rail shipment of the livestock, the Nebraska Stockyard was located just across from the depot. Because of that, it wasn't a very long walk.

"If Mitchell is behind this, I believe I will know it the moment I lay eyes on him," John said as they approached.

There were several large pens crowded with cattle, and the air was filled with their mooing and bawling. But sound wasn't the only thing that filled the air.

Mary Beth frowned and waved her hand in front of her nose.

"Oh, Papa, that smell is horrible!"

John laughed. "No it isn't, darlin'. It's not bad at all, once you understand that what you are smelling is money."

Matt laughed as well.

Matt, John, and Mary Beth stepped into

the low building that sat in the middle of the yard, and once inside they heard a sound that had become familiar to Matt since he started on this trip. It was the sound of ticker tape, with the latest update on the cattle market being sent from Chicago. And like John's teleprinter, the returns were printed on a long, narrow strip of tape. There was, however, someone reading the ticker tape, then writing the returns on a large blackboard that was on the wall at the back of the room.

"Yes, sir, can I help you?" someone asked.

"Is Mr. Mitchell in?"

"He is. May I tell him who is asking?"

"Morgan, that's John Gillespie," another man said. "He owns this place."

"Oh, I beg your pardon, Mr. Gillespie, I didn't know."

"That's all right. Hello, Mr. Carter, how are you doing?" John asked, speaking to the man who had identified him.

"I'm doing fine, sir. If you'll wait for just a moment, I'll get Don for you."

It was only a few seconds later when Mitchell himself came from his office. A large smile spread across his face, and he extended his hand as he approached them.

"Mr. Gillespie! What an unexpected, but very pleasant surprise! What brings you to

Omaha?"

"I'm on my way to Chicago, and the train is going to be delayed for a couple of hours, so I thought I might pay you a visit."

"Well, I'm certainly glad you chose to do so. Will you be here over lunch? Could I buy lunch for you and your friends?"

"Is it somewhere away from the smell?" Mary Beth asked.

"Smell? What smell?" Mitchell replied.

"What smell?" Mary Beth replied in a shocked voice.

Mitchell laughed. "I'm sorry, Miss, but I'm here ten to twelve hours per day, every day. The truth is, I'm so used to the smell now, that I don't even notice it. But yes, we can have lunch at the Stockman's Club, and it is far enough away that I think you won't notice it."

"Mr. Mitchell, this is my daughter Mary Beth. You'll have to excuse her sensitive nose."

"That's all right. Young ladies should have a sensitive nose," Mitchell replied.

"And this is my friend, Matt Jensen." John didn't mention that Matt was also his bodyguard, and Matt thought it was wise that he didn't.

"It's good to meet both of you," Mitchell said, shaking their hands.

346

"I appreciate the invitation to the Stockman's Club, but if you don't mind, I would rather have lunch in the depot," John said. "That way we will be close enough so that if they call the train, we won't miss it."

"All right, sure, that'll be fine by me," Mitchell said. "Terry, look after things while we're gone, would you?"

"Yes, sir, Don, I'd be glad to," Carter said.

As they left the stockyard office, Matt saw three mounted men riding behind a dozen or more cows, herding them into a pen with whistles and shouts, and it reminded him of the few times he had been a cowboy.

"Oh," Mary Beth said. "That looks like so much fun!"

"I thought you didn't like the smell," John said.

"It's like you said, Papa. It's the smell of money."

The others laughed.

"I'll tell you the truth, Mr. Gillespie," Mitchell said over lunch. "Selling the stockyard to you was the best business move I ever made. It has been a huge success, and I'm making money hand over fist, more money than I've ever made in my life."

"You don't wish you still owned it?"

"Oh, I admit, from time to time I sort of wish I did. But almost as soon as I have that thought, I think better of it. The truth is, I would never have been able to afford the investments necessary to make it the success it is today. If I still owned it," he stopped and laughed, then continued, "If I still owned it, I *wouldn't* own it. I would have already lost it by now."

The conversation continued in a congenial tone until the end of the meal. Then, Mitchell stood.

"I hate to run off and leave such good company," Mitchell said. "But I have a stockyard to run, and if I don't do a good job, you won't be making any money from it, and if you don't make money, then there's no way I can make money."

John laughed. "You know, Mr. Mitchell, I like the way you look at that."

Mitchell laughed as well. "It's the only way a sane man can look at it."

"He has nothing to do with all these attempts on my life," John said after Mitchell left.

"I get the same feeling," Matt said.

"With Keaton tied up by the police, and Mitchell in the clear, that leaves only Morris."

"The coal mine owner?"

"Yes. I think, when we get to Davenport,

Iowa, I'll have the car detached from this train and attached to an engine I will hire. We'll go down to Assumption. I would very much like to meet Mr. Raymond Morris face-to-face."

"But, are you sure you want to leave the train in Davenport?" Kelly asked, surprised when John told him of his plans. "I thought you were going to Chicago."

"I am going to Chicago," John said. "But I'm going to Assumption, Illinois, first."

"I'm not sure about the train schedules from Assumption. You may have a difficult time finding one to take you there, then get you to Chicago on time."

"I'm not worried about catching a train," John said. "I've got my private car, I'll just lease an engine. I'll get there in plenty of time."

"But you will be going on to Davenport with us, will you not?"

John chuckled. "Yes, I'm afraid we aren't out of your hair yet. We'll be a bother for a little while longer."

Before they left Omaha, Kelly sent a telegram.

GILLESPIE LEAVING TRAIN IN

DAVENPORT STOP WILL BE GO-
ING TO ASSUMPTION ILLINOIS
BY PRIVATE CAR AND LEASED EN-
GINE

When he heard the key clacking, he looked
over at the telegrapher.

"I expect this is the one you've been waiting for," the telegrapher said, as he began
recording the message.

THE TIME HAS COME TO GIVE
THE JOB TO JC STOP ONE HUN-
DRED FIFTY DOLLARS WILL BE
WIRED TO YOU TO CLOSE THE
DEAL

"Thanks," Kelly said, after he read the
message.

The telegraph key began clicking once
more, and again the telegrapher took the
message.

"Here is your money transfer," he said.

Kelly found Julius Calhoun folding sheets
in one of the three Pullman cars that were a
part of the *Chicago Limited*.

"Is the car empty?" Kelly said.

"Yes, sir, it is," the porter answered.

Kelly looked into every seat, and even
checked the restrooms, one at either end of

350

the train, before speaking.

"It's your turn," Kelly said.

Julius looked around at him, flashing a satisfied smile.

"When do I get my money?"

"You'll get your money the same time I get my money," Kelly said. "As soon as the job is done."

"We'll reach Davenport by ten o'clock tonight. They will be dead before we get there," the powerfully built black man promised.

"You do understand that you'll have to kill all three of them, don't you?"

"Yeah," Calhoun said. "One of 'em, three of 'em, it makes no difference to me."

At about seven o'clock that evening Matt was in the private car with John and Mary Beth. The car was brightly illuminated with gas lamps, and though Matt and John were engaged in casual conversation, Mary Beth was reading the latest issue of *Harper's Weekly*.

"Oh, my, listen to this, Papa!" Mary Beth said, reading from the periodical. *"It has been suggested that some clever person will, no doubt, discover a means of connecting Mr. Alexander Bell's telephone to Mr. Thomas Edison's talking machine. Should such a union become possible, one could then make a telephone call, and if the party isn't available to receive the call, a message could be recorded on the talking machine. Then, when the party returns home, he would need only to play the recording and thereby retrieve any message left."*

Mary Beth put the issue down and looked at her father with her eyes glowing in excitement.

"Oh, we do live in such a marvelous age, Papa," she said.

"Indeed we do, darlin', indeed we do," John replied. "We have covered in less than five complete days a distance that, before the railroad, would have taken from four to five months."

Their conversation was interrupted by a light knock on the door, and Matt got up from his chair to answer it. When he opened the door, he saw the porter standing in the vestibule with a small, wheeled cart. The cart had several silver dome-covered serving dishes.

"The dinner for you gentlemen and the lady," Calhoun said.

Matt stepped aside to allow Calhoun to push the cart on into the car. When he reached the table, he began removing the silver domes from each dish, doing so with relish.

"Oh, that looks so good!" Mary Beth said, enthusiastically. "Thank you, Mr. Calhoun."

"You are mighty welcome, Miss," Calhoun said.

"Apple pie," Matt said with a smile, as he picked up a slice and held it under his nose. "There is nothing in the world that smells better than apple . . ." he stopped in mid-sentence, frowned, and took another sniff.

John had just cut off a piece of the pie with his fork and was about to take a bite.

"Hold it, John!" Matt said sharply. "Don't eat that!"

"What?"

Matt forced a grin and held his pie out toward Calhoun.

"Mr. Calhoun was so good as to bring the pie to us, I think he should have my piece. And he should take the first bite."

"Mr. Jensen, I don't know what you're talkin' about!" Calhoun said.

"I'm just offering you a piece of pie, that's all. And you can have the first bite."

"I wouldn't want to eat your pie, sir."

"Take a bite!" Matt said more forcefully.

Calhoun slapped the pie from Matt's hand, then he grabbed Mary Beth and pulled her to him.

"Take your pistol out of the holster and hand it to me," he said. " 'Cause if you don't do what I say, I'll break this girl's neck."

Suddenly and unexpectedly, Mary Beth brought her heel down sharply on the top of Calhoun's foot. He let out a howl of pain and loosened his grip on her. When he did, she ducked under his arm and stepped away from him.

Calhoun was a big and powerful man, and Matt knew that it would be difficult to handle him in a face-to-face fight, so he drew his pistol, and using it as a club, swung at Calhoun's neck, catching him in the Adam's apple.

Calhoun made a choking noise and put both hands to his neck. When he did that, Matt brought the butt of his pistol down sharply on Calhoun's head.

The big man went down like a sack of flour.

"What was that all about? Why did you try and make him eat the pie?" Mary Beth asked.

"I was testing to see if he was responsible for it, and his reaction told me that he was."

"Responsible for what?'

"The pie is laced with cyanide."

"What? How did you know that?"

"When you smell a pie, what do you normally smell?"

"Cinnamon and apples," Mary Beth said.

"Smell this," Matt said, holding the pie up to her nose.

Mary Beth took a whiff, then made a face.

"Does that smell like any apple pie you've ever smelled before?"

"No. There's sort of a bitter smell to it."

"That's the cyanide."

"What made you suspicious enough to smell it?" John asked.

Matt grinned sheepishly. "I wish I could say that I'm a good enough detective to be suspicious. But I just happened to smell it, because I like the smell of apple pie. That's when I smelled the cyanide."

"What do we do with him now?" John asked.

"I'll tie him up and leave him in the baggage car. They'll discover him after we're gone."

"You don't think we should turn him over to the law in Davenport?"

"Nothing happened, we can't prove he is the one who put the poison in the pie, and we would get so tied up in the court that you would miss your appointment in Chicago," Matt said.

"Yeah, you're probably right. Just leave him in the baggage car."

CHAPTER TWENTY-NINE

Davenport, Iowa

"Mr. Kelly," John said. "I would like for you to make arrangements for my car to be disconnected."

"I know, you told me that back in Omaha. But are you sure you want to do this? I thought it was important for you to go to Chicago."

"It is. But with an engine dedicated just to my need, I'm sure I will be able to make it in time."

"You do understand, don't you, that in order to disconnect your car from the rest of the train, I will need permission from the railroad?"

"Yes, I understand. But if you will come with me, I will secure the permission before your eyes, so that you will be satisfied that you have done no wrong."

"All right," Kelly said. "Of course I will come with you. I do hope you aren't doing

357

so because you have been displeased with your service. I have gone out of my way to be accommodating to you."

"Yes, I'm sure you have," John said.

Kelly accompanied John to the stationmaster's office, where arrangements were made to separate the private car from the *Chicago Limited*. There, too, John made arrangements to lease a locomotive and crew, as well as to secure track usage between Davenport and Assumption, Illinois. He was told that it would be at least noon of the next day before an engine and crew could be located and the tracks cleared.

"Thank you," John said.

"Mr. Kelly, sir, as soon Mr. Gillespie's private car is disconnected, you will need to get the *Chicago Limited* underway in order for all the schedules to be maintained," the stationmaster said.

"Yes, all right, I'll do that."

"Oh, by the way, Mr. Kelly," Matt said as Kelly started to leave. "If you are looking for your porter, I left him tied up in the baggage car."

"You did what?" Kelly gasped. "Why would you do such a thing?"

"The meal he brought us was unsatisfactory."

■ ■ ■ ■

At the Western Union desk in Davenport, Kelly sent a telegram to Lucas Conroy.

JC FAILED IN HIS TASK STOP JG GOING TO ASSUMPTION ILLINOIS BY PRIVATE TRAIN STOP SITUATION IS NO LONGER IN MY HANDS

DK

San Francisco
Lucas Conroy stood on the end of the pier looking out over the dark water of San Francisco Bay. A lighthouse beam swept across the bay, illuminating in stark black and white the empty masts of the sailing ships at anchor.

He heard footsteps behind him, then turned. He was a little nervous until the person spoke.

"Mr. Conroy?"

"Yes."

"I represent the consortium."

"You aren't the one I met with before."

"No. But they asked that I represent them for this meeting."

"Why couldn't we have conducted this

meeting in my office? Why did you want to meet here and at this time of the night?"

"We thought it might be best if we kept as much distance between you and us as possible."

"Yes, I suppose that is so."

"We . . . that is the consortium . . . thought you would have this situation resolved by now. Why is it that John Gillespie is still a problem?"

"You have to understand that the operation has proven to be much more difficult than I was led to believe."

"What is difficult about it? You were given one task to do. You were to kill one old man and a young woman."

"But it isn't just Gillespie and his daughter. He has hired someone to protect him, and the man he has hired has proven to be rather formidable. In fact, he has become quite an obstacle."

"You were hired, Mr. Conroy, because we were led to believe that you were adept at overcoming obstacles."

"Yes, and I am, because I plan for every contingency. And to that end I put men in place at key stops all along the route to Chicago, because I was told he would be going directly to that location. However, I now learn that Gillespie and his daughter have left the main line and are going to someplace called Assumption, Illinois. I have no one in place in Assumption, Illinois. In fact, I don't even know where Assumption is."

"No, you don't, but fortunately we do know where it is, and we do have someone in place there."

"Good, tell me who they are and how to get in touch with them, and I'll make all the arrangements."

"I'm afraid your services are no longer needed."

"Are you telling me I have been fired?

"Yes, that is exactly what I'm telling you. You are being terminated."

"All right, if you don't intend to use me anymore, that's fine. But don't expect a refund. I've already spent almost as much as you gave me to do the job."

"We won't be asking for anything back."

"Good, good, then I can assume that our business here is concluded."

"You may assume that."

Conroy nodded, then turned and started back up the long, dark pier. In the next instant the night was illuminated by the muzzle flash of a pistol shot, but Conroy wasn't aware of it, because he was dead before it could register in his brain.

The shooter had made arrangements to have Gillespie killed in Assumption, but if past experience meant anything, the attempt in Assumption would be as unsuccessful as all previous attempts had been. There was only one way to handle this, and that was to take personal charge. He would leave by express train tonight and would be in Chicago within three days. He hadn't wanted it to come to this, but this was a job he was going to have to handle himself.

Rockford, Illinois

Kelly began collecting the tickets as soon as the train left the station in Rockford. One of the men handed him an ace of spades along with his ticket.

"You're too late," Kelly said. "Didn't you notice that Gillespie's private car is no longer attached?"

"That's not why I'm here," the passenger said.

"Then why are you here?"

"I'm here to settle up with you and Mr. Calhoun."

"Settle up?"

"Yes. Apparently you are still owed something."

"Yes," Kelly said. He wondered if Conroy had forgotten that he had already given him the entire five hundred dollars in advance. "Yes, I'm owed five hundred dollars. And I'm sure Julius is owed some money as well."

"Is there someplace we can go to meet in private? I don't want to do business here in this car."

"Yes, we can go to the baggage car," Kelly said.

Five minutes later, Kelly and Calhoun were meeting with the passenger in the baggage car.

"I'm glad Conroy understands that it wasn't my fault that Gillespie left the train before the job could be completed," Kelly said.

"Oh, Conroy is no longer around," the passenger said.

"What do mean he is no longer around?"

"He was hired to do something, and he failed, so he was killed."

"What?"

"You two failed as well."

"Now, hold on there," Kelly said. "I didn't fail! All I was supposed to do was . . ."

The sound of two gunshots filled the baggage car. Then, with Kelly and Calhoun lying on the floor, the passenger slid open the door, and dragging the two bodies to the door, pushed both of them off the train.

After that, he returned to his seat.

Davenport, Iowa

John Gillespie's private car was backed onto a sidetrack at the Davenport depot where they had arranged to spend the night. John and Mary Beth were sleeping in their private rooms, and Matt slept in one of the comfortable chairs. He slept well enough, though he was awakened several times during the night by the arrival and departure of all the trains.

Early the next morning, a shrill whistle awakened him and he yawned and stretched, then got up and stared out into the darkness, wondering what time it was. His internal clock told him it was probably about five, but he couldn't be sure. When the door to Mary Beth's roomette opened, he looked over toward her.

"Oh, my, it's still dark outside. What time is it?"

"I think it is about five o'clock," Matt said.

"I don't believe I've ever been up this early. Or if so, I certainly don't remember it."

"This is my favorite time of day," Matt said.

Mary Beth laughed. "Yes, you strike me as someone who would be an early riser. Oh, would you like me to make a pot of coffee?"

"That would be most welcome, yes, thank you," Matt said.

Within a few minutes, the car was permeated by the rich aroma of coffee. Mary Beth poured two cups and brought one over to Matt.

"Thanks," Matt said as he accepted the cup.

Mary Beth sat on the couch with her legs folded under her, the position causing her knees to make little tents in her skirt. Lifting the cup to her lips, she smiled at Matt.

"Tell me, Matt, why is it that you have never married?"

"How do you know that I haven't?"

"Oh?" Mary Beth's eyes grew wide. "I didn't know."

Matt laughed. "I've never been married, because the life I live doesn't support being married."

"You can't support it? But I know my father has paid you very well to be our bodyguard for this trip."

"I wasn't talking about money. I mean I've never settled down in any one place. One month I'll be working as a railroad detective, the next I'll be deputy sheriff in one place, and a month later a deputy U.S. Marshal somewhere else. I'm afraid I wouldn't make a very good husband."

"Oh, I think if you found the right woman, she would be happy to take you, any way you are."

"What's all the talking out here?" John said, coming from his roomette then. "How is a man supposed to get any sleep?"

"It's just that some of us don't intend to sleep until noon," Mary Beth replied, teasing her father.

"What time is it, anyway?" John asked. He examined the watch that he had pulled from his pocket. "Good heavens, it's only five thirty. No wonder it's still dark outside."

John bent down to look through the window. "It's not only dark, it is also very foggy," he said.

"I made coffee," Mary Beth said.

"Yes, it smells good. It's too early for breakfast, but I think a cup of coffee would be very welcome."

The three talked until sunup, with Matt finding humorous ways to be self-deprecating in the stories he told.

"Papa, tell Matt how you met Mama," Mary Beth said. "I think that was so romantic."

"I saw a man berating her in Central Park, I stepped in between them, told him if he struck her, I would beat him to within an inch of his life."

"Ah . . . then you became her hero," Matt said.

"Not immediately. Turns out he was her fiancé, and for him to be berated like that in front of her was more than he could take. He broke off the engagement." John laughed. "After that, I felt that the only gentlemanly thing for me to do was to step up and propose to her."

"You mean, right there, right then?" Matt asked.

"Yes."

"And she accepted your proposal?"

"Not right away. But over the next two weeks I was persistent enough until finally she did. She was a beautiful woman, and it was a wonderful marriage."

John was quiet for a moment, and he bowed his head and pinched the bridge of his nose. "I miss her more than I can say."

"Oh, Papa, I'm so sorry I brought up a painful memory," Mary Beth said.

John looked up at his daughter with a sad smile. "Nonsense, my dear," he said. "No memory of your mother is painful."

There was a knock on the door then, and cautiously, Matt got up to answer it. It was the engineer for the leased locomotive.

"Could I speak to Mr. Gillespie?" the engineer asked.

"Yes, Mr. Sharp, what can I do for you?" John asked, stepping up to the door then.

"I just thought I should tell you that we won't be able to leave until one o'clock tomorrow afternoon. Since we aren't on the regular schedule we'll have to take our turn at getting track clearance."

"All right. Assuming we can leave by one, what time would that put us into Assumption?"

"Well, that's another problem. We're going to have to spend tomorrow night in Peoria. The way they have us scheduled now, we won't get to Assumption until seven o'clock on the eighth."

"My speech is to be given on Friday the eleventh. You have no doubt but that you will be able to get me there in time, do you?"

"No, these delays are because I didn't try and get the track scheduled far enough in advance. But I'll start getting us clearance into Chicago as soon as we get to Assumption. I don't figure we'll have any trouble with it at all."

"Good. Thank you, Mr. Sharp."

Assumption, Illinois
Muley Sullivan read the telegram that had just been delivered to him.

368

JOHN GILLESPIE AND DAUGHTER
TO ARRIVE IN ASSUMPTION ON A
PRIVATE CAR ATTACHED TO A
LEASED LOCOMOTIVE STOP
PLEASE REINSTATE PLAN AS DIS-
CUSSED WITH YOU IN A PREVI-
OUS MEETING BETWEEN US
STOP FIVE HUNDRED DOLLARS
HAS BEEN WIRED TO COVER EX-
PENSES

Muley smiled at the news. The plan mentioned in the telegram was to kill John
Gillespie and his daughter, but after the coal
miners' strike was settled, the plan was
dropped. Then, the offer had been two
hundred and fifty dollars. Now, it was five
hundred.

With the telegram tightly clutched in his
hand, Muley went to the Western Union office to see if the money had actually been
wired.

"Yes, sir, Mr. Sullivan, the money has
been transferred," the telegrapher said when
Muley inquired. "All you have to do is sign
this receipt. That's a lot of money. What do
you have to do for this, kill someone?"

The telegrapher laughed at his own joke.

"That's enough to kill for, ain't it?" Muley
replied, laughing as well.

It was dark when the train rolled into Assumption, and as had been done in Davenport, the car was backed onto a sidetrack. A few minutes later, there was a knock on the car door.

"Mr. Gillespie, it's me, Sharp, the engineer."

John opened the door. "Yes, Mr. Sharp, what can I do for you?"

"I was just wonderin' if you got 'ny idea when you'll be wantin' to leave here? Reason I ask is, I'll need to get started right away on settin' up the track schedule."

"Oh, I'd say Thursday afternoon sometime," John replied.

"Good, that gives me two days. That's plenty of time. But if you don't need me 'n Benny now, we're goin' to go over to the Track House to get us some supper and a bed for the night."

"You go right ahead. We'll see you in a couple of days."

"Yes, sir, good night, Mr. Gillespie. Good night, ma'am, and sir," Sharp said.

"Good night," the three replied.

"Papa, you've been here before," Mary Beth said after Sharp left. "Do you know any good restaurants?"

"I know a French restaurant that's pretty

370

good," John said. "Would you like to have dinner there?"

"Yes," Mary Beth said. "That is, if you don't mind, Matt. You might not like French food."

Matt laughed. "So far I haven't discovered any food that I don't like."

CHAPTER THIRTY

Ned Stone and Ruben Harrell had watched the abbreviated train arrive, a locomotive pulling a single car. Through the lighted windows they could see three people in the car, and they knew that because the car was brightly lit inside, and it was dark and foggy outside, that the people in the car would not be able to see them. And that was just the way they wanted it.

"You think that's them?" Ruben asked.

"How many trains has come in here today with there bein' just one car attached to it?" Ned replied.

"Far as I know this here 'n is the only one," Ruben said. "Onliest thang is, they's three people in that car, and we was only told about two people."

"More'n likely this here is the one, on account of we was told it would be only one car attached 'n it would be comin' in tonight. It don't make no nevermind to me

372

whether it has two people or three. We was told there'd be a man 'n a woman in it, and there's a man 'n a woman, which you can plainly see through the winder lights."

"I expect you're right."

"Who is it you reckon that wants 'em dead?" Ruben asked.

"It's Muley Sullivan that's payin' us to do the job. But I don't think he's the one what actual wants it done, I think he's just arrangin' it. Anyhow, what difference does it make? The money spends just as good no matter who it is that wants it done, don't it?" Ned said.

Ruben laughed. "Yeah, you got that right. The money spends just as good, no matter where you get it. Do you think he'll really pay us?" Ruben asked.

"Sure he will. We've done things for him before 'n he's always paid. What makes you think he won't pay this time?"

"I don't know. It's just that he ain't never offered to pay us this much before."

"He'll pay. Shh! Here they come."

"Where we goin' to do it?"

"I don't know yet. We'll follow 'em until we figure out the best place."

When Matt, John, and Mary Beth took a table in the restaurant, none of them noticed the two men who came in right behind them. Ned and Ruben sat on the opposite side of the room. They chose a table that was far enough away so as not to be noticed, but one that was positioned so as to allow them to keep an eye on their prey.

"Oh, good," Mary Beth said as she picked up the menu. "I'm going to get an opportunity to try my French."

"How is the lamb?" she asked when the waiter approached their table.

"It is quite good, madam."

"Then I think I will have *agneau aux petits pois à la crème,*" Mary Beth said.

"Excellent choice, madam," the waiter said. "The creamed peas are excellent today. And you, sir?" he asked John.

"Roti de boeuf avec pommes de terre," John said.

"You will enjoy it, sir. Our beef is superb. And you, sir?"

Matt looked at the menu and saw the words *saumon au four.* He assumed that was salmon, though he wasn't sure how it was being prepared. He knew for sure that he wasn't going to try and pronounce it.

"I'll have the salmon," he said.

"Au four?"

Matt had no idea what *au four* meant, and he looked up at the waiter.

"Baked?" the waiter asked.

"Yes."

"I would like to go see Morris tomorrow," John said as they waited for their meal. "As I knew when I spoke with Mitchell, I believe I will know when I see him, whether or not he is the one who is trying to kill me."

"If he isn't the one, who would that leave?" Matt asked.

"Well, I don't want to be tooting my own horn, but Gillespie Enterprises is one of the largest enterprises in America . . . if not in the world. I have well over one thousand employees, it could be any one of them, I suppose. And it could also be someone who isn't a part of the company at all, but feels that I might be competing unfairly with them, in some way."

"But you chose Morris, Keaton, and Mitchell as your primary suspects," Matt said.

"Yes. Well, I didn't, Drew did. But I think he was quite justified in making those choices."

The conversation grew more casual until the waiter returned, pushing a cart that held their meals, each plate under a silver dome.

Across the room from Matt and the others, Ned and Ruben were eating their own supper, all the while keeping an eye on the three they had seen leave the private car.

"They're fixin' to leave," Ruben said after a while.

"Wait until they are out of the restaurant before we get up," Ned suggested.

The darkness and the fog made it very difficult to see more than just a few feet.

"Oh, I hope we don't get lost," Mary Beth said.

"We won't get lost. This is the way we came," Matt said. "All we have to do is walk back this way, and when we get close enough to the depot, there will be enough lights to guide us the rest of the way."

"This is a very spooky night," Mary Beth said. "If I were by myself, I would be scared to death."

The words were no sooner out of her mouth before two men suddenly jumped out in front of them. Both men were holding pistols.

"Oh!" Mary Beth gasped.

"Are you planning on robbing us?" John asked. "I have to tell you, I never carry much money on my person. I think you might find robbing us could get you into more trouble than it is worth."

"Robbin' you?" one of the men said. "Well, I hadn't thought none about that.

What do you think, Ruben? Think we should rob 'em after we kill 'em?"

"Kill us?" Mary Beth asked in a frightened voice.

"Why do you want to kill us?" John asked.

"We're gettin' paid to. That's why."

"Who is payin' you? Morris?"

"No, it ain't Morris."

"Hey, Ned, it could be. You said that Muley was gettin' paid by someone else to have these folks kilt, didn't you?" Ruben asked.

"Yeah, that's right, Muley did say that," Ned replied.

He looked back toward Matt, John, and Mary Beth. "I don't know whether Morris is the one that paid Muley or not, but it sure as hell ain't goin' to make no difference to you nohow."

"Why won't it make any difference to us?" Matt asked.

"On account of 'cause you're all three goin' to be dead."

"I don't think so," Matt said.

"What do you mean, you don't think so? Are you crazy?" Ned asked. He held his gun up. "Do you see this gun?"

In a move that was so fast that it left Ned gasping in shock, Matt reached out and snatched the gun from his hand. "Do you mean do I see *this* gun?" he asked.

Cocking the pistol, he pointed it toward Ruben.

"Drop that gun," he said.

"Are you crazy, mister? Can't you see that I'm pointing this gun right at this feller?" Ruben said.

"Yes, and that's where you have made your big mistake. You see, you're pointing your gun at him, instead of me, while I'm pointing this gun right at you."

"Matt, if he kills me, I want you to kill him," John said.

"Oh, I will, you can count on that. In fact, I will kill both of them."

"I mean it. I will kill him," Ruben said.

"Oh, I'm sure you do mean it. Go ahead and do it, but just understand that if you shoot him, I'm going to kill you, and then I'm going to kill your friend here. So is it worth you dying, just to see my friend killed? You and your friend can live, or you can both die. Now, which will it be?"

Ruben held the gun for a moment longer, licking his lips nervously.

"For God's sake, Ruben, drop the damn gun!" Ned shouted.

Ruben dropped the gun, and Matt bent down to pick it up. Then he threw Ruben's gun and the gun he was holding into the storm drain. That done, he drew his own gun and pointed it at the two men.

"Now, Ned, Ruben, that's your names?"

"Yeah," Ruben said, the reply little more than a growl. "That's our names."

"Ned and Ruben, I want the two of you to take off your clothes."

"You want us to do what?" Ned asked, surprised by the demand.

"You heard me. I said take off your clothes, both of you."

"What the hell, mister? We're right in the middle of town! Don't you know that?"

"Yeah, but it is dark and foggy, so maybe nobody will see you. And if you don't have any clothes on, you aren't likely to follow us, are you?"

"I ain't takin' off my clothes," Ruben said again.

"Me neither," Ned said.

"Oh, I think you will," Matt said.

"The hell you say. There ain't nothin' you can say that's goin' to make me take off my clothes," Ruben said.

"Oh, I think I'm going to be able to talk you into it."

"Just how are you goin' to do that?"

"I'll shoot both of you, then I'll take your clothes off. On second thought, maybe I don't have to shoot both of you. Maybe I

379

only have to shoot one of you to make an example," Matt said. He pointed the gun at Ned. "I believe you are Ned, right? Ned, I hate to do it, but if I kill you, I'm pretty sure it will convince Ruben to take off his clothes."

"No! No! We're a' doin' it! Take off your clothes, Ruben! I think this fool really would shoot us!" Ned shouted as he began unbuttoning his shirt. Ruben joined him, and a moment later the two men stood before Matt, John, and Mary Beth wearing only their underwear.

"Mister, you got no call treatin' us like this," Ned said. "Makin' us strip down in front of a woman ain't proper."

"But killing us would have been proper, in your opinion?" Matt asked.

"Well yeah, I mean, we wasn't goin' to strip you down nekkid or nothin'. We was just goin' to kill you is all," Ruben said.

Matt laughed. "You know what? I think that, somehow, that might even make sense in your mind. Drop your clothes down there." Matt pointed to the same storm drain where he had thrown the two pistols.

"You're crazy if you think . . ."

A moment earlier Matt had eased the hammer down on his pistol. Now he cocked it again.

"All right, all right, we're a-doin' it!" Ned said as he and Ruben dropped their shirts and pants down the drain.

"Boots, too," Matt ordered.

Ruben started to protest, but when he saw Ned drop his boots down into the drain, he dropped his as well.

"Now, both of you go that way," Matt said, pointing in the opposite direction from the depot. "If I see you following us, I'll shoot you both dead."

Mary Beth laughed out loud as the two men, barefooted and wearing nothing but their long-handle underwear, started padding off in the opposite direction.

"Mary Beth, you can laugh about this?" John asked. "Those men would have killed us."

"I know that, Papa. But you have to admit, seeing them run off into the night, barefoot and dressed only in their underwear? That was funny."

John laughed as well. "You're right," he said. "It was funny."

"What do we do now, Ned?" Ruben asked. "We can't go runnin' around like this."

"We're goin' to get us some more clothes," Ned said.

"I ain't got no more clothes 'ceptin'

another shirt."

"We'll go to a store."

"There ain't no stores open now, 'n even if there was, we couldn't go in dressed like this. Besides which, how we goin' shoppin' when I ain't got no money to spend on clothes anyhow?"

"Ruben, think about it. For the kind of shoppin' we're goin' to do, we don't want the store to be open, 'n we won't need no money."

"Oh," Ruben said. "Yeah, I hadn't thought about that. Oh, 'n after we get some clothes, do you think maybe we could break into Sikes' Hardware Store 'n get us another gun 'n maybe some bullets?"

"I would say we are going to have to, wouldn't you?" Ned replied.

"Yeah. And that way, we can go back to the boardin' house without lookin' like such a couple of damn fools," Ruben said.

"We ain't goin' back to the boardin' house. We're goin' to finish the job we started out to do," Ned said.

"You seen how that fella was. You want to go up ag'in him again?" Ruben asked.

"Yeah, well, he caught us by surprise 'cause there wasn't neither one of us expectin' him to do nothin' like that. But he won't surprise us a second time," Ned said. "Fact is, we'll more'n likely be surprisin' him, 'cause you know damn well he won't be expectin' to see us again. Leastwise, not tonight. But if you don't want to come with me, you don't have to. I'll kill all three of 'em myself and keep all the money."

"No," Ruben said. "There ain't no need in you a-thinkin' nothin' like that, 'cause I'll be comin' with you."

"Here's Blum's Mercantile," Ned said.

Forty-five minutes later the two men, now wearing new clothes, new boots, and because they had also visited Sikes' Hardware, new pistol and holster sets, moved through the night fog toward the private railroad car that was parked on a sidetrack at the depot.

CHAPTER THIRTY-ONE

It wasn't totally dark now, because the fog had rolled away and the moon was full and bright. As a result, the depot, the tracks, and the railroad cars were all gleaming in a soft, silver light.

The night was alive with the long, high-pitched trills and low viola-like thrums of the frogs. For countermelodies there were crickets, the mournful sound of a hooting owl, and from the nearby stable, a mule braying and a horse whickering.

With guns in hand, and staying in the shadows of a string of empty freight cars, the two men moved toward John Gillespie's private car.

Inside the private car, Matt was sleeping in one of the chairs, the back of it tipped to a comfortable angle. He woke from a sound sleep, though he wasn't sure what had awakened him. He knew it wasn't some sound that had intruded into his slumber.

But something had awakened him.

He listened carefully for any sound that was anomalous to the night, but he heard nothing.

Matt had survived for as long as he had despite being so often a target, because he was able to depend upon a sensory perception that went beyond sight, sound, touch, smell, or taste.

"Matt, people who live their lives the way we do learn to depend on this feeling, and if you ever get it, pay attention to it," his mentor, Smoke Jensen, had told him. "It could save your life."

Smoke was right. That feeling had saved Matt's life more than once. And because he was experiencing that sensation now, there was no way he was going to ignore it.

Slipping on his boots, Matt took his pistol in hand, then eased out the door of the car. He climbed on top of the tender so he would be able to see in all directions. He chose the tender, rather than the car, because if there was anyone out there, he intended to challenge him, and if shooting started, he would rather them direct their bullets toward the coal tender than the car.

That way there would be less chance of either John or Mary Beth being hit by a stray bullet.

That was when he saw them . . . two men coming through the dark, passing for only a brief moment through the greenish glow of light cast by a gas lamp. It was obvious that they were walking toward the car. He didn't know for sure, because he couldn't make out their faces in the dark, but he suspected it might be the same two men he, John, and Mary Beth had encountered earlier in the night.

He could see a sliver of silver flashing dimly from the moon's reflection on the guns they were carrying. If these were the same two men, somehow they had managed to clothe themselves and acquire new guns.

"I see you men managed to find clothes and another gun somewhere," Matt shouted from the top of the car.

"What the hell? Where did that come from?" one of the men called. Matt recognized Ruben's voice, which told him for a fact that the two men approaching were Ned and Ruben.

"I'm up here, Ruben," Matt called. "I'm really disappointed in you two. I thought I told you and Ned not to come around again."

"Shoot him! Shoot the son of a bitch!" This was Ned.

The two men shot at Matt, and they came dangerously close. He returned fire and hearing the sound of two men falling, jumped down quickly from the tender. Then with his gun held at the ready, he walked toward the two still forms, his feet making crunching sounds on the cinders that were strewn between the tracks.

He knelt beside the two men and held his fingers to the neck of first one, then the other. They were both dead.

"Matt?"

The call came from John Gillespie, who had stepped out into the rear vestibule of his private car.

"Get back inside, John, please," Matt called back to him. "I'll be right there."

Matt picked up the two pistols, then walked back to the car. By the time he stepped inside, John had lit a lantern, and both he and Mary Beth were standing there in the soft light. There was an expression of concern and curiosity on both their faces.

Mary Beth was wearing a nightgown, which was unbuttoned low enough that Matt could see the gleam of the rise of the bare tops of her breast. It was a most agreeable sight, and Matt had a sudden memory of having seen much more of her when he had walked in on her in the bath.

Mary Beth had caught the glance, and realizing that she was showing a bit more of herself than she had intended, she slid two of the buttons through the holes, somewhat restricting the view. Matt couldn't help but notice a small smile playing across her lips as she did so and realized that she must be sharing the same memory.

"Were they the same two men who accosted us earlier tonight?" John asked. His question brought Matt's attention back to him.

"Yes."

"I thought it might be them. Are they dead?"

"Yes," Matt said. "I had no choice."

"I'm sure you didn't, and please believe me, my question wasn't a challenge. What do you think we should do now?"

"Now? I think we should all go back to sleep. In the morning we can go to the sheriff and tell him what happened and where he can find the bodies."

"Yes," John said. "I think we should do that." John pinched the bridge of his nose. "The number of men killed just keeps piling up, thanks to me."

"What do you mean, thanks to you, Papa?

388

I'm the one who has actually killed someone."

John put his arms around Mary Beth and pulled her to him. "And that's my fault," he said.

"You can't be blamed for any of this," Matt said. "All you are doing is going to Chicago. All these men have brought about their own deaths."

"I know, and when I'm thinking reasonably, I realize that. But sometimes my thoughts go beyond reason." John sighed. "Please, Matt, do not construe my . . . self-recriminations as any kind of disapproval of you. I know well that if you weren't traveling with us that Mary Beth and I would have been killed a long time ago."

"John, if you didn't have doubts about all this, you wouldn't be human," Matt said. "You would be like me. Long ago I learned to put such feelings aside, and now I live in a dark place that I wouldn't recommend for anyone. We'll go see the sheriff tomorrow morning."

"I know the sheriff in this town, and he knows me. When we go to see him, I'll explain everything. And I'll tell him why I am here in Assumption."

"No, I don't think you should do that," Matt said.

"No?"

"Oh, you can tell him you are here to see Mr. Morris. After all, you own the mine and he works for you, so that would be expected. But I don't think you should tell him that you suspect Morris. And I don't think you should even tell Morris the real reason for your visit."

"Why not? If you think I shouldn't tell Morris, or anyone else, I won't of course. But why do you think I shouldn't?"

"If Morris is behind this, he'll give himself away as soon as he sees you. You said yourself, you would be able to tell whether or not he is the guilty party, didn't you?"

"Yes, I did say that."

"And if he is behind it, who is to say that the sheriff isn't in on it as well? We should tell the sheriff as little as possible, make him think that we believed the two men had come to rob us."

"Yes," John said, nodding his head in agreement. "Yes, I think you are right, that is a good idea. I shouldn't tell the sheriff any more than I have to, and I won't let Morris know that I suspect him."

When they stepped into the sheriff's office the next morning, they saw him sitting on a stool near the only occupied cell of the three that made up the jail. The sheriff and the prisoner who was the occupant of the cell were both drinking coffee. In addition, they were playing a game of checkers through the bars.

"Now, damn it, Stu, you touched that man, and that means you have to move it," the sheriff said.

"No, I didn't touch it, Henry," Stu said. "All I done was put my finger real close to it, but I didn't touch it."

"You know, I can keep you in jail for lyin' just as easy as I can for being drunk in public," the sheriff replied.

"I wasn't drunk in public. I was drunk in the saloon. I was sleeping in public."

"You were passed out drunk. Now move that man, or I'll add three more days to your sentence."

"Go ahead. I eat better in jail than I do anywhere else."

"Yeah, but you don't get any whiskey here."

"That's true," Stu said, reaching down to move the man being questioned.

"Sheriff Goodbody?" John said.

The sheriff looked around and, for a moment, showed some curiosity as to who had addressed him. Then, he recognized John, and a broad smile spread across his face.

"Well, I'll be, if it isn't the man who saved our town," he said, standing and approaching Gillespie with his hand extended. "Hello, Mr. Gillespie, what brings you to Assumption?"

"Oh, I'm on my way to Chicago, and I thought I would just drop in and pay a visit to Ray Morris."

"Well, sir, I'm sure Mr. Morris will appreciate it," Sheriff Goodbody said. The sheriff looked, curiously, at Mary Beth and Matt.

"Oh, where are my manners? Sheriff, this is my daughter, Mary Beth, and my friend, Matt Jensen."

"Mrs. Jensen?" the sheriff asked.

Mary Beth laughed, the laughter a pleasant sound. "No," she said. "I'm not married."

"Oh, Miss Gillespie, please forgive me."

"Don't be silly, there is nothing to forgive."

"Mr. Jensen," the sheriff said, extending his hand.

"Sheriff," Matt replied, taking the proffered hand.

"Henry," John continued, clearing his throat. "I have another reason for coming to see you."

"Oh?"

"My private car is parked on a sidetrack down at the depot. During the night two armed men came around, apparently to rob me. Mr. Jensen engaged them in a gunfight."

"I see. And you want me to find out who did it and put them in jail?"

"That won't be necessary," John said.

"What do you mean, it won't be necessary?"

"I know who they are. At least, I know their first names. Ned and Ruben."

"Ah, yes, that would be Ned Stone and Ruben Harrell. And you are right, they most likely were coming to rob you. They aren't either one of them worth the cost of a rope it would take to hang them. I'll see if I can find them for you."

"They will be easy enough for you to find," Matt said. "They are both lying down at the rail yard, about a hundred feet or so from Mr. Gillespie's private car."

"Lying there? You mean they are dead?"

"Yes," Matt said. "I killed them both."

"I assure you, Henry, Mr. Jensen fired in self-defense. Ned and Ruben shot first."

"All right, I'll get Mr. Dumey down there to pick them up. If you'll both sign a statement as to what happened, I'm sure it will go no further than that. Like I said, they were a couple of ne'er-do-wells."

"What about a man named Muley?" Matt asked. "Do you know anything about him?"

"Muley? Why are you asking about him?" the sheriff asked.

"The two men I shot, Ned and Rubin, mentioned him. Do you know Muley?"

"Yes, I know Muley. His real name is Martin Sullivan."

"Sullivan?" John asked. "Look here, Henry, are you talking about the union boss?"

"Yes, that's right, you *do* know him, don't you? He's the one that near 'bout broke the town with his infernal strikes. That is till you come along 'n bought the mine."

"There's no union trouble now, is there?" John asked. "I mean, if there is, Ray hasn't mentioned it."

"Oh, there's no real trouble, but that doesn't mean that Muley Sullivan don't keep the miners stirred up all the time. He's always tryin' to make trouble, but the miners is all mostly satisfied with the pay 'n the workin' conditions now, so they don't always listen to him. Sometimes Sullivan gets a little rough with them, and when he does, he'll often use Stone and Harrell to enforce his policies. Well, I suppose I should say he used them, since they're dead now."

"Where would we find Sullivan?" Matt asked.

"What do you want him for?"

"I just want to ask him a few questions."

"Look, Muley Sullivan is not a very friendly man, and some of the shenanigans he's pulled with the miners have come very close to breaking the law. But so far he's managed to stay on the right side of the line. Barely, I admit, but he hasn't done anything I could get him for. And just because Stone and Harrell may have mentioned him, doesn't really mean anything."

"I suppose you're right," Matt said.

"You said something about us signing a statement?" John asked.

"Yes, let me get a paper and the two of you can say what happened. You don't have to be too specific, just enough so the judge is convinced that the killing was justified."

Sheriff Goodbody sat at his desk taking down the statement that John dictated. When he was finished, he stood and picked up the paper.

"We'll take this over to the bank. Mr. Montgomery is a notary public, and you can sign it in front of him."

"All right," John said.

The sheriff took some keys from the middle drawer of his desk and tossed them over to his prisoner.

"Let yourself out, Stu, then leave the keys layin' on my desk."

"Sheriff, can I wait until Maggie brings over the lunch? Kirby is havin' fried chicken for lunch today, and I wouldn't want to miss it," the prisoner replied.

"Yeah, go ahead."

As the four walked from the jailhouse to the bank, the sheriff pointed out some new buildings.

"Ever'one of these here businesses was built since you bought out the mine," he said. "Yes, sir, you buyin' that mine is the best thing that ever happened to Assumption."

"What does Ray think about it?" John asked.

"Are you kiddin'? Why, ever'body is treatin' him like he's a hero, 'n him runnin' the mine so well now, I reckon he is."

Matt, John, and Mary Beth signed the statement in front of the banker, Bob Montgomery, who then notarized it for them. He was as profuse in his appreciation of John buying the mine and his praise of Ray Morris as had been the sheriff.

"Papa, the way everyone is talking about all the good the mine is doing and how happy all the miners are, do you think this man, Sullivan, might be the one who has been trying to kill us?" Mary Beth asked. "I mean if he's the union leader, and the miners don't really need him, maybe he's blaming you."

"I don't know," John replied. "I do know that after I bought the mine and broke the strike, he was quite upset with me."

"How did you break the strike?" Matt asked. "Did you bring in new workers?"

"No, I didn't have to do that to keep the mine working. I paid Morris and the supervisors their salaries and informed Sullivan that I was ready to negotiate, but if we couldn't come to a mutually agreed-upon contract, I was prepared to wait it out indefinitely.

"It was the miners themselves who finally put enough pressure on Sullivan to force him into a settlement. I suppose it could be him."

"But do you think a union boss for a coal mine here in Assumption would have enough reach to be behind all the previous attacks?" Matt asked.

John shook his head. "No, I don't think he would. And now that you mention it, those two did say that they thought someone else was paying Sullivan. That shifts the suspicion back to Raymond Morris, doesn't it?"

CHAPTER THIRTY-TWO

The Assumption Coal Mining Company

The mine was a busy place. Small cars pulled by mules were rolling back and forth across the network of rails that crisscrossed the area. Some of the cars filled with coal were heading for the huge piles of coal; others were empty, returning to the mine. Smoke spewed from the towering stacks over the steam-operated crushing mill, and men, their faces so blackened with coal dust that their eyes stood out, hustled busily about.

John Gillespie, along with his daughter and Matt, stepped into the coal office unannounced.

"That's him," John said quietly, pointing to a man who was standing at a drafting table talking to the man who was standing alongside. "That's Raymond Morris."

"The new shaft looks like it's going to be

pretty productive," Morris was saying to the man.

"That'll mean hiring more miners," the man replied.

"Do it, the increase in production will more than pay for it."

"Yes, sir, Mr. Morris. What with the good wages that you're payin', that's goin' to make a lot of folks pretty happy."

"But before we start pulling coal out of there and putting pressure on the seam, I want you to make another check of all the shoring. I want this shaft to be strong and well-constructed."

"Good for you, Ray," John said. "Safety first, that's always been my motto."

Startled, Morris looked around. For just a moment there was a look of total surprise on his face, but the surprise was quickly replaced by a smile.

"Mr. Gillespie!" he said, coming toward him, with his hand extended. "What a surprise! It's a pleasant surprise, but it is a surprise! What are you doing here?"

"I have to go to Chicago, so I figured why not come down here for a visit."

"Well, I'm very glad you did. Come, let me show you around the place. As you can see, business is booming, and we've opened up a new shaft. Well, it's open, but we aren't

400

mining it yet. I plan to start tomorrow." He paused for a second. "That is, if it is all right with you. Before I actually started anything, I was going to send you a telegram telling you about it and getting your permission."

"Of course it's all right with me," John said. "I told you when I bought the mine and left you in charge that you would have a free hand to make any decision you thought might be necessary."

"I know you did, but still, I like to keep you informed on what's going on." Morris glanced toward Mary Beth and Matt.

"Oh, this is my daughter, Mary Beth, and a friend who is going to Chicago with me, Matt Jensen."

"I'm very pleased to meet you," Morris said, extending his hand to each of them.

"Mr. Morris," Matt replied.

"How long are you going to be here?" Morris asked.

"We'll be here until sometime tomorrow," John said.

"Good, good! I was going down into the shaft tomorrow morning for one final inspection before we started mining. Why don't you come with me? It's a beaut!"

"I'd be glad to," John said.

They ate at the same French restaurant where Gillespie, Mary Beth, and Matt had

401

eaten the night before, but that was not a surprise, John said, since the only reason he knew about it, was this was where he and Morris had eaten the first time John was in Assumption.

"I've been wanting to write to you, anyway," Morris said over their meal.

"Oh? Why? Is something wrong?"

"Wrong? No, nothing is wrong," Morris replied. "Everything is right. Why with the money you've invested, we are now operating the biggest coal mine in Illinois and one of the biggest mines in the entire country.

"Our workers are all satisfied, and the mine is making so much money that the entire town is benefiting from it. Why, did you know I've been asked to run for mayor?" Morris added with a proud smile.

"No, I didn't know. I hope you turned them down, but I have to admit, that's selfish of me. I want you to turn them down, because I don't want to lose you as manager of the mine," John said.

"Don't worry, I'm not going to run. Besides, as I pointed out to the people who asked, I'm able to do a lot more for this town where I am right now as manager of the Assumption Mining Company than I could as mayor. It was an honor to be asked, but I'm making too much money where I

402

am. And I'll stay right here in this position for as long as you are willing to keep me on. That's what I was going to say to you in the letter."

John smiled, then stuck his hand across the table. "And I'll keep you on for as long as you are willing to stay," he said. John laughed. "That reminds me of a contract between Harry and Clem Studebacker. Harry said, *'I will build as many wagons as you can sell,'* and Clem said, *'I will sell as many wagons as you can build.'* It was a good contract, since you see Studebaker wagons all over the country."

They continued with their conversation until Matt brought up the subject of Martin Sullivan.

"Mr. Morris, what can you tell me about Martin Sullivan?"

"Mulcy Sullivan," Morris said, twisting his mouth into a sneer. "He is one of the dregs of the earth. Why did you ask about him? Have you had trouble with him?"

"You might say that," Matt replied. "We were accosted by two men named Ned Stone and Rubin Harrell. They said they were sent by Sullivan."

"I wouldn't doubt it. Stone and Harrell used to work in the mine, but I fired them. Sullivan tried to organize the rest of the miners to strike to save Stone and Harrell's jobs, but it didn't work. Now they do Sullivan's dirty work for him. What did they want?"

"They wanted to kill us," Matt said.

"What?"

"More specifically, they wanted to kill me," John said.

"Why on earth would they want to kill you?"

"Apparently, Sullivan was paying them. I was hoping you might be able to tell us why," Matt said.

Morris shook his head. "I have no idea why he would want such a thing. What did Stone and Harrell say? Where are they now? Are they in jail?"

"They are in the morgue," Matt said.

"The morgue?"

"Yes."

"Well, I can't say that I'm sorry. I suppose, if I had to guess, it would be that Sullivan blames you for his loss of power. Before you bought the mine, the union was strong, and because Sullivan is the head of it, he wielded a lot of power. But now that things are going well, all of the miners are satisfied, and the union has practically no power at all."

"Yes, I suppose that could be the reason,"

John said.

They didn't take a hotel room, but spent the night in the private car.

"I'm absolutely convinced that Morris isn't the one who has been trying to kill me," John said that evening. "And I am equally sure that it isn't Keaton or Mitchell either. We're going to have to start all over."

"There's not another name you can come up with?" Matt asked.

John shook his head. "I don't have another name, but maybe Drew does. I'll ask. He probably needs to know that I've altered my travel plans anyway. If he contacts the hotel in Chicago and learns that I'm not there, he's likely to get worried." John chuckled. "I swear, he looks over me like an old mother hen."

"Well, can you blame him, Papa? He works for you," Mary Beth said. "You might say that gives him a very good reason for keeping you alive."

"I suppose so, but nobody has a stronger incentive in keeping you alive than I do," Matt said. "After all, you're paying me five thousand dollars. That's more money for this trip than the average cowboy would make in five years."

"Matt, are you telling us that you have

actually been a cowboy?" Mary Beth asked with a little laugh.

"What's the matter? You don't think I could be a cowboy?"

"Yes, I think you could be a cowboy, if you wanted to be. I've never known anyone quite like you. I think you could be anything you chose to be," Mary Beth replied.

"Well, being a cowboy is not my normal occupation, I admit, but I have punched cattle from time to time. And I once helped drive a herd of Black Angus from Wyoming to Texas."

"You took cows from Wyoming to Texas? That's backward, isn't it? I thought Texas shipped cattle out; I didn't know they brought cattle in."

"It was someone starting a new herd with a new breed," Matt explained.

"I think I'll send Drew a message while I still have the teleprinter connected," John said.

All the time they had been talking, reports had been coming in straight from the stock market in New York and the commodities market in Chicago. John cut off the long narrow strip of paper that was now lying in a pile on the floor in front of the bell jar, then he began tapping in the message to Drew Jessup.

NOW IN ASSUMPTION ILLINOIS. ANOTHER TRY ON MY LIFE LAST NIGHT BUT JENSEN HANDLED IT WELL. I VISITED WITH MORRIS. AM CONVINCED THAT HE IS NOT BEHIND THIS. NEITHER IS KEATON NOR MITCHELL. LEAVING FOR CHICAGO TOMORROW. WILL ARRIVE LATE TOMORROW NIGHT. IF NOT KEATON MITCHELL OR MORRIS WHO?

A response was received quickly.

JESSUP UNAVAILBLE NOW STOP HE ASKED ME TO RESPOND TO ANY FUTURE MESSAGES YOU MAY SEND STOP HE WILL BE IN TOUCH SOON

JAKE FOWLER

"Hmm, that's odd," John said.

"Maybe he had to go shopping for something," Mary Beth said.

"It isn't just that he isn't there, it's the wording of Jake's telegram. He says he is to respond to any future messages, as if Drew's absence isn't just temporary. I hope everything is all right."

407

CHAPTER THIRTY-THREE

The next morning Matt accompanied John and Mary Beth to the Assumption mine. Around the mine shaft, which was sunk into the ground to a depth of several hundred feet, were clustered the mine buildings: the mine office, the engine house, the machine and repair shops, and the sheds and other out-buildings. Towering above all these buildings was the tipple tower, a tall skeleton of structural ironwork that covered the mouth of the main mine shaft, which lowered cages down into the mine as well as bringing them back up.

They were met as soon as they arrived by a smiling Ray Morris.

"Come on," he said, heading toward the mouth of the mine. He handed each of them a cap, to which an oil wick lantern had been attached.

"There are also lanterns down in the mine, but this will give you light wherever you might need it," Morris explained.

After going down in the elevator, they reached the bottom of the main shaft. Here there was a network of tunnels. The tunnels led to the rooms at the end of which were the headings and the blank, black face of the coal seam where the actual mining was done.

"This is our new shaft," Morris said, pointing to one of them. "Come on down, and I'll show you what a rich seam we've hit onto."

The tunnel was a little less than six feet high, and though the other three had no problem walking in it, Matt had to stoop over slightly.

"What's that cracking sound?" Mary Beth asked.

"That's the coal talking to you," Morris replied with a little smile.

"What?"

"There is tremendous amount of pressure put on these seams, so the coal snaps, pops, and creaks all the time. The miners get used to it."

"I see you've got new shoring up," John said.

"Yes, sir, I intend to keep my miners as safe as I can. Why, this shoring . . ."

Morris was interrupted in midsentence by

the sound of a blast. A cloud of coal dust came whipping through the tunnel.

"What was that?" Mary Beth asked, coughing and waving her hands in front of her face.

"It was a dynamite blast," Morris replied. He, like Mary Beth and the others, had to cough a couple of times as the billowing cloud settled to the floor. "But I don't understand. We aren't doing any blasting today."

The four of them hurried back to the opening of this shaft where they saw that part of the wall had collapsed. The shoring, however, held enough of the shaft up that they were able to get through. That's when they saw a man, lying on his back, with a large part of the wall on him. His eyes were open and bulging, and blood had come from his mouth.

"Oh!" Mary Beth said, turning away from him. "That poor man!"

"That's Martin Sullivan, isn't it?" John asked.

"Yes. But what is he doing here?" Morris asked. Morris looked at part of the wall. "Look, here is a borehole." He stuck his finger in it, then pulled his finger back and smelled it.

"I'll be damned! Sullivan set off that blast!

But why?"

"It's fairly obvious, isn't it?" Matt asked. "He wanted to kill us."

Morris shook his head. "I know we've had trouble with him. But I never expected him to take it this far!"

Later that same day, cleaned up from all the coal dust, Matt, John, and Mary Beth waited in the car for track clearance so their trip could resume.

"I'm wondering now if it might not have been Sullivan all along," John said. "And now that he's dead, maybe, at last, Mary Beth and I really are out of danger."

"Morris might have been right in suggesting why Sullivan wanted you dead, here, but I doubt seriously that he had a long enough reach to have been behind your coach accident or any of the incidents on the train," Matt said.

"Yes, I guess you're right. But I have no idea where to go now."

"How about Chicago?" Mary Beth suggested.

John laughed. "Yeah, how about Chicago?"

A few moments later they heard the engine whistle, then they began moving.

"It must look strange to people to see a

one-car train," John said, as they were looking through the windows and saw the curious expressions on the faces of the people who were watching them pass by.

"Yes, but seeing as we are the only ones on the train, at least we know there isn't anyone on board now who is trying to kill us," Mary Beth said.

Paxton, Illinois

Two men, Hank Pearson and Mo Carson, were waiting by the Illinois Central tracks, just south of Paxton. There was a railroad switch here for the purpose of being able to shuffle a freight train off to a sidetrack so that a fast-moving passenger train, called "varnish" by railroad people, could pass on by.

Mo had climbed a nearby tree and was looking south along the tracks.

"I see somethin' comin'!" Mo shouted down.

"What is it?"

"It's a locomotive 'n two . . . no, there's only one. A locomotive 'n one car."

"That's got to be it," Hank said. "We was told there would only be one car. Come on down. I'll throw the switch, then we'll ride up to the next switch."

"You think he'll be able to stop?" Mo

412

asked, as he scrambled back down the tree.

"No, he'll be goin' too fast when he hits the first switch, ain't no way in hell he'll get stopped afore he hits the next 'un," Hank replied. "And since that switch won't be throwed, it'll wreck the train."

"Damn, now ain't that goin' to be a fun thing to see?"

"Yeah, it'll be somethin' all right. Most likely it'll kill 'em all, but we'll hang around till afterward, just to make sure they're dead."

"All of 'em? Or just Gillespie 'n his daughter?" Mo asked.

"I expect all of 'em will be kilt. But the only ones we'll worry about is the Gillespies," Hank said. He pulled the lever to move the tracks.

"Hey," Mo said. "When you moved them tracks that sign moved too. You think that means anything?"

"Yeah, it'll tell him that the track has been switched."

"That ain't good, is it?"

"No, but I can take care of that."

It took a little doing, but Hank managed to move the little circle sign back to indicate that the track was clear ahead.

Dooley had the steam pressure at the maxi-

413

mum, and Sharp had the throttle to the full-open position. The engine, pulling only one car, was going so fast that when Sharp looked down, he couldn't make out individual cross ties, and all he could see was a blur.

"Look at this, Dooley," Sharp said, tapping his finger on the speedometer. The needle was quivering near sixty miles per hour. "Whoowee, in all my days of railroadin', I ain't never gone this fast before."

"Lord, if there was wings on this thing, we'd near take off 'n fly," Dooley said.

Sharp was leaning out the window, staring at the long straight track in front of him when, all of a sudden, the engine lurched hard to the left, doing it so unexpectedly that Dooley, who had just picked up another shovel full of coal, was thrown down. He started sliding across the engine deck and might have gone all the way out if Sharp hadn't seen what was happening and grabbed him by the leg at the last minute.

In the private car Matt was immediately aware of the drastic change of direction, because centrifugal force pressed him back against the chair in which he was sitting.

Mary Beth had been reading on the side of the car opposite Matt, which was also

414

opposite the curve. As a result of that, the same force that had pressed Matt back into his chair threw Mary Beth from her seat, all the way across the car, and she wound up in Matt's lap.

"Oh!" she said. "I'm sorry!"

"Don't be, I'm just glad I was here for you," Matt replied.

John had been in his bedroom, and because he was lying on the bed, he was tossed somewhat but was uninjured.

"What in the world is wrong with that engineer?" John asked, angrily.

Almost immediately they were aware of a severe braking action by the train.

"Better grab something and hold on," Matt said. "I don't know if we're going to get stopped in time or not."

"In time for what?" Mary Beth asked.

"In time to keep from hitting whatever it is that Mr. Sharp is trying to stop for."

Even as the train was skidding along the track, Matt went out the front door and climbed over the tender. Gleaming gold sparks spewed up from the sliding wheels, steel on steel as the train dissipated its high speed, and finally ground to a stop. Matt had just dropped down onto the deck of the locomotive when, with a final bump, the train came to a complete halt.

"What happened?" Matt asked. "Why the sudden stop?"

Sharp pointed to the right through the window of the cabin. "You see that track?" he asked.

"Yes. What about it?"

"That's high iron. That's the track we're supposed to be on. Someone left the switch track throwed, 'n here we are. If I hadn't got us stopped in time, we woulda hit the closed switch, 'n gone off the track. Anyone hurt back there?"

"No, thrown around a bit, but nobody was hurt."

"Here's the thing," Sharp said. "If the switch was throwed, the warning sign shoulda told us. Only the sign was turned like as if the track was clear."

"Then that means it was deliberate," Matt said.

"Yeah," Sharp replied. "Yeah, I hadn't thought about that, but you're right. Someone throwed that switch, then turned the sign so as to make it look like nothin' had happened."

"Harry," the fireman said. "We better back up. The engine is sittin' over the switch 'n I can't throw it with the engine sittin' here."

"All right," Sharp replied. "I'll back us up, then you jump down and throw the

416

switch for us."

Sharp put the engine in reverse, and they backed away from the point where the two tracks joined.

"Sumbitch! How the hell did he get that thing stopped in time?" Mo asked.

"We forgot to figure that it wasn't a whole train, it was just one car," Hank replied. "If it had been a whole train, it woulda never got stopped in time, and it woulda gone off the track for sure 'n certain."

The two men were lying down in a dry ditch, about fifty yards from the track.

"What do we do now?"

"They're goin' to have to throw that switch to get back out onto the main track," Hank said. "When they do, we'll shoot 'em."

"What good will that do?" Mo asked. "Hell, you know it ain't goin' to be Gillespie hisself that's goin' to change the switch. It'll more 'n likely be the engineer or the fireman."

"We'll kill whoever comes out," Hank said. "If the engineer or the fireman gets kilt, then we know for damn sure, the train won't be goin' nowhere. And with they train stopped, why there won't be nothin' to keep us from a-goin' aboard the car 'n shootin' the passengers."

"Yeah," Mo said. He giggled. "Yeah, that'll be the way to do it."

"Shh! There comes one of 'em."

Dooley climbed down from the engine and went forward to the switch. He was just about to move it when gunfire rang out, and he went down.

"Dooley!" Sharp's calling of his fireman's name was more of an anguished cry than it was a shout.

Sharp started to climb down from the engine.

"Sharp, no!" Matt shouted, but his warning was too late. Again shots rang out, and Sharp fell from the train and rolled down the ballast-strewn berm.

This time Matt had seen where the shots came from, and he saw two men lying in the ditch. They may have thought that their position afforded them some cover, and it would have had Matt been on the same level as they. But Matt was in the cabin of the engine and thus elevated. He could see both of them from his position.

"You men come out of there with your hands up!" he shouted.

"The hell we will!" one of the two men called back. Their response was augmented by more gunfire as the two, realizing now that there was a third man in the engine, began shooting.

Although the two men in the ditch fired many times, Matt fired only twice.

That was all it took, and the men, both with head wounds, were lying dead in the same ditch from which they had conducted their ambush.

Matt jumped down quickly and saw the engineer grimacing in pain.

"Where are you hit?' Matt asked.

"In my hip," Sharp replied. "I don't think none of my vitals was hit. Check on my fireman, would you? How bad hurt is Dooley?"

Matt hurried over to the switch to check on the fireman. It didn't require much of a check to see that he was dead. He walked back toward Sharp, who was now sitting up, holding his hand over his wound.

"Dooley?"

"I'm sorry, Mr. Sharp. Dooley is dead."

"Did you say Mr. Dooley is dead?" The question came from Mary Beth who had climbed down from the car.

"I'm afraid so," Matt said.

"That means I'll have to stoke the boiler myself," Sharp said, and he tried to stand but fell right back down with a groan of pain.

"You won't stoke and you won't drive,"

Matt said.

"Who will?"

"I will," Matt said.

"Have you ever stoked or driven a locomotive?" Sharp asked.

"No."

"Well, I'll tell you right up front, you won't be able to do both. You might be able to stoke it, but I'm going to have to drive." Again Sharp tried to stand up, and again he fell back in pain.

"How are you going to drive the engine when you can't even stand?"

"Well, someone has got to drive it, and like I said, you can't stoke and drive it, too."

"I'll drive," Mary Beth said.

CHAPTER THIRTY-FOUR

"That's impossible. A woman can't drive a locomotive," Sharp said, in response to Mary Beth's offer to act as the engineer.

"Why not?"

"Because it just ain't done. It wouldn't be fittin'. It wouldn't be fittin' at all. And besides, you wouldn't even know what to do."

"That's no problem. I'll have a real good teacher."

"Who?"

Mary Beth smiled coquettishly at Sharp. "Who do you think?"

"You're talkin' about me, ain't you?"

"I don't know who else I can get to teach me."

"All right," Sharp said. "When you think about it, I reckon that's about the only way we're goin' to be able to get out of here."

John stepped out of the car then and glanced over toward the ditch where the two shooters had been.

"Dead?" he asked.

"Yes," Matt answered.

"Good."

"Papa, Mr. Dooley is dead, and Mr. Sharp is hurt."

"Dooley is dead?" John asked.

"I'm afraid so," Matt replied.

John looked at Sharp. "I'm very sorry about your friend," he said. "How are you doing?"

"Didn't hit no vitals, so I reckon I'll be all right," Sharp replied.

Matt helped Sharp to his feet, made a preliminary assessment of his wound, then helped the engineer into the cabin. After that, he hoisted Mary Beth up to the mounting step.

"Mary Beth, what are you doing climbing up there?" John called up to her. "This is no time to get in the way."

"I'm not getting in the way, I'm going to be driving this thing."

"Don't be ridiculous," John said.

"She's not being ridiculous, John," Matt said. "We need to get this train out of here now."

"It will be all right, Papa. Mr. Sharp is going to tell me what to do."

John shook his head and shrugged his

shoulders. "Do it if you must. I'm just glad your mother isn't here to see such a thing. I would hear no end of it." John turned and climbed back into the private car.

"All right, what's the first thing we do?" Matt asked after he, Mary Beth, and the engineer were all in the engine cab.

"First, we have to open the switch to let us back on the main track. Check the gauge; what's the steam pressure?"

"The needle is on one seventy," Matt answered.

"It needs to be a little higher. It needs to be at least one ninety. Throw a few more shovels of coal. It'll come back up."

"Oh, wait!" Matt said. "I expect we had better get that other switch put back, too, hadn't we?"

Sharp smiled through his pain. "Good memory," he said.

While waiting for the steam pressure to recover, Matt walked out to look down at Dooley, then he picked him up, draped him over his shoulder, and carried him back. He laid him out in the front vestibule of the private car, then he opened the door.

"John, I have Dooley's body. I don't want to just leave it out here for the wolves and the buzzards, do you mind if I bring him in here?"

"No," John said. "I don't mind at all. What about the men who shot him?"

"Well, the wolves and the buzzards have to have something to eat, don't they?"

"We've got enough pressure," Sharp said when Matt returned to the engine cab. "I think Miss Gillespie is about ready to give it a try."

"What do I do first?" Mary Beth asked.

"Turn this shuttlecock to direct the steam in such a way as to make us back up," Sharp directed. "Now, reach up there and grab that Johnson bar. That's your throttle. Squeeze the release handle and shove it forward."

"Oh, we are moving!" Mary Beth said excitedly. "We are moving, and I'm the one making it happen!"

Once they were back on the main track, Sharp showed her how to change the shuttlecock so that they could move forward. "Better keep it at about twenty miles per hour," he suggested.

Mary Beth adjusted the shuttlecock, then moved the Johnson bar into position. As the train started forward, she stuck her head through the cab window and let the wind blow through her hair.

"This is fun!" she said. "I could take us all the way to Chicago!"

"I think we need to get Mr. Sharp to a hospital first, don't you?" Matt asked.

"Oh, yes, of course. Mr. Sharp, I'm sorry."

"No need to apologize, Miss Gillespie," Sharp said. "I agree with you, it is fun. That's why I do this for a living."

"Anyway," Matt said, as he threw another shovel of coal into the fire. "I don't think I want to do this all the way to Chicago. What is the next town we come to, Mr. Sharp?"

"Decatur," Sharp replied.

When they pulled into Decatur less than an hour later, they attracted some attention, because the engine was pulling only one car, and it was a highly varnished private car.

"I'll be damned! Would you look at that?" someone shouted, and he pointed to the engine as it rolled by. Mary Beth, with her left hand back on the Johnson bar, was leaning out the window, looking ahead of the engine. Her auburn hair was hanging down across her shoulder.

"That's a woman drivin' that machine!"

"No, it ain't. It's just a man with long hair," someone else said.

"If it is, it's the prettiest man I've ever seen," another added, and by now everyone standing alongside the track realized that it was, indeed, a woman who was driving the locomotive.

With Matt's job of shoveling done, he was standing on the deck just behind the engine cab. He laughed when he saw the reaction of the people who had noticed Mary Beth at the throttle of the locomotive.

"Mary Beth, you seem to be attracting a lot of attention," he said.

Mary Beth looked out toward the men who, with mouth agape, had been watching, and with a broad smile, she waved at them. Only one of the men at trackside had the presence of mind to return the wave.

Sharp was sitting on a bench in the cab, still giving instructions.

"Stop here until the track is switched to put us onto the side," he said.

Mary Beth stopped, then when the track was switched, started up again. The trackman gave a casual wave, thinking it would be a regular engineer, but did a double take when he saw that the driver was a woman.

Mary Beth proceeded slowly to the end of the sidetrack, then stopped.

"Now, open that valve to vent off all the pressure," Sharp directed, and Matt did so.

By now, nearly a dozen trackmen, most of whom were merely curious, had gathered around the engine, having followed it up the sidetrack.

"What's a woman doing running that engine?" someone asked.

"She's driving it because our engineer is hurt and our fireman dead," Matt called down to them. "Please, if you will, get an ambulance in here to take Mr. Sharp to the hospital."

Fifteen minutes later Dooley's body was removed from the private car, and a couple of attendants came into the cab to put Sharp on a stretcher. Matt, Mary Beth, and John were standing down on the ground alongside the train as Sharp was being loaded into the ambulance.

"Mr. Sharp, I've made arrangements with the hospital," John said. "You are to be given the best care possible, and I will be paying for all of it."

"I appreciate that, Mr. Gillespie," Sharp replied then, with a smile, he looked over at Mary Beth. "And young lady, if you ever want to work as an engineer, I'll be glad to give you a recommendation. You did a fine job bringing us in."

Mary Beth leaned down and kissed Sharp on the cheek.

"Well now," Sharp said with a big grin. "That was almost worth getting shot for."

Matt, John, and Mary Beth watched the

team pull the ambulance away. Then, more somberly, they saw the hearse take Dooley away.

"Poor Mr. Dooley," Mary Beth said.

After the hearse left, Mary Beth wiped tears from her eyes, then noticed that her face was blackened with soot.

"Oh, I bet I look just like I did when we came out of the coal mine," she said. "Papa, is there any way I can get cleaned up before we go on to Chicago?"

"Yes, I'll have to make arrangements for Mr. Sharp and Mr. Dooley, and I'll have to get a new train crew. You'll have plenty of time."

Chicago

Lou Borski ground the rest of his cigar out in an ashtray, then leaned forward.

"I hear what you're sayin' about how ever'body else has been unable to get the job done, but here's your problem. You've been dealin' with amateurs. You shoulda come to me in the first place."

"I didn't expect them to ever get this far. But from what I understand, they'll be here tonight. Gillespie is going to be giving a speech at Northwestern University tomorrow."

"No he ain't," Borski said. "That is, unless you want him to give the speech. How soon do you want the job done?"

"When you do it isn't as important as that you do it. Tonight, tomorrow, I don't even care if you wait until after he gives the speech. The point is I need him and his daughter dead."

"What about this man that's been lookin' after him and the girl? You want him dead as well?"

"I don't care whether you kill him or not. Although you might find it necessary to kill him before you can take care of Gillespie and his daughter. I won't lie to you, this man, Matt Jensen, has proven to be quite a formidable adversary."

"He's a what?"

"He is a most resourceful man. He, alone, is the reason that all the previous attempts have failed."

"He's some rube, ain't he? I mean from somewhere out West?"

"I believe he is from Colorado."

"Ha!" Borski replied. "Well, he ain't never encountered anyone like my boys. You just come up with the money, then put it all out of your mind. Ten thousand dollars, I believe you said."

"Yes."

"Hand it over."

"No, I've already paid others to take care of them, and they failed. I won't pay for any more failures. You do the job, then you get paid."

Borski smiled, though it was a smile without humor. "You know what, mister? You have just made a big mistake. You don't have a choice. You have to pay me now, or I will go to the police and tell them that you are trying to hire someone to kill John Gillespie. And Gillespie, being a rich and famous man, is going to get their attention just real fast."

"What? Why, you wouldn't dare!"

"Oh, yeah, I would. Trust me, I really would."

There was a moment of silence.

"All right, I'll pay you. But you absolutely must assure me that you will be successful. We've come too far now. John Gillespie and his daughter must both be killed."

Borski smiled as the money was counted out.

"Well, I'll tell you what. You and your people can put your minds at ease, because the job will be done. Just think of all the money and worry you would have saved if you had come to see me and my boys in the first place."

CHAPTER THIRTY-FIVE

Decatur, Illinois

When Matt returned to the private car, Mary Beth, now having cleaned up and changed clothes, was already there.

"Where's John?"

"He's having to sign some papers to get track clearance for us to go on to Chicago. He'll be right back."

"I suppose so, but I don't like letting him out of my sight for too long."

"You're supposed to keep me in sight, too," Mary Beth said. "Don't I count?" She pouted, coquettishly.

"Sure, you count."

"Well, that's certainly good to know."

Matt took a seat where he could look through the window.

"There's something I've been wanting to ask you," Mary Beth said.

"What is that?"

"Why?"

"Why? Why what?"

"Why have you never been married?"

"I told you why."

"I know you said because you didn't think that the way you lived would let you settle down and get married. Have you never found a woman that you liked?"

"Yes, I've found women that I like."

"You know, Papa really thinks a lot of you. I know he would give you a job, a good job that would pay very well, one with a lot of responsibility. You could settle down then."

"Mary Beth, I . . ." Matt wasn't certain how he was going to answer that but, fortunately, there was no need for him to, because at that moment the door to the car opened, and John Gillespie stepped in.

"John, I'm glad you're back," Matt said. "I was a bit uneasy with you off by yourself like that."

"I wasn't really by myself. I was in the depot in front of a lot of people. And even coming out here to the car, I had one of the railroad detectives walk with me. I told him that someone had seen the private car and tried to rob me at one of the earlier stops. He was glad to do it."

"How much did you give him, Papa?" Mary Beth asked.

"Twenty dollars."

She laughed. "Then, of course, he was glad to do it."

"I got another telegram from the office. Drew is still gone. I have no idea where he is."

"You know Uncle Drew, Papa. He's always finding things that need to be done."

"That's true. I'm not sure I could run the office without him."

"Of course, you could," Mary Beth said.

"Well, yes. But I must confess that Drew takes responsibility for so many things that he just about makes himself indispensable."

"Have you ever thought that he might be doing that on purpose, just to make certain that you keep him around?" Mary Beth asked.

"Ha! Even that shows how smart he is."

"Did you get track clearance for us?" John asked.

"That I did, and a new engine crew. They're building up steam now."

"Why, you didn't need a new engine crew, Papa. Matt and I could have taken you on to Chicago."

"Sure we could have," Matt teased, "if you had been willing to trade jobs with me. You shovel and I drive."

"Come to think of it, maybe it was a good idea to get a new crew," Mary Beth agreed, with a laugh.

Half an hour later, they left Decatur.

Chicago

It was eight o'clock that evening when they rolled into the Central Depot located in the middle of the city. They left the car, then waved to the engineer as he moved it to a sidetrack where it would wait the few days to be attached to the train that would take them back to San Francisco.

The depot was a curious mix of architectural styles with several restaurants and spacious waiting rooms. When they stepped inside the building, Mary Beth smiled and called out to someone she saw.

"Uncle Drew!" She rushed toward him with her arms extended, and he embraced her.

Drew looked toward John. "Hello, John," he said.

"Drew!" John replied with a happy smile, greeting his friend with an extended hand. "What are you doing here?"

"I couldn't just wait anymore for your telegrams telling me you were all right. I had to come here and see for myself that you made it," Drew said. "Hello, Mr. Jensen," Drew said, extending his hand. "You don't know how thankful I am that you have

434

been able to keep my friend in one piece."

"You have no idea what all he has done," John said. "He has saved Mary Beth and my life more times than I can count. I don't know where all these would-be assassins have come from, but whoever it is that wants me dead has certainly gone all out to get the job done."

"We were wrong in suspecting Keaton, Mitchell, or Morris," Drew said. "None of them have a thing to do with it."

"Yes, I've learned that as well. But tell me, Drew, how did you get to Chicago so quickly? I know we left before you did."

"I took an express, and unlike you, who wound up gallivanting all over the country, I came straight here. I've discovered who is behind all these attempts on your life."

"Who are they? Have you sent the law after them?"

"Well, I misspoke when I said I know who it is. I should have said that I know what it is. It is a consortium of businesses who are in competition with us. The problem is, I don't know which businesses, or any of the people who are actually involved."

"How did you find out that it was a consortium?"

"Jefferson Emerson's Detective Agency found out. He's still trying to learn just which businesses are behind it."

"Yes, of course, I should have realized Jeff would be doing that. Good for him. Well, shall we arrange for transportation to the hotel?"

"I've already hired a coach, the driver is waiting for us. And I have four rooms at the hotel."

"Rooms? I thought you had arranged a suite for Mary Beth and me."

"Yes, but we had to give it up when you didn't arrive on your original schedule. I do have one for you for tomorrow night."

"Yes, of course, I didn't mean to be critical."

The lobby of the Palmer House Hotel was just as nice as Matt remembered from his last stay here. The frescoed ceiling was done in gold and red, and the walls were festooned with electric lightbulbs. Cushioned chairs were set around low tables that were scattered throughout the lobby, and several of them were occupied by well-dressed men and women, many of whom seemed to be engaged in animated conversations.

The desk clerk was standing behind a carved, mahogany counter, and he greeted Matt and the others as they approached.

"My name is Drew Jessup," Drew said.

"We have four rooms reserved."

The clerk looked at the registration book and nodded. "Indeed you do, sir. You have rooms on the second, third, fourth, and fifth floors."

"I specifically said I wanted all four rooms on the same floor," Drew said.

"Sir, I wasn't here when you checked in and don't see any such notation," the desk clerk said.

"How can a hotel like the Palmer House be so incompetent? Change it now, please. I want all four rooms on the same floor."

"I'm afraid that is impossible, sir. We are completely booked up."

"This is unconscionable," Drew said angrily.

"It's all right, Drew," John said. "We're all tired and any room sounds good. Let's have our dinner and go to bed."

Picking up the keys to their rooms, the four went into the dining room, a large, oak-paneled room with matching oak tables, each table situated under a hanging chandelier. They had the evening special, which was a spinach salad, smoked trout, and wild rice.

"I will say this about the consortium who is after Mary Beth and me," John said as they ate. "They are very determined. I have

437

lost count of the attempts."

"Yes, but thankfully you have survived every one of them," Drew said.

"There is something about these attempts that I don't understand," Matt said.

"What's that?" Drew asked.

"It is a question that has perplexed me from the very beginning, and I have asked it of John, but now I will ask it of you. I can understand how business competitors might want John out of the way. But why are they trying to kill Mary Beth?"

"Are you sure they are trying to kill her? Or is it just that she has been there for every attempt?" Drew asked. "I'm sure that when they cut the tongue pin on John's coach, they had no idea Mary Beth would be with him."

"You may be right," John said.

"No, I don't think so," Matt said. "John, you remember back in Assumption, those two men told us they were being paid to kill you *and* Mary Beth."

"That's right, they did say that, didn't they?" John said.

"Which brings me back to my original question. Why do they want to kill Mary Beth?"

"But what happened in Assumption might not even be related to all the other attempts," Mary Beth said.

"Why do you say that?" Matt asked.

"Remember, they said that a man named Sullivan was the one who was paying them. And Mr. Morris said that Sullivan was upset because the mine is doing so well, and he blames Papa."

"I think Mary Beth is right," John said. "I don't think the attempt in Assumption had anything to do with any of the earlier attempts. And Sullivan was just evil enough to want to kill Mary Beth as well, because he knows how much she means to me."

"Instead, he wound up killing himself," Mary Beth said.

"Sullivan killed himself?" Drew said. "How so?"

John explained how, while Morris was showing them a new seam in the coal mine that Sullivan had set off an explosion, intending to cause a cave-in that would trap them.

"But he miscalculated," John concluded, "and he brought a large part of the wall down on himself."

"Well, thank goodness, none of you were hurt," Drew said. "And that is the important thing. And Mr. Jensen, you are certainly to be congratulated. You have been most successful in your obligation to get John and

Mary Beth here safely."

"Jeff Emerson certainly deserves every cent we pay him for keeping him on retainer," John said. "His suggestion that we hire Matt was, quite literally, a lifesaver."

"Oh, I agree," Drew said. "By the way, Mr. Jensen, I have taken the liberty of securing first-class passage for your return trip to San Francisco. Your train leaves at six o'clock tomorrow morning."

"What?" Mary Beth asked, with a surprised gasp. "Uncle Drew, why did you do that?"

Drew got a surprised look on his face. "Have I erred? I thought the idea was for Mr. Jensen to get the two of you here safely. That he has done, so I assumed he would be anxious to get on his way." Drew laughed. "After all, he does have five thousand dollars to spend."

"Yes, of course, his job is finished," John said. "But I assumed he would have a couple of days of rest before he started back."

"Mr. Jensen was going to take me to the theater while we were here," Mary Beth said.

"Mr. Jensen, I assure you, it was not my intention to hurry your departure," Drew said.

"Don't worry about it," John said. "I know you did what you thought was best. Matt, it's up to you. You may stay a few days longer or start back tomorrow."

"It's just that I've already purchased the ticket," Drew said.

"Oh, for heaven's sake, Drew, the decision certainly doesn't turn upon the price of a railroad ticket. If he doesn't use it, we can turn it in and get the money back," John said. He laughed. "And even if we can't, I'm sure we can afford to take the loss."

"Well, it's like Mary Beth said, I did promise to take her to the theater," Matt said. "So, if it's all right with you, John, I'll stay a few days longer."

"Oh, Matt, they have a bar here, one that serves ladies as well as gentlemen," Mary Beth said. "Would you have a glass of wine with me?"

"Oh, but we can have wine right here at the table," John said.

"Papa!" Mary Beth said.

"Of course, what was I thinking? You young people go ahead. Drew and I will have our wine here."

Mary Beth smiled. "Thank you," she said. Getting up, she kissed her father lightly on his cheek, then held her hand out toward Matt. "Shall we?"

CHAPTER THIRTY-SIX

John watched Mary Beth and Matt as they headed toward the hotel bar.

"Do you think that was wise, John?" Drew asked.

"Do I think what was wise?"

"Letting Mary Beth go off with Jensen like that."

"Drew, what in the world are you talking about? Our lives have literally been in Matt's hands for the last several days. Why should I be in the least concerned about letting Mary Beth go into the bar with him?"

"It isn't her safety I'm concerned about. Surely it is obvious to you that Mary Beth is taken with him. You are a very wealthy man, what is to say that Jensen won't see some advantage in the situation? Surely you wouldn't want someone like that as a son-in-law."

"I don't think that thought has crossed his mind. Matt Jensen is one of the finest and most dedicated men I have ever met."

"But don't you worry about his character? From what I understand, he has killed several men just since you left San Francisco."

"Yes, he has, but in every case the men he killed were men who were trying to kill Mary Beth and me."

"I'm not criticizing the killings, I'm sure they were all justified. But it takes a certain kind of man who can kill so easily, don't you think?"

"Drew, Mary Beth killed one of those would-be assassins," John said quietly.

"Mary Beth did?"

"Yes, and she has had a hard time of it. I would very much appreciate it if you didn't talk about this subject around her."

"Well, yes, of course. I won't mention it anymore. As I say, I was just thinking about her well-being, is all."

"I'm glad that Mary Beth is showing some interest in anyone. Ever since her mother died, she seems to think that, somehow, she would be deserting me if she showed any interest in a man. I don't expect anything to come of this, but I do want her to enjoy the opportunity of spending some time with him."

"Of course, John, please forgive me,"

Drew said. "I'm sorry I ever brought the subject up."

"There is nothing to forgive," John said with an easy smile. He reached over to put his hand on Drew's arm. "We have been friends for far too long to be worried about what we say to one another."

There was a piano in the bar and a pianist wearing long tails was playing music.

"Matt, let's go over there and sit next to the piano," Mary Beth suggested.

They did so, and while Matt knew that piano players in the saloons almost always had an empty beer mug for tips, he didn't know what the proper protocol would be for a place like this. When he saw, not an empty beer mug, but a decorated bowl for the same purpose, he added a dollar.

"Thank you, sir," the pianist said, without missing a note.

"You're welcome," Matt said.

"That's Mozart's Piano Concerto Number Nine," Mary Beth said.

"Very good, madam, indeed it is," the pianist said. "I am always happy to play for someone who not only appreciates the music but recognizes it."

"I love classical music, and you are playing beautifully."

Pleased by the compliment, the pianist smiled and nodded his head.

"Do you like Mozart?" Mary Beth asked Matt.

"Well, I like this," Matt said. "But to tell the truth, I've never really had the opportunity to listen to this kind of music. I know that Sally likes it, though."

"Sally? Who's Sally? You've never mentioned Sally."

"You asked me once if I had ever found any women that I like. Well, Sally is such a woman. She is a very beautiful lady, and like you, she knows the manners of good society."

"Are you in love with her?"

"Am I in love with her? Well, no, I couldn't say that. She is a wonderful lady, and I do think the world of her. But I'm not sure how Smoke would take it if I said I was in love with Sally."

"Smoke?"

"Smoke Jensen. Sally is Smoke's wife."

"Oh, she's married!" Mary Beth said with a broad, relieved smile. "I thought . . . well, never mind what I thought."

After finishing the wine, Matt walked Mary Beth up to her room.

"Would you like to come in?" she invited with a seductive smile.

"Mary Beth, you have no idea how much I would like to come in," Matt said. "But I couldn't do this to your father."

"Why, Matt, are you afraid? I didn't think you were afraid of anything."

"Let's just say I'm cautious."

"Too cautious for this?"

Mary Beth put her arms around Matt's neck and pulled him to her for a deep kiss. Then, pulling away, she smiled at him, her eyes reflecting the light of the hall lamp.

"You'll be sorry you didn't accept my invitation," she said.

"I know I will be," Matt agreed. "Now, get on in there before I change my mind." He pushed her, gently, back into her room, his rejection ameliorated, however, by a broad smile.

Once Mary Beth got inside and went to bed, she was asleep within minutes. She had no idea how long she had been asleep when she woke with a start. She felt someone put something over her face, a cloth with a strong, cloying smell. She tried to call out and to fight against it, but her head began to spin, and she passed out.

When Mary Beth came to later, she found herself, not in the well-furnished hotel room, but in a small room that consisted of four bare walls. Rather than the large comfortable bed she had gone to sleep in, she was now lying on a cot. She wasn't covered with silk sheets and a woolen blanket, and all she had to push back the cool, morning air was her cotton sleeping gown and a single quilt. There were no sheets between her and the bare canvas of the cot.

Frightened, she looked around the room and saw as the only furnishings a table, a chair, and a chamber pot. Where was she? And how had she gotten here? She sat up on the cot and looked for her clothes but didn't see them.

Why would she have come here without her clothes?

Then she remembered the frightening scene in her bed when she had been awakened, then passed out again.

"Hello?" she called. "Hello, is there anyone here?"

Padding barefoot across the floor, she walked over to the door and tried to open it, but it was locked. She knocked on it.

"Hello?" she called again. "Is there anyone out there?"

She was a prisoner. But who had brought her here and why?

She knocked on the door again, and when

the knocking got no response, she banged on it as loudly as she could.

"Let me out of here!" she shouted at the top of her voice.

She saw the doorknob turn slightly, then she heard the sound of a key being pushed into the keyhole from the other side.

"Step back away from the door, miss," a woman's voice said.

Mary Beth did as she was asked.

When the door opened, a middle-aged woman with unkempt hair came in carrying a bowl and a spoon.

"Here's your breakfast," she said as she started toward the table.

Mary Beth waited until the woman had reached the table, then she jerked the door open, intending to escape the room.

There was a large man standing in the hallway, right in front of the door. His arms were crossed over his chest, and doing so flexed them in such a way as to disclose powerful biceps.

"Where do you think you're goin'?" he asked in a low, gravelly voice.

Matt, John, and Drew were sitting at a table in the dining room.

"I have no idea what's keeping her this morning," John said. "Mary Beth is normally an early riser."

"Well, it had to have been a tiring trip for her," Drew said. "If you would like, I'll go up and knock on her door."

"Would you?" John asked. "Tell her there are three hungry men waiting for her."

Matt didn't say anything, but he drummed his fingers on the table as he watched Drew leave the dining room.

"He's a good man," John said. "I never worry about getting anything done with him around."

"You say you met in college?"

"Yes. We had what you might call a symbiotic relationship."

"A what?"

"It means I looked out for him in areas where he wasn't very strong, and he looked out for me in areas where I wasn't very strong."

"Oh?"

"Yes." John laughed. "I'll be honest with you, Drew wasn't that strong of a student, and I helped him with his class work. On the other hand, even then, he had a way of getting things done."

"What do you mean by getting things done?"

"He just seemed be able to go around the rules if he needed to. For example, we weren't allowed to have liquor in the fraternity house, and some of our parties would have been terribly dull if Drew hadn't come through for us. I don't know where, or how he did it, but he always had liquor available."

"By available, you mean he sold it?"

John laughed. "Oh, yes. Even then he was a good businessman."

Drew came back into the dining room then, alone, and with a concerned look on his face.

"I knocked, pretty loud, and I called out to her, but I didn't get an answer."

"Are you certain you knocked loudly enough?" John asked.

"I was loud enough that some of the other guests on the same floor opened their doors to see what was going on," Drew replied.

"Why don't we get a key from the front desk and check on her?" Matt suggested.

"Yes, that's a good idea," John said.

"Now, that is very odd," the desk clerk said.

"What is odd?" John asked.

"I don't have another key for that room. I have two keys for every room, one that I give to the hotel guest, and one that I keep here at the desk just for such a reason as this. But I can't seem to find the other key."

"Don't you have a skeleton key?" John asked. "How do the maids get into the rooms to clean them up?"

The desk clerk smiled. "Yes, of course, I do have a skeleton key. Just a moment."

The clerk stepped into the room behind the check-in desk, then returned a moment later with the key.

"I'm afraid I'm going to have to send the concierge up with you," he said. "This key grants access to any room in the hotel, and I can't just give it to any guest."

"I understand," John said. "But I do need to get into my daughter's room."

The three men and the concierge went up to Mary Beth's room, which was on the fourth floor. John pushed past him almost as soon as he opened the door.

"Mary Beth?" he called. It took but a second for him to see that she wasn't there. "Matt!"

Matt rushed into the room, followed by Drew.

"She's gone!" John said.

"Maybe she went shopping," Drew suggested. "I know that women like to do that."

"She wouldn't have gone without telling me, and she certainly wouldn't have gone without her clothes," John said. He pointed to her dress and shoes. The suitcase was

451

nearby and unopened.

"Here is something," Matt said, picking up a piece of white paper that was folded over on the dresser.

Gillespie, if you want to see your daughter alive again, meet me near the railroad tracks on the lake shore in Lake Park by ten o'clock this morning. I will give you further instructions then. Come alone.

"Oh, my God! Someone has taken her!" John said in shock and fear.

"There is no way I'm going to let you go alone," Matt said. "I'm going with you."

"No!" Drew said sharply. "You'd better not. They said come alone. If they see someone with John, they might . . . kill her." He added the last two words ominously.

"I'm not so sure that they would," Matt said. "It seems to me like they are using her as a bargaining chip. They are going to ask for money, and in order to do that, they are going to have to keep her alive."

"Yes, they are going to ask for money, aren't they?" John said, with a sense of relief in his voice. "This has nothing to do with the consortium wanting to kill us."

"It is obvious that they know who you are," Matt said. "That means they know that

452

you are a very wealthy man. It also means they are going to ask for a great deal of money."

"I don't care how much money they ask for. All I care about is getting my daughter back alive," John said.

"I still don't think you should go alone."

"Don't go with him, Jensen," Drew said. "That young woman means almost as much to me as she does to John, and I'll not stand by and watch you do anything that would put her life into jeopardy."

"Her life is already in jeopardy," Matt said.

"All right. I'll not let you put her life in further jeopardy."

"Matt, please," John said. "I think that Drew is right. I know you mean well, but I would much rather go by myself."

Matt sighed, then nodded.

"All right, John," he said. "If that is the way you feel about it, I won't interfere."

When Matt went back downstairs, he stepped into the bar and ordered a beer. He was angry with himself. Mary Beth had invited him into her room last night, and if he had accepted her invitation, this wouldn't have happened.

He was also angry with himself because he had been hired to protect John and Mary

453

Beth, and he had failed. Matt thought about the message. It contained no instructions as to where money should be left, nor did it mention money at all. The only instructions were for John to meet someone at Lake Park.

Mary Beth sat on the edge of the canvas cot. She knew her father would be worried sick about her, and she was more concerned about the distress her father must be in than she was about her own situation. Who were these people, and why had they taken her? She knew that someone had been trying to kill her and her father for the last month, starting with the sabotage of their coach. But if they were going to do that, why was she still alive?

The door to her room opened, and the same woman who had brought her a bowl of oatmeal earlier came in.

"You have a visitor," she said.

"Who?"

The woman said nothing, but stepped back out of the room, leaving the door open behind her. A couple of seconds later, her visitor came into the room.

"Uncle Drew!" Mary Beth said excitedly. "I've never been so happy to see anyone in my entire life!"

Mary Beth jumped up from her cot and started toward him, but he held his hand out toward her. Puzzled by his odd reaction she stopped.

"Bring her her clothes," Jessup said.

"Oh, thank you!" Mary Beth said. "I don't mind telling you, I have been very uncomfortable wearing only my nightgown."

The man who Mary Beth had seen standing guard outside the little room when she tried to leave earlier came in then, carrying a sack. He handed the sack to her, and looking into it she saw her clothes as well as a pair of shoes.

"Get dressed," Jessup said.

"I will, and gladly so. Where is Papa? Does he know you have found me?"

Mary Beth removed the clothes from the sack, then looked toward Jessup and the man who had brought them to her.

"Well, aren't you going to step outside?" Mary Beth asked, with a little laugh.

"No. Get dressed."

Jessup's reply was clipped and cold.

"Uncle Drew? What is this? What is going on?" Mary Beth was confused by Drew's odd behavior.

"What is going on is you are going to get dressed, and you aren't going to give me any more back talk," Jessup said.

455

Mary Beth's joy had turned first to confusion, now she was experiencing fear.

"I don't understand. Why are you doing this?"

"Take off her nightgown," Jessup said to the muscular man who was in the room with them.

Mary Beth looked around, hoping to see the woman she had seen earlier, but the woman was gone and now only the two men were present, and one of the men she had known her entire life. The fact that she knew him so well made the current situation even more bizarre and more frightening.

Back at the hotel, Matt studied his beer and drummed his fingers on the bar.

Damn! he thought. They aren't after money! The consortium is using Mary Beth to get John there, and when they get him there they will, no doubt, kill both of them.

Why? Why would the consortium want to kill both of them?

A memory of something Mary Beth said suddenly popped up in his mind.

"Well, what difference does it make, Papa, whether I spend it now, or I spend it later? It will all be mine someday anyway. You told me so yourself."

That's it! he thought. That's why Mary Beth must be killed, because she will inherit the business after John is gone. But why would that matter to a consortium who is trying to get even, or get a business advantage over . . .

The unfinished question died in thought.

There is no consortium. The only one who would profit by both of them being dead would be Drew Jessup! It all made sense now. Jessup had arranged for Matt to catch a train by six o'clock this morning, and if he had left, he would have been gone before Mary Beth's abduction was discovered. That is also why there were four separate rooms on four different floors, and that was why there was no second key at the desk. Drew Jessup had gotten the second key and provided it to someone to give them access to Mary Beth's room.

Matt glanced up at the clock that was between the two mirrors behind the bar. It was already 9:40.

"Hey!" Matt called to the bartender.

"Yes, sir?" the bartender replied, then noticing that Matt had not drunk all his beer, got a worried expression on his face. "Is something wrong with your beer, sir?"

"No, the beer is fine. Tell me how to get to the lakeshore in Lake Park."

"Oh, that's very easy, sir. You go out the front door, turn left, and just keep going until you reach the lake."

"How far is that?"

"About a mile, I would say."

"Thanks," Matt said.

He thought, for a moment, about going up to check John's room to see if he had left yet, but he was sure he had. No time to check on Jessup either.

When Matt stepped out of the hotel, he saw a mounted policeman dismount and tie his horse off at a hitching rail out front. The policeman went into the hotel.

Matt untied the horse's reins.

"I'm sorry about this, boy," Matt said to the animal. "I've never stolen a horse before in my life, but this is an emergency."

Matt swung into the saddle, then headed east at a gallop. Within a few blocks he was onto a large grassy area, filled with trees, low-lying shrubbery, and blooming flowers. Pulling his pistol, he urged the horse into a gallop across the park. Then, when the lake came into view, he stopped and dismounted.

"Go," he said, slapping the horse on the rump, and the horse turned and began trotting away. Matt didn't know if he would be returning to the hotel or going back to the police barn, but it was obvious that he had some destination in mind.

Matt began running toward the lake, keeping a low profile behind a long hedgerow. When he reached the edge of the hedgerow, he saw them. John was standing with his arm around his daughter. Drew Jessup and three men were standing across from them. The three men were holding pistols pointed at John and Mary Beth.

"Drew, I can't believe you are doing this to us," John said. "Do thirty years of friendship mean nothing to you?"

"It wasn't thirty years of friendship, you old fool," Drew replied with a harsh sneer. "It has been thirty years of 'Drew do this, Drew do that.' I've never been anything but your personal servant."

"But that's not true! I have paid you very well all these years. I put you in charge of my entire operation. Why, I even set it up so that if anything happened to me, you would be next in line after . . ." John stopped in midsentence. "Drew, no, my God, no. It's you, isn't it? It's been you all along. You want the business."

"Ha! Figured it out, have you? Putting me next in line after your daughter was a totally meaningless move. I'm much older than Mary Beth. What were the chances I would ever wind up inheriting anything?"

"Drew, Drew, Drew." John shook his head. *"Et tu, Brute?"*

"I don't even know what the hell that means," Jessup said.

"Well I know what it means, and I didn't even go to college like you did," Matt said.

"What the hell?" Jessup shouted. He pointed toward Matt. "Shoot him! Shoot him!"

Borski and the two armed men with him spun toward Matt, but it was too late. Matt fired three times, the shots coming so quickly on top of each other that it sounded like one sustained roar. All three of Matt's bullets found their mark, and only one of the Chicago thugs, Borski, managed to get off a shot. But that shot occurred after he was hit, and as he was twisting around while going down. As a result of that, Borsky's shot hit Drew Jessup in the middle of his chest.

Matt kept his eye on the three armed men to make certain that none of them posed a threat, but he saw, quickly, that they did not.

"Oh, I was so scared!" Mary Beth said, running to Matt to wrap her arms around him. Matt embraced her, pulling her close to him.

"John, I'm sorry."

The words were quiet and strained, and they came from Drew Jessup, who like the others, was lying on his back.

"Drew, how could you have done this?" John asked, squatting now alongside Drew's prostrate form.

"I'm sorry," Drew said again.

"But the attack on your house," John said.

"I set it up to draw attention away from me," Drew said, barely able to get the words out.

"Don't you understand, Drew? You didn't have to draw attention away from you. I never suspected you, and I would never have suspected you."

Drew raised his hand toward John, and John grasped it. "Please forgive me, old friend."

John was quiet, then he opened his mouth to speak, but he didn't have to. With a last gasping breath Drew died.

"Were you going to forgive him, Papa?" Mary Beth asked.

"I don't know," John said. "Lord help me, child, I don't know."

"He . . ." Mary Beth started, then she halted after only one word. She was going to tell her father about the humiliation she had suffered when Drew forced her to strip naked in front of him and another man. But

Drew was dead, and her father was obviously distraught over the betrayal by the man he had thought was his best friend, so she remained quiet.

"What were you going to say?" John asked, standing up and putting his arm around her.

"Nothing, Papa. I wasn't going to say anything," Mary Beth replied.

Somewhere in Nebraska

There were three bedroom compartments in the private car, and on the way back to California, now with the threat to John and Mary Beth over, they had talked Matt into taking one of them.

Matt was lying awake in his bed, looking through the small window at the open countryside. They were running parallel with the Missouri River, and Matt could see a steamboat out on the water, the only lights being those in the pilothouse. He heard a light knock on the door.

"Mary Beth," he said in surprise, when he opened the door.

"I wanted to thank you for saving my life."

"No need to. It was my job. Besides, you've already thanked me."

Smiling, Mary Beth slipped the nightgown off over her head, revealing the same beautiful body Matt had seen when he stepped in on her as she was taking a bath.

"Yes," she said. "But I want to thank you again."

The employees of Thorndike Press hope you have enjoyed this Large Print book. All our Thorndike, Wheeler, and Kennebec Large Print titles are designed for easy reading, and all our books are made to last. Other Thorndike Press Large Print books are available at your library, through selected bookstores, or directly from us.

For information about titles, please call:
(800) 223-1244

or visit our Web site at:
http://gale.cengage.com/thorndike

To share your comments, please write:
Publisher
Thorndike Press
10 Water St., Suite 310
Waterville, ME 04901